The Marriage Clock

The Marriage Clock

a novel

ZARA RAHEEM

WILLIAM MORROW
An Imprint of HarperCollins*Publishers*

This is a work of fiction. Names, characters, places, and incidents are products of the author's imagination or are used fictitiously and are not to be construed as real. Any resemblance to actual events, locales, organizations, or persons, living or dead, is entirely coincidental.

Grateful acknowledgment is made for permission to reprint an excerpt of "Venus" from *Wild Embers*, copyright © 2017, by Nikita Gill.

HarperCollins books may be purchased for educational, business, or sales promotional use. For information, please email the Special Markets Department at SPsales@harpercollins.com.

FIRST EDITION

Designed by Diahann Sturge
Title page and chapter opener art © Lovely Mandala / Shutterstock, Inc.

Library of Congress Cataloging-in-Publication Data has been applied for.

ISBN 978-0-06-287792-5

19 20 21 22 23 LSC 10 9 8 7 6 5 4 3 2 1

Dedicated to every woman who's ever been told she wasn't enough.

She hasn't a single moon
to worship her
or to cloud her judgment.

She is alone.
And oh
how brilliantly she shines.

—from "Venus" by Nikita Gill

A Bollywood State of Mind

As a young girl, when I thought about life in my mid-twenties, I envisioned a glamorous profession like being a principal dancer for a prestigious New York ballet company, living in a fabulous penthouse apartment overlooking a city skyline, and being married to a tall, dark, and mysterious musician whose beautifully written love songs were the inner soundtrack to my beating heart. If I had known that my mid-twenties would actually consist of a less-than-desirable career working as an underpaid English teacher, a modest-sized room in my parents' suburban home, and a total sense of ambivalence regarding the notion of love, I probably would have signed up for someone else's life.

Growing up in a semitraditional Muslim household, I believed in love wholeheartedly. Love, after all, was Shah Jahan's inspiration for the Taj Mahal. Love was the underlying theme in every Urdu *ghazal* or *shayari* ever written. Love was the reason my mother left behind her entire life in India to start afresh with my father—a man she barely knew—in America. Love was the sole reason the world turned; why bluebirds sang and fireworks shot into the warm summer sky. It was not just an idea; it was something tangible—felt within my grasp. A whimsical notion looming in the distant future, anxiously waiting to be discovered, like a present still wrapped.

My years of dissecting on-screen Bollywood romances provided me with enough insight to know *exactly* what to look for when it would finally happen. I was desperately waiting for that random run-in with a total stranger with unbelievably good hair with whom I could slow-motion run through a meadow as we dramatically proclaimed our love for each other through nonsensical lyrical metaphors and perfectly synchronized dance routines—with multiple colorful outfit changes. In my mind, that was what was *supposed* to happen. You meet someone, fall in love (in the aforementioned fashion), get married, and live happily ever after. Unfortunately, the screenplay written for my life was not quite as predictable as I had hoped. There were no meadows in close proximity to Los Angeles, and my lack of coordination limited my dance moves to the Robot and the Inebriated Baby. The only random run-ins I had were with nosy South Asian aunties inquiring about my marital status. Finally, after twenty-two delusional years and a brief yet eye-opening conversation with my college roommate, I was temporarily plucked out of my Bollywood fantasy and brought back to harsh reality.

"What if you turn out to be one of those people who are incapable of falling in love?" Annie said as she leaned back in her chair and took a sip of her coffee.

"Of course I'm not going to be one of those people." I scoffed, appalled by this idea. "Why would you possibly think *I* could be one of *those* people, Annie?"

"Because you push away every nice guy you've ever met and refuse to date anyone longer than two weeks. I mean seriously, Leila, we have produce in our refrigerator with longer life spans than most of your relationships."

"That . . . is not true." I was completely taken aback by the blatant verity behind her words; a realization that I was not quite ready to acknowledge in that particular moment. So what if I was a "serial" dater and not a "long-term" dater? Before I went away for college, I was a "never allowed to" dater. I grew up Muslim. My conservative parents made sure all my free time was occupied with homework from AP classes, community activities, and tennis. Annie was being slightly unfair given that the whole concept of dating was still fairly new to me in comparison to my non-Muslim peers.

"Fine." Annie lifted one of her eyebrows accusingly. "Then remind me of the last time you were in a long-term relationship."

I hesitated as I thought for a moment. "That's beside the point," I said dismissively when nothing immediately jumped to mind. "Besides, I'm not just looking for a nice guy," I stated firmly. "I'm looking for the *right* guy."

"The right guy?"

"Yes, the *right guy.* And I don't need to waste my time on a long-term relationship when it's pretty obvious I haven't found what I'm looking for yet."

"Okay, Leila," Annie said, shrugging. "Then tell me, what makes someone the *right guy*? Let's make a list."

"A list?" I half laughed. "I'm not shopping for groceries, Annie," I said, leaning back with my arms crossed. I couldn't help but feel irritated by her interrogation of my love life.

My decision to attend college outside of Los Angeles—away from my parents—had given me four years of unrestricted freedom to date without having to deal directly with the aftereffects of fear, guilt, or the risk of bringing shame upon my family. But my hopes of attaining a bona fide Bollywood romance at school were destroyed freshman year when I realized that aside from myself, not many other Muslim *desis*—aka, people from the Indian subcontinent—chose to attend my small liberal arts college. Even the Muslim Student Association on campus was more just a club consisting of five overly zealous bearded guys who seemed more interested in planning protests and food drives than talking to the opposite gender. So while I had plenty of opportunities to meet "nice guys" over the next few years, my dating experiences were chiefly restricted to non-*desis*, which—to my dismay—was much less glamorous than the sizzling on-screen story lines entrenched in my mind.

Even just the memory of my first real date caused me to cringe with embarrassment. It was sophomore year, and I had been asked out by Chad Edelstein from my Literary Theories class. Our first—and only—romantic engagement ended with him leaning in for a kiss outside my dorm room, and me shyly yet teasingly turning my head to gaze into a nonexistent camera, causing him to make out with my right earlobe for a solid ten seconds. I eventually got better at these types of interactions, yet whenever I would be introduced to another blond-haired, blue-eyed guy, a small voice, which sounded eerily similar to my mother's, would sound off in my head like a broken fire alarm—never ceasing to remind me that I was failing my culture, and essentially myself, somehow.

I tried my best to ignore that voice, but despite my efforts, in the end, I couldn't imagine running through a meadow with any of the non-*desi* guys surrounding me—no matter how unbelievably good their hair was. As much as I hated to admit it, I too had subconsciously imagined my future to be with someone closer to my counterpart—an American-born South Asian man. Who shared my affinity for Bollywood romances. And who also happened to be Muslim—or was at least willing to convert to Islam to prove his undying love for me. Being with someone who not only understood my culture but also lived it as I had would definitely have its perks. I wouldn't have to explain things like why my mother called me five times a day just to remind me to eat, or why I couldn't go out twice a week because my hair was slathered in amla oil. Plus, it wasn't worth going to war with my parents over.

So I ended relationships before they even started. I pretended that love was merely a social construct that failed to exist outside a silver screen. I convinced myself that my feelings were an inevitable side effect of all the Bollywood movies watched during my impressionable years as a youth, but the truth was, I wanted to experience love. It was just that I had yet to find someone who mirrored the dashing image of the Bollywood hero who had stolen my heart from that very first pelvic thrust.

"Look, Annie." I sighed. "When I do meet the right guy, I'll just know. I don't need some list to tell me what I want."

"I'm sure you *do* know what you want, Leila," Annie replied with a hint of frustration in her voice. "The list is just there to keep you focused on the qualities that are important, and a few of the ones that you may need to . . . compromise on," she continued with such an intense look that I couldn't help but smile.

"Fine," I groaned. "Let's make a list. But just so you know, *all* the qualities I'm looking for are important, so there's no need for any compromising." I grabbed a napkin off the table.

For the next hour or so, I rattled off every trait embodied by my Bollywood crushes as Annie frantically tried to jot them all down. I wanted someone who had *#4:* Govinda's *SENSE OF HUMOR*, *#17:* Shah Rukh Khan's *CHARMING* demeanor, *#23:* Salman Khan's *MUSCULAR* build, and *#38:* Akshaye Khanna's *SENSITIVE* side. As Annie wrote out the final quality—*#46: SEXY*—on the seventh napkin, I started to see why she may have thought I needed to scale back on my vision of love . . . just a little. However, the idea of giving up any of the qualities listed made me feel like I would be cheating myself out of finding "the one." So I quickly pushed the thought out of my mind. Besides, this was the person I was supposed to spend the rest of my life with. So what if I had forty-six items on my list? Why should I settle for anything less than my idea of perfect?

As we walked out of the coffeehouse that afternoon, Annie handed me my Mr. Right on seven napkins and left me with her last piece of advice:

"Leila, it's good to have expectations. There's nothing wrong with that. All I'm saying is life is not a movie and not everyone experiences that moment you're so hopelessly waiting for. The longer you hold on to these notions of perfection, the more disappointed you're going to feel when you don't find it."

While I quickly brushed aside the probability of her prediction at the time, looking back on this moment four years later, I now realized that Annie—my annoyingly wise and astute college roommate—might actually turn out to be right after all.

Arrange This

After graduating college, I moved back in with my parents, found a part-time teaching gig, and resumed my casual dating habits—albeit much more discreetly, since my mother and father were still not keen on the whole noncommittal-outings-for-the-sake-of-getting-to-know-each-other idea. My excuses to "hang out with friends" were always met with their silent disapproval. My parents simply couldn't understand another purpose for dating aside from marriage. They also couldn't understand why any decent "friend" would choose to pick their daughter up in anything other than a Toyota Camry.

"They really are the most dependable cars," my mother would casually remark at the breakfast table the morning after my late-night trysts. "You should let your *friend* know."

Despite their failed attempts to feign ignorance, I appreciated my parents' efforts to stay out of my love life. And as a compromise, I made a greater effort to meet more

South Asian men, not only to make up for my past non-*desi* pursuits, but also because I was still harboring hopes of finding my perfect Bollywood hero. I figured if I couldn't find him in college, now was my chance. Even if my living situation added another layer of complication to my search.

While my quests for love were consistent, they unfortunately did not go as smoothly as I had initially anticipated. It seemed the more I chased after love, the more confused I felt about it. So after a couple of years of numerous failed attempts and crumpled-up napkins, I eventually accepted my fate as "one of those people who are incapable of falling in love," and decided to surrender myself, voluntarily, to a life of singlehood. That plan, however, quickly changed the night of my twenty-sixth birthday, when my parents excitedly informed me of *their* plans to arrange my marriage during my home-cooked celebratory dinner. This was not exactly what I had wished for when I blew out the candles on my cake.

While the idea of my parents arranging my marriage might seem preposterous, I had listened in on enough conversations at the mosque and community gatherings to know that this was a pretty normal topic of discussion in Muslim American households like mine. In traditional South Asian culture, marriage was considered the climactic point of one's life. Most Indian parents equated marriage to happiness. Marriage was the ultimate goal. Once you reached this goal, you had not only attained happiness but had also completed the first half of your filial duties as an Indian son or daughter. (The second half completed only after the successful birth of a grandchild.)

I was always subconsciously aware of the importance of marriage in my culture, even though it was never directly stated by either of my parents. Even as a child, I had a slight inkling that all the hours spent in the kitchen with my mother held a far greater purpose than simply practicing the art of cooking. Looking back on it now, it was obvious that my mother was preparing me to become a "good" wife so I could one day honor my family by making impeccably seasoned *biryani* and rolling perfectly round *chapatis* for my future husband. The same way if I were a boy, I would've been taught early on to get good grades and prepare myself to apply to a respectable (non–liberal arts) college so I could study either medicine or engineering and become a more desirable candidate as a husband.

The signs were all there, so I probably should not have been quite as surprised by my parents' plans for my future. The only problem was that I had never—at least not until that exact moment—considered my parents to be such staunch traditionalists. They had grown up in India and were both practicing Muslims, but despite being religiously conservative, they had made great efforts to assimilate to American culture when they immigrated almost thirty years ago.

For as long as I could remember, my mother wore high

heels, watched *Wheel of Fortune*, and prided herself on her "international" cuisine. My father was a Dodgers fan. For all I knew, I was American. At least as American as a Starbucks chai tea latte. They had even agreed to let me go away for college and did a commendable job of pretending they didn't know about all the Chad Edelsteins and the non-Camry-driving dates over the years. I could only assume they were kidding with this proposition . . . at first. But as soon as I saw my mother pull out a carefully organized portfolio of "bio-datas"—a collection of résumés containing the names, birth dates, family histories, and professions of all the South Asian Muslim potential grooms residing in the greater Los Angeles area—during dessert, I suddenly realized that this was no joke.

"How did you get all of these?" I asked incredulously as I watched my mother unclasp a one-inch stack of "applications" from the black portfolio.

"Oh, never mind all that," she said, shrugging off my question. "Now that you are twenty-six, *beti*, it is time to think of our future." She took a seat next to me at the table. "Remember, Leila, marriage is half your *deen*."

I cringed. This was not the first time I had heard this saying. All Muslims grew up hearing some version of this: "Marriage is half your religion" or "Marriage will complete you" or "Your life doesn't truly begin until you get married." With each year that passed, these phrases were tossed around more frequently; often being used as a guilt tactic by Muslim parents to remind their children of their priorities.

"Here are just a few *rishtas* we thought might be good matches for you." My mother pointed to a bulleted list with each name highlighted in one of three colors—most likely organized in order of compatibility. The sheer excitement in her voice matched the degree of dread steadily rising inside of me.

"Leila, you remember the Dhakkars, right? Well," she continued before I even had a chance to respond, "one of their close family friends, the Rehmans, have a son who is around your age. Can you believe that?" she squealed, as if this were the most exciting news since the inception of JadooTV. "He is just finishing his last year of residency at County General, and your father and I were thinking of inviting them for dinner." I instantly knew where this was headed, and I did not like it one bit. "What do you say, Leila?"

As she eagerly searched my face for a response, I turned to my father in hopes that his innate sensibility would kick in at this precise moment and work to my advantage. "*Abba*," I said. "Please tell me you're not trying to set me up on a blind date?"

"Of course not, *beti*," he said calmly. I let out a deep sigh of relief. "We would never force you to do a blind date. Come look, see here is a picture of him." He removed a page from the stack and pointed to a two-by-three head shot stapled to the bottom.

I knew then it was time to make my exit. I quickly excused myself as my mother continued to pull out other options from the portfolio whom I could choose from "if the Rehmans' son is not your type." As I walked to my room—in utter confusion and disbelief at what had just occurred—I could not help but think that my parents had absolutely lost their minds. Yes, I had heard them engage in conversations over the years with other aunties and uncles in the community who had arranged marriages for their children, but never before had they brought up the topic with me. I had just assumed they considered the practice to be outdated.

And while it was true that my own belief in love had somewhat fluctuated over the years, there was still no way I could bring myself to abandon my long-held fantasies of a Bollywood love story and agree to an arranged marriage. Besides, I was perfectly content being single for the time being. Was there still a part of me that shared their hopes of my one day being married? Sure, but I needed to go through the process in a way that didn't involve my parents or their ridiculous color-coded portfolio. Whether I would ever experience love or not, who knew? But the mere possibility of it was enough to convince me to reject my parents' offer. And once I came to this conclusion, I knew that there was nothing they could say or do to make me change my mind.

Never Say Never

The weeks following my decision were trying ones, to say the least. My parents—particularly my mother—did not take my refusal well, and she made certain I felt the gravity of her disappointment.

"*Ammi*, can you pass the sugar?" I asked at breakfast one morning, pouring myself a cup of chai.

My mother pushed the sugar jar in my direction, her eyes refusing to meet mine.

"The eggs are extra creamy today," I raved, taking a generous bite. It was a cheap move, but I knew how much she enjoyed compliments.

Silence.

My father cleared his throat, darting discomfited glances from my mother to me. "Yes, *jaan*, the eggs are very tasty."

"Thank you." My mother turned to him, smiling sweetly. "It's nice to know *someone* appreciates what I do."

"I believe I'm the one who said they were creamy," I said, lifting my hand.

My mother rolled her eyes and scooped more eggs onto my father's plate.

"I was thinking I might go out tonight with a friend. Would that be okay?"

More silence.

I looked over at my father. He gave me a helpless shrug.

"So you're just not going to talk to me?" I eventually blurted. My mother looked at me, her mouth slightly agape.

"*Jaan*," she finally said, her voice slow yet firm. "Would you please tell your daughter that if she has not reconsidered our offer, then I have nothing to say?"

This time, I rolled my eyes. My mother could try to guilt me as much as she wanted; my mind had been made up. I had no intentions of reconsidering. In fact, I felt quite confident with my decision . . . or so I thought.

I tried to ignore my mother's silence, but less than a month in, I suddenly started seeing signs of love and marriage everywhere. Whether it was a HAPPINESS IS MARRIAGE bumper sticker, a two-for-one couples discount at the local diner, or the obnoxiously incessant "Love Your Spouse" challenges on my social media feed, it was as if my mother had convinced the universe to conspire against me. Like they had combined powers and joined together to put *nazr* on my new independent self. How could I fight against two such powerful forces?

And if that alone wasn't bad enough, when an acne-riddled sixteen-year-old accidentally addressed me as "Mrs." in the school cafeteria, I finally decided to concede to my fate.

"I'll do it," I said to my mother at breakfast the following morning.

She dipped a piece of cake rusk into her teacup and remained silent.

"*Ammi*, I'll let you arrange my marriage." As soon as the last of these words left my mouth, I knew there was no turning back. If someone had happened to walk into our kitchen at that exact moment, they probably would have thought my mother had just won the California Lottery from the look on her face. Her eyes were sparkling, and she was grinning from ear to ear like a deranged maniac. It was practically the same expression she had every time there was a "buy one, get one free" sale on basmati rice at the Indian grocery.

"Oh, Leila!" she shrieked excitedly as she leaned over the table to give me a hug. "You have made your mother so very happy," she said, pressing me into her neck.

"Okay, *okay*," I said, trying to pry her body off my face.

"All right." She clasped her hands together. "First things first. We must create your bio-data."

I groaned.

"Leila!" she exclaimed. "What do you expect me to send when people ask for your information?"

"I don't know. Can't you just tell them to do a Google

stalk—I mean, search—like everyone else?" My mother shot me an unamused look. "Besides," I grumbled, "haven't you already collected a whole stack of applications in your portfolio thingy?"

"No, no, no." She shook her head back and forth. "Those were just some sent to me here and there. But we must now do this the proper way." She looked at me, her eyes gleaming with anticipation.

The thought of my bio-data making its rounds through the Muslimverse made me slightly queasy. I could already imagine the sea of judgmental aunties, their writhing tentacles picking apart every single detail from my weight to my skin color to my career choices. My stomach seething, I opened my mouth to take it all back, but the words didn't dare escape my tongue. After weeks of the silent treatment, my irrational desires to please my mother clouded my better judgment. It was the curse of the Indian daughter. How could I have the heart to take away her excitement now? I sank into my chair. "Fine. Why don't I just email you my résumé? Better yet, I'll send you my CV."

"Great!" my mother exclaimed, completely unfazed by my lack of enthusiasm. As she got up to finish cooking breakfast, I debated whether I was doing the right thing by handing so much power to my mother, of all people. Since it was too soon to tell, I quelled my doubts by reassuring myself that if all else failed, it might at least buy me some time to discover love on my own while my parents scoured the western region for a husband for me. Just because I had agreed to an arrangement didn't mean I actually had to go through with it. I could just give them the illusion of power; give them some time to live out their lifelong dreams of doing the one thing they were explicitly born to do—control my life—while I continued a separate search for my own Bollywood romance. I tried to convince myself that this would be a win-win situation, but as I watched my mother cheerily chopping onions for my Spanish omelet with that maniacal grin on her face, I couldn't help but wonder if the only deranged person in that kitchen was me.

* * *

"So we hear you are in your final year of residency at County General. How do you like it?" my mother asked as she spooned an extra-generous serving of vegetable pilaf onto Anwar's plate.

My mother had been slaving away all afternoon preparing the menu for tonight's dinner. Given the immaculate array of fancy copperware filled with vegetarian and non-veg curries, spiced lentils, aromatic saffron rice, soft oven-baked flatbreads, a side of cucumber yogurt, and a variety of pickles and vegetables, the dining table looked as if it were set for the prime minister of India himself. My parents were dressed in their traditional best on either side of me, while I was conveniently seated directly across the table from my potential husband. Next to him were his parents, the Rehmans, along with Mr. and Mrs. Dhakkar, longtime acquaintances of my parents who were the ones responsible for this awkward matchmaking. While I carefully nudged a neat pile of pilaf from one side of my plate to the other, I wondered if I was the only one who thought it was strange to be on a first date with my parents and four of their friends.

I pondered the incommodiousness of my situation during Anwar's monotonous description of the "fascinating" ins and outs of being a chief medical resident at the sixth-largest hospital in the state. As the sound of his voice gradually faded into a dull drone, I found myself carefully examining his physical features—in between lowered gazes, of course. His dark eyes were deeply set behind thick square-rimmed glasses, and framed beneath broad, unkempt eyebrows. His wide, rectangular forehead was starkly accentuated by the horizontal sweep of his wavy black hair. I noticed his long hooked nose, tanned skin, narrow lips, and receding chin —*A clear indication of a nonassertive personality*, I thought. Although he was not entirely *un*attractive, his stiff demeanor visibly lacked the natural charisma to which I was typically drawn. As I watched him nervously adjust the starched collar of his peach-colored button-down shirt, I mentally crossed *#46: SEXY* off my list.

I must have gotten lost in my thoughts because the next

thing I knew, my mother was clearing the table while my father was carrying in a large platter of creamy rice pudding topped with golden raisins and chopped pistachios and almonds. I leaned over to pour myself a bowl of *kheer*—my all-time favorite dessert—thinking that this evening might have a silver lining after all. That is, until my father tapped me on the arm and said, "Leila, *beti*, why don't you take Anwar into your room so you two can chat for a bit."

I stared with my mouth open. This was the same man who had refused to let me date, attend school dances, or receive phone calls from all members of the opposite gender until the age of eighteen; my ears were having a difficult time processing the words that were actually being spoken. The only explanation for why my father would *ever* ask his only daughter to escort a man—whom she had just met only two hours earlier—into the privacy of her bedroom so they could "chat" was that my mother's absurd logic had finally rubbed off on him. I remembered countless teenage arguments with my mother over why it was *haram* to wear tank tops during the uncomfortably hot west coast summers, yet entirely *halal* to attend public cultural functions in form-fitting saris that exposed my entire midriff through the thin chiffon fabrics. And though I had grown accustomed to her irrational ways over the years, my father had always been the one person I could rely on to keep things sane. Until now.

I reluctantly led Anwar down the hallway toward my

lavender-walled bedroom. Before stepping inside, he politely excused himself so he could wash up. The hallway bathroom was situated directly across from my bedroom, and I noticed that he left the bathroom door slightly ajar. My curiosity quickly got the better of me, and I found myself watching as he meticulously rolled up each sleeve of his button-down and slowly yet thoroughly rubbed water over his arms all the way to the elbows. Then he grabbed the soap and carefully scrubbed each forearm in a circular motion before rinsing off the lather. It was almost as if he was getting ready to prep me for surgery. I shuddered at the thought. I was pretty sure that *OBSESSIVE* and *COMPULSIVE* were two qualities I had *not* mentioned on my list; however, I did not have much time to reflect on these thoughts because before I knew it, Anwar was making his way directly across the hall and into my room.

He walked around my bedroom silently, studying the various objects that were scattered across the floor and shelves—piles and piles of books, a stack of essays that had yet to be graded, old high school yearbooks, trophies from various tennis matches and the spelling bee I won in the fourth grade, and a wide assortment of picture frames highlighting special memories such as the spring break I spent in Cancún with my college roommates five years ago. When he finally finished his thorough examination of the contents of my room, he slowly made his way to the edge of my bed and sat down next to me.

We both stared uncomfortably at the purple wall in front of us, the slow ticking of the wall clock becoming louder with each passing second. I started to think about what my parents could have found appealing about him. I mean, it was true that on paper, he was exactly the kind of guy *they* would want me to be with—a star student who had gotten into medical school; came from a respectable family; and, most importantly, did everything his parents expected—including agreeing to participate in this old-fashioned matrimonial process. However, it seemed highly unlikely that Anwar had dated many girls in the past. My parents probably saw his lack of experience as a sign of decent values and traditions, but I saw it as yet another cultural flaw. As awkward as he was, I couldn't really blame him. Until I moved away for college, the only conversations I was allowed to have with boys involved homework or smack talk on the tennis courts. It was no wonder that most South Asian men and women were far more stunted when it came to social interactions of these kinds. We were taught our whole lives to avoid any specimen of the opposite sex like the plague; yet the instant we reached a "marriageable" age, we were suddenly expected to skip the whole dating process and go directly into lifelong commitment. It was probably unreasonable of me to expect Anwar to know how to "woo" a woman when the only girls he had probably ever talked to were ones he was related to.

If this conversation was going to go anywhere, I had to figure out a way to get the ball rolling. So when the silence finally became unbearable, I turned to Anwar and asked him what kinds of things he did for fun. He looked at me and furrowed his bushy eyebrows, which up close seemed to be magnified behind the thick lenses of his glasses. I could tell by his expression that I had already lost him at the word *fun*. "Let me rephrase," I said, trying not to let my discomfort show. "What do you do when you're *not* working?"

"Well," he began in that same monotonous tone, "the life of a medical resident is quite intense. When I'm not at work, the majority of my time is spent studying and reviewing terms and procedures, filling out paperwork, and catching up on my beauty sleep." He chuckled and pushed back his glasses. I smiled politely and mentally crossed *#4: SENSE OF HUMOR* off the list. It was becoming apparent that the qualities my parents found appealing in Anwar didn't share the same order of importance as the ones on my list. While most American women, like myself, considered a sense of humor to be an important aspect of determining compatibility, South Asian parents felt this trait was far less significant in comparison to a groom's profession or height.

"I also enjoy watching medical dramas," Anwar continued.

"Medical dramas?"

"Yes, like *Grey's Anatomy*, *ER*, and *Scrubs*."

I looked at him quizzically. "So even your hobbies are somehow related to work," I stated rather than asked.

He grinned. "I mean, I'm sure you're the same. Aren't you thinking about your students all the time?"

I thought for a moment. Typically, when that two thirty bell rang, I jetted out of my classroom at full speed—sometimes even knocking over a student or two in the process. I liked my job an acceptable amount, but once the school day ended, work was the last thing on my mind.

"Well, I wouldn't say all the time," I finally said. I found it odd that Anwar was so obsessed, for lack of a better word, with his job. He seemed so sheltered. Completely caught up in his own little bubble. I wondered if he even had room in his life for anything other than work.

"Hmm" was all he said as he rested his index finger against his chin and frowned. The silence indicated that he was just as confused by my response as I was by his.

After a few more awkward, uncomfortable minutes, I remembered that it was my job to carry the dreadful conversation, so I said, "Surely you must have some questions for me?"

"Yes, of course," he replied hesitantly. "I've actually been quite curious about your family history."

"Oh, really?" I said, surprised. I was expecting that he

might be more curious to learn about *me* before delving into my family; however, I figured it was at least a good sign that he was showing some interest in something other than his profession.

"So, let's see. I'm an only child," I began, "however, I do have a *ton* of cousins and relatives . . . well, you're Indian, so I'm sure you can relate . . ."

"Actually," he interrupted, "I meant more like your family *medical* history."

"Huh?"

"Are there any medical problems in your family? Like cancer, heart disease, high blood pressure, chronic flatulence?"

"Um," I replied, trying to ignore the fact that he'd just mentioned flatulence in my presence. "I suppose none of the above. Although I do have an uncle on my dad's side who is known to spit excessively when he talks. I don't know if that's considered a medical problem, but he should definitely get that checked out."

"I see," he said, clearly not amused by my lack of seriousness. "So what about you? Do you have any allergies or conditions?"

"Conditions? Oh God, not that I know of. Why, what did you hear?" I asked, feigning concern. While I suffered from bouts of intermittent asthma, I figured it was in my best interest to withhold any information that might cause Anwar alarm.

"Nothing. Well, what about your habits? Do you smoke,

drink, or partake in any . . . uh, how shall I phrase this . . . recreational drugs?" he asked, shooting a quick glance toward my spring break photo collage. Although I was not as religiously conservative as my parents, I did manage to steer clear of cigarettes and alcohol. The cigarettes were primarily due to my mild asthmatic symptoms, and the alcohol owed to a single incident back in college when I accidentally downed two bottles of Mike's hard lemonade during a barbecue and ended up vomiting for thirty-six consecutive hours. If that was my punishment for going against the religious teachings imparted on me in Sunday school, then it worked, because any desire I once had to drink instantly disappeared after that weekend. In terms of recreational drugs, aside from the snorts of Flonase I was known to inhale every now and then, most of my activities were pretty *halal*.

"No." I rolled my eyes, not willing to provide any further explanation. This was definitely not going in the direction I had expected. At this rate, it would only be a matter of time before Anwar asked me about my next menstrual cycle. If there was ever a place for an out, this was it.

"Maybe we should make our way back to the living room," I suggested as graciously as I could.

"Oh, but I still have a few more questions for you," Anwar replied eagerly.

"As much fun as I've had with this brief consultation, I think that's about all the questions my insurance covers." I smiled. "Besides, I think the other six members of our date might be waiting for us," I added, feeling a sense of relief as I finally saw him get up. I shut the bedroom door behind us, and we made our way down the hall. I couldn't help but think that if this was the caliber of potential grooms available, then this process was definitely going to be a lot more painful than I had predicted. What had I gotten myself into?

* * *

"Well, that was a very nice evening," my father said. The three of us were standing on the doorstep waving goodbye to our guests as they backed out of the driveway. My cheeks were starting to numb, and I wondered how much longer I would have to keep the fake smile plastered across my face.

"Yes, it could not have gone any better." My mother beamed as the glare from the headlights turned onto the road. We shut the door behind us, and I stealthily backed out of the room while my parents continued gushing about what a wonderful night it had been. Just as I was about to reach the hallway, my mother's voice called after me.

"Leila, *beti*, can you help me with the dishes?"

I groaned. *So close.*

"Coming," I said, dragging my feet into the kitchen.

"So, how did it go with Anwar?" my mother finally asked.

"Okay," I said, stacking the dirty plates in the sink.

"Just *okay*?" My mother turned to me. "You two were talking for a very long time."

"He was asking me if you guys were chronic tooters."

"Tutors?" She scrunched her face. "Did you tell him about the after-school tutoring you started for your students? He will be very impressed to learn that!" She bobbled her head.

"No, *Ammi*, that's not what I meant," I said, annoyed. "Never mind."

"Don't worry if you didn't get a chance to say everything, Leila. We will see the Rehmans again next weekend, *insha'Allah*. You can mention the tutoring to him then."

"What?" I turned to her, my soapy hands dripping onto the floor. "What do you mean we're seeing them next weekend?"

"Mona aunty invited us for dinner. *Beti*, we cannot say no," she said, pouring the leftover curries into clear Tupperware containers. "I think you should wear your light pink *salwar kameez*. And go a little easy with the eyeliner next time." She pointed to my face. "How can we see your eyes with all this black stuff?"

I sighed. "If they invited you, why do *I* have to go?"

"Because Anwar will be there!" she exclaimed. "Leila, what is the problem?"

"I'm not interested in him," I stated flatly.

"Not interested?" my mother repeated, her voice surging. "Leila, he is smart. He is good-looking. *And* he is a *doctor*. Really, what is the problem?"

I shrugged, feeling irked by her debriefing. She couldn't possibly have thought Anwar was the one for me. This was only a first date, and she was already planning the wedding.

"He's a nice guy, but we just didn't connect," I said.

"Connect? What is this, a Wi-Fi signal?" My mother glared at me.

"*Ammi*, didn't you say if I didn't like someone, I would have other options?" I asked. "You've only introduced me to one prospect, and you're already putting all this pressure on me."

"No pressure, Leila." My mother held up her hands. "But he is really a very good boy—"

"I know, *Ammi*."

"Even his parents are both very nice—"

"Yes, I know."

"And you're now saying you're not feeling the same—"

"I don't know, *Ammi*."

"I mean, it makes no sense, Leila! How can you not like—"

"I just don't," I snapped.

My mother and I stared at each other, the tension mounting above the silence. Neither of us spoke a word.

"Can we move on?" I finally asked.

"Fine," my mother said quietly, placing the Tupperware in the fridge. "I will let them know."

"Thank you," I said, breathing a sigh of relief. But when I turned to offer her a smile, she was already gone.

The Marriage Clock

If my mother was disappointed by my decision about Anwar, she didn't show it. Instead, she kicked her matchmaking duties into overdrive and made sure to give me every "option" she could find. The next few weeks could only be described as a classic Bollywood flop. Each morning, I awakened to a freshly printed stack of bio-datas on my nightstand with certain phrases like *cardiovascular surgeon*, *computer engineer*, and *close to his family* highlighted. Other times, I would just receive a random text message with a guy's picture and the words *Harvard educated* below it. How my mother managed to acquire so many prospects, I had no idea. It was as if she was a card-carrying member of an elite, underground *rishta* network comprising middle-aged suburban aunties with a lot of time on their hands. Needless to say, I quickly realized that it worked in my favor to not question the process.

Meal conversations were spent with my parents quizzing

and grilling me on the information listed in the bio-datas in attempts to determine PGC—potential groom compatibility.

"Did you see what was listed under hobbies, Leila?"

"No, *Abba*, I didn't."

"It says that he played tennis in high school."

"Cool."

"You also played tennis, Leila. Remember?"

"Yes, *Ammi*. How could I forget?"

"And he also enjoys watching movies, just like you!"

"I'm pretty sure everyone enjoys watching movies, *Ammi*. That's like saying you like french fries."

"No, Leila, it is very rare to have *so* many things in common. What do you think, *jaan*?"

"I think he sounds perfect."

"Yes, I agree. What do you think, Leila?"

These discussions would typically end with my parents staring at me eagerly until I finally gave them a response. If I showed the slightest bit of interest, they would jump on the phone to schedule a meeting. If I voiced any concerns, though—even if they were valid—they would be quickly dismissed as "unimportant" and replaced with solutions.

"So what if he is a little overweight, Leila? He can always get a gym membership."

"But what about the fact that he hates animals?"

"It's okay, you can get a bird."

"And why does he only wear clothes in different shades of brown?"

"*Ya Allah!* He went to Yale, Leila! Stop being so picky!"

I swallowed it all, surrendering to the fact that my weekends now consisted of a steady stream of awkward dinners followed by parental interrogations. My mother had developed quite a knack for selecting the dullest men in the South Asian Muslim community. And while I tried to remain optimistic, after my last date with a computer programmer who sounded strangely like Apu from *The Simpsons* despite growing up in West Covina, I finally decided, for the sake of my sanity, that it was time to take matters into my own hands.

"What do you mean you don't want us to find any more *rishtas* for you?" cried my mother when I broke the news to her. "How else will you find a husband?" She clutched one hand to her heart and waved the other in the air. "*Ya Allah!* What will we do with a twenty-six-year-old unwed daughter? This is my life's curse!"

I sighed and prepared myself for the drama I had known would inevitably follow the announcement of my decision.

"Look, *Ammi*. I met more than my share of potential grooms from your portfolio these last few weeks, but I'm going to need extensive therapy if I have to sit through any more of those horrible dinners."

My mother shot a look of confusion across the table at

my father. "Horrible *dinners*?" My father shrugged, his face mirroring the same uncertainty as my mother's. "I thought the dinners all went exceptionally well, no?"

"I agree, *jaan,* they went very well." He nodded in agreement. "In fact, the *kheer* was especially delicious last night with the Khans."

"Oh, really, you thought so?" My mother switched off her hysteria as swiftly as she'd switched it on, suddenly beaming with pride. There was nothing she loved more than a food-related compliment. "You know, I added some condensed milk in there for a little extra sweetness," she stated proudly, wobbling her head.

What is happening right now? I thought as I watched my parents discuss their mutual affinity for condensed milk. The only thing I could even remember about last night's dinner was the enormously long, wiry black hair protruding from my potential groom's fleshy left nostril—never mind the dessert. Now, if they had wanted to have a conversation about *that* monstrosity, I would have been on board, but, the last thing I wanted to do was discuss cooking techniques. "Are you even listening to me?" I finally interrupted with an exasperated sigh. "I'm talking about needing therapy and all you guys can talk about is the *kheer*?"

"Leila, *beti*, we are not 'guys,' we are your parents. Do not use this term with us," my father said with impatience. "And tell us now, what exactly is *your* plan for finding a good boy, who fits all our requirements, without our help?"

"I don't know, *Abba*. But maybe we could spend some time reevaluating how well your requirements match with mine to reach some sort of . . . compromise." I stumbled over the final syllables as they hastily left my mouth. My parents stared at me with doubt etched across their faces. A reevaluation of any kind was definitely out of the question.

Who am I kidding? I thought miserably. My requirements, my wants, my tastes meant nothing to my parents. All this time, they simply pretended they didn't know about my dating history because it was far easier than having to admit that I could actually have preferences of my own. Maybe I hadn't found what I was looking for yet, but I had gone out with enough guys—*desi* and non-*desi*—to at least know what I *didn't* want. If they would only be willing to hear my opinions, this process could go so much smoother. But as far as they were concerned, they already knew what was best for me and my future. I was just interfering. As frustrating as it was, I knew I had to play this smarter if I was going to convince them to let me do this on my own. I had to hit them with an angle they didn't expect.

"What if you just gave me a little bit of time to find someone on my own? And in return"—I rushed through without giving them a chance to interrupt—"I give you my word that I will find someone who you *both* approve of. I mean, based on all the *promising* prospects you've already found, how hard can it be, right?" I said, flashing them my most convincing smile.

"It is very hard, Leila! Don't you understand, *beti*, you are already *twenty-six*!" my mother cried, hysterical once more. I rolled my eyes at the emphasis placed on the *twenty* and the *six*. Any time age was referred to in an Indian household, it was a reminder that the marriage clock was ticking. The fact that my age had already been announced twice in a span of five minutes suggested that mine was not only ticking but was on the verge of falling off the wall. While twenty-six was still considered young in American years, in South Asian years, I was almost past my expiration date. Fortunately for me, my mother never hesitated to point this out.

"I've only been twenty-six for a couple months, *Ammi*. It's not that big a—"

"But tomorrow, you will be thirty!"

"That's not how aging works, *Ammi*."

"And what will we do when that day comes? Who's going to marry you after thirty? Have you thought about that? *Ya Allah!*" my mother wailed as she placed her palm over her forehead for extra effect. "We have waited too long!" She turned to my father despairingly. "We are going to be old and without grandchildren! Our noses will be cut!"

"*Arey, arey*," my father interjected, reaching across the

table and taking my mother's hand. "Leila, your *ammi* is right. Your time is short. If we don't act quickly, this will not end well." My mother let out another wail.

I tried to appear sympathetic, but I couldn't understand why they were being so dramatic. I had *just* turned twenty-six. And mentally, I felt even younger. I didn't own a home yet. I had just started my career. Aside from Cancún, I had never traveled outside the country, and my mother still did my laundry—I was barely an adult! I still had my whole life ahead of me, yet my parents were acting as if I had been diagnosed with a terminal illness and given only a few weeks to live. Sure, I was slightly older than more traditional Indian girls in starting the process of finding a husband, but I still had plenty of time. Most Americans in their mid-twenties were still in the "discovery" phase. They were traveling, partying, enjoying the single life. None of my other non-Muslim friends were panicking about dying alone yet. What my parents' generation didn't understand was that it was much more common for people to marry later in life these days. Besides, everyone knew that South Asians didn't raisin, so they had nothing to worry about.

"Listen, Leila," my father continued. "I know you think you can do this alone, but please, *beti*. There is too much at stake. Allow us to help you," he said in a hopeful tone.

"No, *Abba*, wait," I cried. All I wanted was to have some say in my future, but they had managed to turn this into stakes and cut noses. Any hope I once had was now seeping through my fingers like tiny grains of sand, and I could feel a sense of urgency roaring in my gut. I had to do something—*anything*—to regain some control over my life. I took a deep breath and tried to stay calm.

"Just hear me out." I looked at them pleadingly. "I'm just asking for a little time to explore this process on my own and for you both to trust me. That is all. Just a little time."

After a few moments of thought, my mother finally spoke up, her voice shaky and small. "Okay, Leila, we will let you try on your own. But listen carefully, you are at a very crucial point in your life." She wagged her finger at me. "We have already waited too long; we cannot risk any more time. If you do not succeed in finding a suitable boy by our thirtieth anniversary, it is in our hands from there," she said warningly, holding up the dreaded black portfolio. "No more excuses."

I exhaled and nodded quickly, trying not to imagine the awful contents remaining in the folder. I had approximately three months before my parents' anniversary in July, and based on what I had just promised, I knew the odds were already stacked against me. At the most basic level, my parents simply wanted someone who was South Asian and Muslim. A sudden flashback of Chad Edelstein quickly reminded me that I had already come to the same conclusion years ago. We were all in agreement on at least two of their requirements. The rest, I wasn't so sure.

I needed to find not only someone whom they approved of, but someone who also checked off all forty-six items on my list. Sexy with a sense of humor; sensitive yet strong; American-born but also cultured—especially in his love of Bollywood. My exact counterpart. The type of person I could fall in love with. Although three months hardly seemed like a reasonable amount of time to accomplish this feat, I knew that if there was anything I was good at, it was a challenge. And this was one challenge I could not afford to lose.

Set in Motion

"What do you mean you have three months to find a husband?" squealed Hannah as she gawked at me with widened eyes. It was a typical Tuesday night, and my girlfriends and I were hanging out in Liv's apartment eating junk food and watching high-quality reality television—in other words, anything playing on the Bravo network. I had been anxiously waiting all evening, trying to figure out the perfect time to tell them about my newfound predicament, and the best I could come up with was during a *Real Housewives* marathon—right after Ramona Singer downed her fifteenth glass of pinot grigio.

"You can't be serious, Leila. That's not a lot of time." Hannah frowned as she tucked a strand of thick red hair behind her ear. Liv muted the television and shook her head with a worried look on her face.

I sighed heavily. If anyone understood how crazy this sounded, it was me; however, the last thing I needed was for my closest friends to point out how cracked I was for agreeing to go through with it. In fact, I needed them to come to my aid and find some sort of solution to this burden of a problem that I had been carrying around for the last seventy-two hours.

"So, what are you going to do?" asked Liv, her brows knitted together.

I shrugged.

"Maybe an arranged marriage isn't such a bad idea," Hannah offered. "At least you're guaranteed you won't end up alone."

I glanced at Tania, who watched us silently from the armchair. She was one of my few Muslim friends, and although she was more *outwardly* conservative—she wore a hijab—I could already tell that her opinions about my situation were a lot less optimistic than Hannah's. "You know, you're never going to be happy if you just do what your parents say," she finally said bluntly.

Tania's lack of trust stemmed from her own past experiences. Her parents had pressured her to marry a distant cousin back in her homeland of Bangladesh when she was just eighteen years old. They divorced four months later—and the "shame" associated with her choice ultimately caused her parents to sever their relationship with her. Despite being subjected to the "*log kya kahenge*" epidemic that often infested the South Asian Muslim community, Tania remained intent on never falling victim to traditional expectations again. She had moved out of her parents' home, went back to school, and managed to carve out a fairly successful career for herself in public relations. She also made certain to steer clear of all romantic relationships and kept a healthy distance from the clutches of prying aunties. While I was not in the least bit surprised by her sentiment, I also knew that no one could truly understand the mess I was in better than her.

Although my parents weren't by any means suggesting a forced marriage, like Tania's, their idea of an arranged marriage, which "generously" offered both the prospective bride and groom a say in who they would spend the rest of their lives with, was still a scary proposition. Just the image of that awful black portfolio racked my body with a shudder as I tried to shake it away.

"I honestly don't know what I'm going to do." I was sitting upright on the carpet with my back against the couch, knees bent up toward my chest. "That's the reason I need your help," I pleaded, burying my chin into my knees. "At this point, I'm open to any suggestions as long as they're legal and don't involve fleeing the country."

As soon as I gave them the green light, they began brainstorming; however, it was only a matter of minutes before I realized they weren't the greatest of ideas.

"What about the Indian guy who works at the coffee shop across the street?" Hannah said.

"The one with the beard who always wears plaid?" She nodded excitedly. "Okay . . . what about him?" I asked.

"Well, he's kind of cute, right?" Hannah turned to the others, receiving only a minor signal of affirmation from Liv.

I shook my head. "I'm pretty sure he's, like, twelve," I said, rolling my eyes.

"No, he's definitely older. He's got a *beard*," Hannah stated.

"I think you're forgetting that Indian boys start growing facial hair at the ripe age of seven," I said, turning toward Tania, who nodded in agreement. "I'm not really into younger guys. And even if I was, I'm not going to date some random guy from the coffee shop just because he's Indian."

Why did people always assume two people would be compatible just because they shared the same ethnicity? I would never walk up to a friend and say, "Hey, you know Joe? He's Caucasian. And since you're Caucasian, I thought the two of you would be perfect for each other!" That would be ridiculous. Joe would only be considered "perfect" if he and my hypothetical friend shared hobbies or interests, or complementary personalities—none of which were being taken into account with coffee shop dude.

"I agree, it is a bit random, but I don't know. Maybe Hannah is onto something. This might be a good opportunity to push past your comfort zone," Liv suggested. "I mean, you'll never know what possibilities are out there unless you try."

"Thank you, Liv," Hannah piped up excitedly. "I think you should really consider it, Leila. Who cares if he's younger? It's scientific fact that women live longer than men. Which means if you marry someone younger, it'll all balance out in regards to life spans."

"You don't plan a relationship based on who will die first," I exclaimed, dropping my head to my knees. I let out a muffled groan. If this was their idea of helping, I might have been better off on my own. The only problem was, I didn't have anyone else in mind.

"This is crazy," said Tania, quickly jumping to my aid. "We can't just set her up with random coffee shop guy. It has to be someone we know and think will be compatible."

We all sat around thinking. After what seemed like hours but was probably only a few minutes, Hannah jumped to her feet. "I've got it," she said with a huge grin on her face. "I think I know someone."

"Really? Because this can't be like the time you set me up with that ex-felon," Liv said, the sudden memory causing me and Tania to break into giggles.

"He wasn't a felon!" cried Hannah as she sat back down in a huff. "He was charged with a misdemeanor, and I told you, I didn't even know about it until *after* I set you up!"

We could barely contain ourselves at that point, and the three of us burst into laughter as Hannah's smile quickly dissolved into a frown. Although her intentions were always good, it was no secret that Hannah's matchmaking skills were a little rough around the edges. In addition to the ex-felon, she had also managed to set up two other friends who coincidentally turned out to be cousins, and her hairstylist Pam with Liv's brother, not realizing that Pam was actually a lesbian. For years, it was a running joke among our friends, and Hannah's oversensitivity to the subject always gave us even more reason to tease her about it.

"Fine, laugh all you want," Hannah finally said, looking defeated. "But I don't hear any of you coming up with ideas of your own."

"Okay, okay," I said once the laughter subsided and I had pulled myself together. I hated to admit it, but she was right. Since neither Liv nor Tania had any other potential options, I had no choice but to at least entertain Hannah's suggestion, regardless of her previous track record.

"So who is this *someone* that you know?" I finally asked.

"His name is Omar. He's a friend of a friend. We were in undergrad together, although I think he graduated a year before me," she said, the smile on her freckled face slowly reemerging.

"Okay . . . well, what is he like?" I asked, trying to sound interested. I still wasn't sure if I fully trusted Hannah's judgment; however, with this three-month deadline looming over my head like an ominous cloud, I knew I had to consider all my options.

"From what I remember, he's really smart, friendly, and I think he was president of the Muslim Student Association on campus, which means he must be pretty in touch with the culture. That might get you some bonus points with your parents." Hannah grinned.

I thought back to the bearded guys from my alma mater's MSA and winced. Hopefully Omar had stronger social skills than those guys, but it was still a gamble. His MSA background would definitely earn him points with my parents, but I wondered how well this trait would hold up to my list. My idea of "being in touch with the culture" meant having a superhuman tolerance for spicy foods, knowing enough Urdu to have basic conversations and watch Bollywood movies without the subtitles, and making semiregular appearances at the mosque. Anything more than this might be too much. Anything less might not be cultured enough—as was the case with the non-*desis* in the past.

My phone suddenly buzzed. I looked at the screen to see a text from my mother. When I clicked on it, an image of a man with wide-rimmed frames, a shaved head, and a red polo shirt outlining his rounded gut popped up. Below it, she had typed PHD. I clicked the screen off.

"Everything okay?" Hannah asked, her face eagerly awaiting a response.

Maybe the guy she had in mind wouldn't turn out to be so bad. I figured as long as he didn't turn out to be a felon . . .

or one of my cousins . . . or a lesbian, there might actually be a chance.

"Okay," I said haltingly. "I guess I'll do it."

"Great!" Hannah jumped up excitedly. "Don't worry, Leila." She grabbed me by the arms and gave me a tight hug. "I'll set everything up; all you have to do is show up."

The clock ticking away, I returned Hannah's excitement with an apprehensive smile and silently prayed that by some divine miracle, my friend, just this once, would somehow turn out to be a better matchmaker than my parents.

Mr. Bollywood

What am I doing? What am I doing? What am I doing? I repeated to myself nervously as I tapped the heel of my navy blue stiletto against the table leg and stared at the gold-embossed vintage clock hanging on the wall directly behind my table. My stomach felt woozy, like I had just stepped off the Tilt-A-Whirl, and I tried my best to calm my nerves. Hannah had stayed true to her word and set up the entire date.

Three o'clock sharp, and don't be late, Leila! she had texted right below the address of the location last night. Although I had gotten to the bistro a little early, I couldn't help but wonder when Omar would arrive. Muslims were notorious for being late—we had even coined the term "Muslim Standard Time" to jokingly refer to our issues with punctuality. Despite this cultural malfunction, I always made the extra effort to dispel this stereotype and couldn't help but silently judge those who didn't do the same. I glanced at the clock once more, watching the minutes tick by. The anticipation was beginning to do a number on my nerves, and anyone who knew me was aware that patience was definitely *not* one of my strongest qualities.

As I sat there, restless, a torrent of questions flooded my mind: *What is he like? Will he like me? Will I like him? Is he cute?* Regardless of all the impressive things Hannah had told me about Omar over the past week, I had never actually had a direct conversation with him. Everything I knew about him came from a secondary source, so although I was hopeful, I tried not to have any expectations. I'd learned in the past few weeks there was no worse feeling than that of disappointment; it was far better to be pleasantly surprised than utterly disillusioned. However, as I watched the small hand pass the fifteen-minute mark on the clock, I couldn't help but think that Omar wasn't making the best first impression by being late to our first date. My hopes of him not running on MST were already dashed.

My thoughts were suddenly interrupted when the doors of the small restaurant opened and a tall, muscular, caramel-complexioned man came striding through. It had to be Omar. I held my breath for a second as I watched him quickly scan the restaurant; his eyes stopped squarely in my direction. He precisely lowered his shades with his right index finger, gave me a slight smile, and strutted toward the table. He was wearing a slim-fitting, white, collared shirt that was unbuttoned down to the middle of his chest, tight-fitted gray slacks, and shiny Italian-leather loafers. His outfit was complete with a gaudy Armani belt and gold-framed aviator sunglasses—which I noticed he still had not taken off.

"Greetings, I'm Omar," he said in a deep, commanding voice as he held out his hand. As we awkwardly shook hands, a glint of bright yellow from his thick gold chain-link bracelet nearly blinded me.

"So sorry I'm late. I got a little lost," he said as he sat down on the stool across from me. "This is not my usual neighborhood." He flashed me a movie-star smile, and I couldn't help but notice that he might have gone a bit overboard with the Crest Whitestrips. I tried my best not to be distracted by how out of place he looked in the midst of the quaint bistro. He wasn't kidding about being in the wrong neighborhood. Nearly everyone around us was dressed in casual spring attire. I was wearing indigo skinny jeans, a white boho blouse, and a floral-printed scarf. After nearly an hour of going through every item in my closet to find the perfect outfit that screamed *sexy without trying too hard*, I was now seated across from this glossy, gelled-up man who looked like he had just taken a detour from the fist-pumping electronic beats at Fuego De Vida.

After we ordered some refreshments—an iced green tea for me, a cup of coffee, straight black for him—Omar finally removed his shades. "It's cozy in here," he said, looking around. "This is a nice place for us to talk and get to know each other." He hit me with another one of his blinding smiles, and I actually contemplated reaching over for his sunglasses for a split second.

"Well, I guess we have Hannah to thank for picking out a good spot. She's convinced she has a future in this matchmaking business," I joked.

Omar laughed. "So how long have you and Hannah been friends?" he asked.

"I've known her for about four years now. We met at a mutual friend's dinner party a few weeks after I moved back to L.A. We dominated the night when we were teamed up for a game of charades, and we've been friends ever since." I smiled. "You guys met in college, right?"

"Yeah, we sat next to each other in a business writing class that we had together during my second year of undergrad. I tried to flirt with her, but she was having none of it. I think I must have been a contributing factor to her changing majors."

I laughed. "Well, she at least thinks you're a pretty good catch, otherwise she wouldn't have been so adamant about setting us up."

"Well, I'm glad she was." His centerfold smile flashed across his face. "But enough about Hannah. I'm more interested to know what *you* think about me." He leaned across the table, and I had to hold my breath for a second as the thick, leathery scent of his cologne overwhelmed my nostrils.

"Um, I'm not quite sure," I said as I slowly leaned back. "I don't think I know you well enough yet, but why don't you tell me a little more about yourself?" I asked, steering the conversation back to him.

"Well, most people who know me would describe me as a very confident person," he began, taking a sip of his coffee. "I believe it's important to carry yourself in the way you want to be seen by others."

I nodded. "So how is it that you want to be seen?" I asked.

"I want to be seen as a man willing to take risks. A man unafraid to pursue his dreams. That is the way I've lived my whole life . . . I'm sure Hannah has told you all about my many accomplishments."

"She mentioned some, but I'm sure you would *love* to tell me about the rest of them." I pursed my lips.

"I go after what I want, Leila," he continued without missing a beat, completely mesmerized by the sound of his own voice. "When I want something, I work hard to get it. For example, when I wanted to start a Muslim Student Association on campus, I pursued it and *BAM*, I made it happen. And then I wanted to be president of the organization, so I campaigned and *BAM*, I got elected. We started with only a few members and by the time I graduated, *BAM*, we had over a hundred. I mean, a lot of people would not be able to accomplish these things, Leila, but I'm a go-getter. *BAM, BAM, BAM*, I get things done," he said, slapping his palms on the table.

With every *BAM*, I jumped slightly in my chair. For someone claiming to be a go-getter, I really wished he would "go get" a new catchphrase. Normally, at this point, I would've been rushing toward the nearest exit. But there must have been *something* Hannah saw in him that made her think we would be good for each other. If anything, I told myself, I should be impressed by Omar's ambition.

It reminded me of my father, who was the OG when it came to ambition. Every birthday, or family gathering, or Tuesday afternoon when he'd pick me up from school, he would tell me the story of how he came to America with sixty dollars in his pocket and a dream. I knew every detail of his story—how he stocked boxes in the back room of Mervyn's and took engineering classes at night until he saved enough to buy a house in the suburbs. My father worked harder than anyone I knew, and my admiration for this quality in him was the reason *#29: AMBITIOUS* was on my list. I felt like I owed it to both Hannah and my father to see this thing out.

"So I gather your college years were quite successful," I interjected, trying not to get clobbered by his heightened sense of self-confidence. "But what are some things you've been doing since graduating?"

"I'm currently a top agent at my father's real estate firm. However"—he leaned in again—"my true passion is music."

"Oh. What kind of music?" I asked, preparing myself for his response. I quickly ran through all the possibilities in my head—hip-hop, hard-core rap, straight-up country, even traditional mariachi—just so I wouldn't be caught off guard again.

"Do you watch Bollywood movies?" he finally asked.

"Yes . . ." I said slowly, my heart gently fluttering.

"Well," he continued—I suddenly noticed a sparkle in his eyes—"my ultimate dream is to become a Bollywood playback singer."

I had to give it to him: that was one possibility that had not even crossed my mind. I was intrigued. What if this was the Bollywood fantasy I had been dreaming of my whole life? I never thought it would happen, *literally*, but I was suddenly pleased with my earlier decision to stick this date out. It would have been a shame if I had let a little gel and ostentation stand in the way of my Indian fairy tale. He was South Asian and Muslim (*check*). He had decent hair (*check*). He had a passion for cheesy love songs (*check*). The only thing missing was a meadow to run through leading us to our happily ever after.

"You're kidding?" I said, taking in a deep breath. I had to remind myself not to get too excited yet. "What got you into that?"

"Well, I grew up listening to old Bollywood soundtracks. Mohammed Rafi, Lata Mangeshkar, Mukesh, that kind of stuff. Both my parents were real enthusiasts. And the older I got, the more aware I became that my own singing voice was up to par with—if not better than—most of the great singers out there."

I took a sip of my tea and smiled pleasantly.

"So," he continued, "I eventually realized that it was my responsibility to share this God-given talent with my people." He pointed his finger toward me and winked.

"Wow. That's so . . . generous of you," I replied, ignoring his pretentiousness. "I haven't met many guys who are into Bollywood music, so that's cool. It sounds like a really unique hobby."

"Hobby?" He chortled. "Dear Leila. It's not a hobby. It's a way of life." He spoke in such a serious tone that I had to cover my mouth to hold in the giggles. "Would you like to hear some of my work?"

"Um, sure . . . Right now?" Before I had my answer, he had already pulled out his cell phone and a set of earbuds from his back pocket. "Oh, do you have some of your tracks recorded on there?" I asked, watching his perfectly manicured fingers skimming through his playlist, his pinkie raised.

"Here, put this on," he said. He seemed pretty psyched as he placed one of the earbuds in his right ear and handed me the other.

I hesitantly stuck it in my ear; the familiar percussive beats mixed with a medley of strings and high-pitched instruments came blasting through the speaker. It took me a few moments to realize that it was the instrumental version of the classic love song "*Dil To Pagal Hai*" which loosely translates to "My Heart Is Crazy (For You)." I glanced over to find Omar with his right hand over the earbud, eyes closed, his head gently swaying to the rhythmic sound of the music. The scent of his cologne too close for comfort, I turned and coughed. I looked around the bistro. Was anyone else noticing how incredibly awkward this date had just become?

Impatient for this moment to be over, I reached out, gently tapping Omar's left hand, and asked him if his vocals would soon begin. He didn't reply. Just as I was about to shake him out of the trance he was in, he suddenly opened his eyes, grabbed my hand, and started belting out the opening verse of the song—in Hindi.

I know I'd agreed to hear his work, but never in my wildest dreams did I think that meant I would be forced to sit through a live show in the middle of a semipacked bistro. Without the lush greenery of the countryside, the elaborately dressed background dancers, the gentle wind blowing in our hair, and the pitch-perfect voice of Udit Narayan, this moment wasn't quite as romantic as I had always imagined it would be. As I sat there completely dumbfounded, mortified, and trying to make sense of exactly what was happening, Omar continued serenading me with each emotional lyric of the song—entirely oblivious to his tone deafness and the dozens of eyes that were curiously pointed in our direction.

Anyone who knows Bollywood music knows that most classic love songs are sung as duets between two enamored lovers. This means there's always a guy's part and a girl's part. However, that gender constraint didn't stop Omar; as soon as he finished the third verse of the song, he seamlessly transitioned into the girl's part, passionately singing his heart out to the man of his dreams. While I could feel the stares continue to pierce through every layer of my skin, I sat there silently, plotting all the different ways I could murder Hannah for this godawful date she had set me up on.

When Omar finally finished, I didn't know whether to clap or run, although I was leaning more toward the latter. Instead, I gave him an embarrassed smile and thanked him for his "performance," relieved that the horror was over.

"So? What did you think of my voice?" Omar asked earnestly, wiping beads of sweat off his forehead with a white napkin.

"What do you mean?" I replied, feeling grateful that we were at least back to talking rather than singing.

"I mean, my tone and pitch. How would you rate them?"

Rate them? Is this guy for real? I'd thought the worst was over, but now he wanted me to critique him? This was definitely not how I pictured my Indian fairy tale panning out. I had imagined me + Akshay Kumar + quaint European village + romantic song + dancing elephants. Instead, I got guy with too much gel + weirded-out looks + tone-deaf singer + a lifetime ban from ever stepping foot into this bistro again.

I stumbled through a few generic compliments, and the remainder of the date was more or less a blur. Omar continued to talk—primarily about himself—and I pretended to listen while silently praying each time he opened his mouth that I would not be subjected to the remix version of his song. At the end of the date, we finally said our goodbyes, and I watched Omar pull away in his shiny red Audi S5 convertible—the shattered remnants of my Bollywood fantasy emanating from the trail of smoke he left behind.

Matchmaker, Matchmaker

"Leila, *beti*, can you come in here?" my mother called from the kitchen. "We need to talk about something." My stomach dropped. I had spent the first half of my weekend recovering from my Bollywood nightmare, and despite the piles of papers that still needed to be graded, all I wanted to do was lie on the couch indulging in romantic comedies and wallowing over my failed love life. Whatever it was that my mother wanted to talk about, I just wasn't in the mood.

"*Ammi*, what is it?" I yelled back from the couch. There was some shuffling in the kitchen and then footsteps. Finally, my mother appeared in the living room wearing a polka-dotted apron and holding a rolling pin in her hand. I picked up the remote and muted the TV.

"Leila, I know you wanted to find somebody on your own, but look at you." She nodded her head toward my oversize T-shirt with holes in the armpits and my long black hair, rolled into a messy topknot. "It just doesn't look like you're off to a very good start." My mother possessed a natural flair for capitalizing on my lowest moments.

I rolled down my sweatpants and picked a single Cheeto off my shirt—examining it thoroughly before placing it in my mouth. "What are you suggesting, *Ammi*?" I said, licking the orange powder from my fingers.

"Well, since you ask . . ." She smiled and pushed my legs aside, making herself comfortable next to me. "Do you remember Rubina aunty?"

I shook my head. In South Asian culture, any person who was middle-aged was automatically referred to as *aunty* or *uncle*. I remember from when I was a kid how confusing this was to my non-*desi* friends, who just assumed that all Indian people were somehow related to one another. As my parents' circle of friends continued growing over the years, even I could hardly keep track of all the aunties and uncles rolling through.

"You remember," my mother persisted. "We met her last *Eid* at Sharmila aunty's house. She brought the lamb *biryani*?" I continued shaking my head. "The rice was slightly undercooked. It ruined the whole taste. Remember? She wore that beaded *salwar kameez* that looked terrible with her maroon lipstick. *Remember?*"

"Oh, yes, the maroon lipstick. I remember," I said, rolling my eyes.

"Well," she continued, my deception going unnoticed,

"Rubina aunty's daughter-in-law, Mariam, has that friend with the boy-cut hair. Well, her mother has a neighbor who is a dentist, Dr. Fareedah, who is friends with another sister who works for the local mosque and does matchmaking in our community. So, of course, I told her about you, Leila." She smiled and patted my leg. "And guess what? She wants to meet us!" And there it was. My mother had scheduled an appointment with a community matchmaker.

"*Ammi*," I protested. "Please tell me you're kidding. Who goes to a matchmaker these days?"

"Leila, matchmaking is a very good way to find an alliance," she said, sounding like the official spokesperson for South Asian matchmakers everywhere. "What is the problem?" She shrugged. "It is the same thing your friends are trying to do, except *she* is a professional."

I sat up in surprise. "How did you know my friends were trying to set me up?"

"Leila." She clicked her tongue. "You forget, *beti*, I know everything."

I sank back into the couch. "Well, this matchmaker lady—"

"Seema aunty," she interrupted.

"*Seema aunty.*" I stressed each syllable for effect. "She doesn't even know me. How can she set me up with someone if she doesn't know anything about me?"

"That is why we are going to meet her, Leila. So she can *get* to know you." I buried my face into the cushion and groaned. "Leila, if you agree to do this with me, I will not interfere anymore." She clasped her palms together. "*Really.* I mean it," she pleaded with hopeful eyes.

"Fine." I surrendered, knowing full well that once my mother set her mind to something, it was impossible to talk her out of it. "When do we meet this *Seema aunty*?"

"Two thirty." She tapped my leg and got up. "You should freshen up." She pushed the hair out of my face as I drew back. My stomach churned as she walked back into the kitchen, humming a little melody.

I clicked off the television and forced myself up. On the way to my room, I caught an unfortunate glimpse of myself in the hallway mirror. My skin was oily and greasy from not having been washed all day. Little bits of mascara from the night before had gathered under my eyes, giving me a freckled-raccoon look. I removed the elastic band from my hair and tried to smooth out the bump. No success. *Freshen up?* I sneered at my mother's words. I had less than an hour. It was going to take nothing short of a belt sander and a miracle to survive the uncompromising scrutiny of a South Asian matchmaker.

* * *

"*Salaams!* Come in!" Seema aunty welcomed us enthusiastically and invited us into her office. She was a large woman in her fifties with a bright smile and a youthful face. As she and my mother exchanged greetings—a standard hug and kiss on each cheek—I hovered near the door, looking around the small office attached to the local mosque. There was a rectangular gold placard on the door, on which was written MATRIMONIAL SERVICES. This was a lot more legit than I had expected. Perhaps my mother was right. It did look very professional. My mother extended her arm and pulled me close.

"This is Leila, my daughter." She beamed.

"*Masha'Allah, beti*, come here and let me look at you." Seema aunty took me by both hands and pulled me toward her. I suddenly felt very self-conscious—despite having had enough time to wash my hair and put on some lip gloss. I glanced over at my mother uncomfortably, not sure what to make of this inspection. She gave me a slight nod, indicating this was perfectly normal.

"Come, come, sit down," Seema aunty said, still holding me captive, her clammy palms handcuffed around my wrists as she steered me toward the chairs in front of her desk. When I was finally released, I took the seat closest to the door and my mother sat down beside me.

Seema aunty opened up the filing cabinet behind her desk and pulled out a manila folder. "I ask all my clients to fill out this questionnaire before we begin." She slid the folder across the desk in my direction. "Now, please be very detailed with your responses as it will give me a chance to know you better, Leila." She gave me a gummy smile. I noticed there was lipstick on her right front tooth. "And Mrs. Abid"—she wagged a chubby finger at my mother—"no helping your daughter with these questions. Let her answer on her own."

My mother appeared shocked by the suggestion but nonetheless nodded in compliance. Seema aunty told us she'd be back in a bit and closed the door of her office on her way out. I opened the manila folder. There was a packet of twenty pages stapled together. I lifted it up.

"You've got to be kidding me," I said, flipping through the pages. It was like the SATs. There was a true/false section, short-answer responses, and even a few essay questions. "*In a paragraph or two, describe the qualities that your ideal partner possesses. Describe how you imagine married life to look. Explain your role as a husband/wife,"* I read aloud.

"*Subhanallah!* These *are* very good questions," my mother stated as she leaned over my shoulder. I could feel her inquisitive eyes surveying every word on the page. "Remember, Leila. Don't hesitate to mention *anything at all* that might be important. For example, if you want a good family . . . or you want a doctor . . . or an engineer. Write down *whatever* is important to *you*."

"*Ammi*, you're not supposed to help me with this."

"I'm only giving you suggestions, Leila, but if you don't

want—" She held up her hands in resignation. "I will sit here quietly." She pretended to zip her lips. I looked back at the packet. I couldn't believe I was being forced to complete this application. This was nothing more than a glorified version of the bio-datas my mother had stacked in her black binder at home. I sighed and glanced at the analog clock hanging on the wall. It was three o'clock. This was going to take me forever and all I wanted to do was put my sweatpants back on and vegetate in front of the TV. My mother opened up her purse and fished out a pen for me. I snatched it miserably and began to write.

Thirty-eight minutes and forty-two questions later, the office door opened and Seema aunty walked back in carrying a box of *chum chums*. She held out the box as an offering, but my mother and I shook our heads, politely declining. "Okay," she said, taking a seat in the leather chair, which creaked under her weight. "Let's see what you have for me."

I watched her anxiously as I rubbed my fingers, trying to squeeze out the cramps. This was the most I had handwritten in years. Imagine how much time would be saved if they had just uploaded the application online. But clearly nothing about this process was twenty-first century.

Seema aunty placed the packet in front of her while simultaneously popping a *chum chum* into her mouth. She spent the next ten minutes flipping her sticky fingers through each page of the packet, grunting every now and then.

I had a difficult time interpreting her thoughts from her sounds, and the whole thing was making me very, *very* nervous. *What if I answered something incorrectly? What if I forgot to mention the great hair? What if I didn't list everything from those seven napkins?* My mind swimming with *what-ifs*, I imagined this was how guests on the *Maury* show felt when they were just about to learn the results of a paternity test.

"So," she said, finally pressing the packet closed. "You are looking for an intelligent, outgoing, adventurous, ambitious, emotionally mature partner"—she drew in a deep breath—"with a great sense of humor, movie star looks"—she raised her brows—"a balance of Indian and American values, and"—she paused and looked at my mother—"who comes from a good family?"

The corners of my mother's lips instantly turned upward and she nodded with approval.

Seema aunty had intentionally left out the part where I wrote that I was *not* looking for a "traditional" husband. I wanted someone who was more evolved in his views of marriage; who did not consider a wife's only role to be that of a domestic guru but who desired an equal partner in every sense of the word. She probably knew that my traditional Indian mother would not approve of those wants, so I appreciated that she left them out.

"Are you sure, Leila, this is what you want?" Seema aunty asked with a knowing look. I hesitated for a moment. I had a feeling she was inquiring about the parts she'd left out. But that was it. I was sure that was what I wanted. I nodded eagerly.

She pushed her bottom lip out and flipped her palms upward. "Okay. Let's see what we can find." She leaned down and pulled out the second drawer of her filing cabinet. It was full of manila folders just like the one she had given me.

"Are those all the applications from potential grooms?" I asked, glancing at my mother, whose eyes were wide with awe.

"Hmm." Seema aunty ignored my question as she flipped through each folder. Every now and then she pulled one folder out—her left index finger keeping tabs—quickly skimmed through the packet inside, and then returned it to its place. My heart rose and fell synchronously. *What if she actually has my perfect match in one of those folders? What if I wasted all this time looking around, and my Mr. Perfect is just waiting for me right here in this cabinet?*

She pulled out folder after folder; the anticipation was making me giddy. My mother was sitting at the edge of her seat, her lips moving in silent prayer. All hope for my future lingered in Seema aunty's sticky hands. *This really could be it. My grueling search might actually be over.*

I held my breath, watching her scan through each folder. The closer she edged to the end of the row, the fewer folders were left, and she had yet to pull one out completely. She finally pushed the drawer shut and leaned back in her chair. She looked at me and my mother intently, her pencil-drawn brows pinched together. For a few moments, no one said a word. The steady ticking of the clock kept time to the thumping in our chests. Finally, she broke the silence.

"Unfortunately, I do not have a match for you at this time," Seema aunty said solemnly. Her words reverberated through the room.

"What do you mean no match? How can that be?" My mother turned toward me. "Leila wants a traditional, straightforward husband. You read her description."

I looked down at my hands, trying not to make eye contact.

"You are telling me there is not a *single* person in your filing cabinet who could be a match?" my mother cried, lines of concern engraved across her forehead.

"Not according to what *she* is looking for."

My mother looked like she was about to cry.

"I'm sorry, Mrs. Abid. I know this is not what you want to hear, but not everyone will necessarily have a match for them."

"I . . . I don't understand," my mother stammered, confused.

"I will keep an eye out in case something comes up. But you must understand, it is not so simple. Sometimes people are unable to find someone who is a good match."

"So what happens in those cases?" I asked, avoiding my mother's gaze and trying to keep my voice steady.

"If no good match is found"—Seema aunty flung her hands out casually—"well then, my advice is to not get married." My mother gasped in horror. Seema aunty looked at her and then over at me sympathetically. "I am just saying, Mrs. Abid, sometimes the duties required in marriage are not right for everyone. In those cases, it may be better to remain unmarried than go the more traditional route—"

"Remain unmarried!" My mother jumped up with disgust. "*She* is my daughter." She pointed in my direction as I sat there confounded. "Marriage is half her *deen*! What do you mean to say she will not marry?"

"Mrs. Abid, please." Seema aunty attempted to defuse the situation. "I'm not saying she will not get married, but keep in mind, marriage is only *one* aspect of one's faith." She paused and popped another *chum chum* in her mouth before turning toward me. "With the divorce rates rising these days, even in our own communities, I think it is wiser to wait until a good match comes up. Someone who shares your values." She lifted her brows. "In the meantime," she continued, "as I said, I'll keep my eye out in case something comes up. I just don't have anyone at this moment." She wiped her fingers on her pants, leaving a syrupy trail on the gray wool, and held out her hand. "It was very nice meeting you, Leila." I shook it, speechless. She then nodded toward my mother and walked us to the door.

"What rubbish," my mother muttered under her breath as we walked out to the parking lot. "No match." She sneered angrily. "Don't listen to that nonsense, Leila. Who is she to tell me my daughter won't marry? Of course you will marry. You are my daughter, after all! That woman has no idea what she is talking about. What kind of matchmaker says marriage is not for everyone?" She shook her head in disbelief.

I was too shocked to respond. How was it possible that a professional matchmaker—with a drawer full of potentials—could not find a match for me? Was what I wanted really so radical? So impossible? I never anticipated this.

As I listened to my mother repeatedly vow to never recommend Seema the matchmaker to anyone and harshly question the judgment of Rubina aunty, Mariam, her friend with the boy-cut hair, her mother, and Dr. Fareedah the dentist during the entire drive home, I leaned my head against the window and stared out at the trees sliding past the glass.

What if Seema aunty was right? What if I was unmatchable? Would that really be such a terrible thing? It wasn't like I'd had much success with the prospects I had been "matched" with these past few months. If Seema aunty had no one in her drawer who shared the same values as me, perhaps it was better to end up alone. I had been alone before. And I was perfectly fine with it . . . *But maybe I was fine with it because I used to think my aloneness was an outcome of my choice. What if it isn't a choice at all? What if it's because there's no one out there for me? What if Mr. Perfect doesn't even exist?* This realization suddenly made my situation seem a lot more tragic.

If it was up to me, my timeline wouldn't be as rigid as my parents', but even so, I did eventually want to get married. I never planned to end up alone. *Forever.* I was just waiting for the right guy. But if there was no right guy, did that really mean that I wouldn't get married? Did that mean that I couldn't?

I closed my eyes, trying to quiet my doubts.

I had been taught all my life that marriage was half my *deen*, so how was I supposed to believe that my life would still be complete or meaningful if I didn't have a husband to share it with? I suddenly felt very lost.

We stopped at a red light, and I looked out at the patches of wild dandelions scattered along the side of the road. Thickets of weeds the color of sunshine.

Seema aunty was wrong.

The one consistent element in every Bollywood film was that it ended with a marriage. Girl meets boy. Girl falls in love with boy. Girl and boy fight off band of criminals, disapproving in-laws, jealous ex-lovers. Girl and boy get married. *Le fin.* This was the only ending I knew. So my story had to end the same way. *Right?* Maybe my views of marriage were a bit nontraditional, but I still deserved the same outcome as every heroine on the screen. A perfect guy and a perfect wardrobe. I wasn't going to let Seema aunty snatch my happily ever after from me by making me feel like my wants were too extreme. I was my mother's daughter, after all! I just needed to keep looking. I needed to find my perfect match and prove Seema aunty wrong. The other "half of my *deen*" *did* exist. He had to, because I *was* matchable—to whom was yet to be known, but I was more determined than ever to find him on my own.

Cyber Suitor

After my newfound resolve following the matchmaker debacle, I found myself back in Liv's living room the following Tuesday night. My friends and I had collectively decided—for the sake of humankind—that Hannah was officially banned from the matchmaking business, and thereby forbidden from setting any two people up on a date. Ever. With that out of the way, the rest of us quickly began searching for other options. The last thing I wanted was to put my fate back in the hands of my parents—or Seema the matchmaker—so whatever we could find, we had to come up with fast.

"You should date online," Liv suggested.

"Oh, c'mon Liv, I'm not that desperate," I said. However, as soon as the last of these words left my mouth, I knew I wasn't convincing anyone. I had just been deemed unmatchable by a person who matched people for a living. With zero prospects on the horizon and less than three months to find a husband, of *course* I was desperate.

In my mind, I knew online dating was a perfectly viable option. Everyone and their mom was online dating these days. It was how most people my age met their significant others. The success stories were there, but for some reason, a part of my brain still reserved online dating solely for losers, social outcasts, and serial killers—even though logically, I knew this was no longer the case. It was just that in all my fantasies of falling in love over the years, I had factored in picturesque meadows, synchronized dance routines, and slow-motion hair flips, but never swiping right. I just imagined I would meet someone the old-fashioned way: in the international foods aisle at the grocery store. Or at a Bombay Jam fitness class as we *thumka*-ed our way into each other's heart. I never thought my real-life circumstances would become so dire that I would be forced to resort to virtual options. But this was ultimately what it had come to.

"Trust me, Leila," Liv coaxed, clearly sensing my hesitation. "Everyone online dates. Even I've tried it."

"You have? When?" I asked, slightly taken aback. For as long as I had known Liv, since our junior year of high school, she was always in a relationship. Even her current relationship with Dreamy Darian had been going strong for more than two years. I'd always assumed she was just lucky when it came to the opposite sex. With her jet-black hair and alabaster skin, men were drawn to her like macaroni to cheese. I never would've guessed that someone like her would have to go online to find a date.

"Remember Alejandro? That Brazilian guy I dated a few summers ago?"

I nodded.

"I met him on eHarmony back when it was trendy," she continued.

"No way," I sputtered in complete disbelief. "You never told me that!"

"Well, you never asked." Liv shrugged. I had presumed Liv had met Alejandro at a club or something, but thinking back on it, I should've known that serendipitous encounters with hot Brazilians didn't just happen by chance in the suburbs of L.A. Once Liv had made this admission, I was surprised to learn that the others had had their own forays into the world of online dating.

"My sister met her boyfriend on a dating app too," Hannah added. "And they've been together for over a year now."

"Yeah, but that's probably because you didn't set them up," I retorted, and we all broke into giggles, even Hannah.

"I've tried it before too."

"Tania?!" we all exclaimed. Since the end of her marriage, I had never heard Tania mention being involved in *any* type of relationship—serious or casual. I figured her ultraconservative upbringing, coupled with her divorce at eighteen, had thwarted her from pursuing other dalliances of the sort. It seemed she was perfectly content on her own without the hassles of *rishta* aunties, meddling parents, and the temptations of online dating. But I was obviously mistaken. At least about the latter.

"I wanted to see what was out there," she said nonchalantly. "It's actually kind of nice."

I raised my eyebrows, still trying to wrap my mind around the idea of Tania on a dating website.

"It gives you access to all these options that you wouldn't otherwise have in real life."

"Like what?" I frowned, still feeling slightly skeptical.

"I'm a twenty-five-year-old divorced Muslim woman, Leila," she said. "Aunties aren't exactly fighting to set me up with their precious, 'virgin' sons, you know."

I knew exactly what she meant. It didn't matter that Tania was strikingly beautiful or intelligent or successful; the fact that she had been previously married was reason enough for many Muslim parents to disregard her as a contender for their sons. Although not all Muslim families shared this mentality, Tania had probably encountered enough of them over the years to feel limited by her preferences.

"I have more control," she continued. "So, for example, I can filter my options to only show me men who have also been divorced. Or who have no issues with women who are divorced. I can hand-select all of the qualities I'm looking for, and it will generate a list of options for me based on my choices. It's almost like . . . shopping. But instead of pashminas and ankle boots, you're trying on husbands for size."

"Huh." I'd never thought about online dating from that perspective, but Tania's analogy suddenly made it sound much more appealing. The more my friends talked about scientific data sets, compatibility algorithms, and sepia-tinted profile pictures, the more excited I became.

"So you mean I can choose all the characteristics I'm looking for, match them up to my requirements, and it'll just *generate* a bunch of options for me?" I asked.

"Pretty much," Tania said.

"And then you just pick the guy you like best." Liv smiled.

A vision of my perfect guy on seven napkins suddenly came dancing through my mind. "This almost sounds too easy," I said, astonished.

"The important thing is that we choose the right website or app, though," Liv said. "They have something for just about everyone these days."

"Literally *everyone*," emphasized Hannah. "Amish singles. Cat lovers. Biker dudes and dudettes. Big-hearted introverts. Singles with food allergies. I even saw a commercial once for a dating app for vegan dairy farmers."

"How does that even—" I began, confused, but Tania interrupted me.

"Leila, what she means is, they have South Asian matrimonial sites that are specifically geared towards Muslims."

"Now *that* sounds perfect!" Liv said. "That'll narrow it down, so you won't waste any time."

"You'd be surprised by how many people are on there," Tania continued. "I actually helped my cousin make a profile on one, and she ended up meeting some really great prospects."

"I guess it wouldn't hurt to check it out," I said hesitantly. I settled into the couch as Hannah and Liv squeezed in on either side of me. Tania grabbed Liv's laptop from the dining table, pulled up a chair next to us, and quickly logged on to the website her cousin had used. Within seconds, she was filling out the five-question survey asking for my name, birth date, height, weight, and skin complexion.

"Skin complexion?" Liv asked as she watched Tania scroll down the list of options ranging from *fair* to *wheatish* to *dusky*. "Isn't that kind of . . . what's the word?" She turned toward Hannah.

"Racist." I helped her out. Sadly, I wasn't all too surprised by this question. It was an often repeated inquiry on every bio-data, and even on the matchmaker's application packet. "Unfortunately, that's pretty common in our culture," I added, looking at Tania with a knowing look. "Basically, a fair-skinned bride has more marriage value than a 'dusky-complexioned' bride."

"But why?" Liv asked.

"Beauty, status . . . ," I began explaining.

"Colonialism," Tania interjected.

Liv and Hannah looked at us, their faces perplexed.

"That's just how it's always been," I said. "Fair skin in the Indian culture is considered more attractive. Which I suppose makes sense when you're a country that has a two-hundred-year history of British rule—"

"And a caste system based on inequality," Tania said.

"And a totally skewed perception of beauty." I sighed. "Whiteness has always been linked to superiority . . . or power . . . or whatever. It's not right, but it's a belief that's embedded deep within the Indian psyche."

"But people don't still believe that, do they?" Hannah asked.

Tania and I looked at each other. As much as I wanted to say no, I knew that wasn't true. It was obvious that these prejudices still existed. I remembered glancing through my mother's *Stardust* magazines on her nightstand as a kid and feeling so confused by all the ads for bleaching creams. Growing up in Southern California, I was used to seeing images of beautiful, tanned people everywhere. I couldn't understand the desire to be "Fair and Lovely!"

While my parents never overtly expressed these views, they would still say things like "Leila! You can't go out to play until the sun goes down!" or "Here, use this *dupatta* to shade your arms" whenever we'd go on long road trips. I just assumed it was normal.

"Do you think men on this website also have to answer these questions about skin color?" Liv asked.

"They do, but it doesn't matter," Tania said as she checked the box next to *fair* on the survey. I looked down at my hands. I could pass for "wheatish," but no way was I fair. "You'll just get more interests that way," she stated matter-of-factly.

I nodded, swallowing the guilt I felt for allowing myself to succumb to these unfair standards. I was certain that males in our communities dealt with some aspect of colorism, but I doubted it was to the same extent as the females.

"So is that it? Is that all they want to know about me?" I asked, slightly irked. For some reason, I'd imagined the online survey was going to be more like a digital version of the matchmaker's questionnaire packet. I thought it would have detailed questions about my personality, my views on life, my wants in a partner. Instead, everything about it felt so superficial. I wondered how my mother would feel about this method. Based on the specificity of the résumés in her portfolio, I doubted she would approve.

"You can always go back and fill out a more detailed version of your profile later," Tania said, her eyes still glued to the screen. "But for now, I think we should just skip past the tedious parts and go straight to browsing the profiles." She looked back at us and wiggled her brows. "Ready to give it a whirl?"

The four of us crowded around the computer screen, scrolling through endless lists of potential grooms in my age range. It didn't take me very long to realize that this dating website was nothing more than an electronic Rolodex of the same options from my mother's black portfolio. It was pages and pages of the same type of guy—well-educated doctors and engineers, good families, traditional values, *blah, blah, blah*. It was not that I didn't recognize the merit behind these qualities; it was just that I was looking for something . . . more. I wanted someone who was *#5: PASSIONATE, #11: ADVENTUROUS, #21: SPONTANEOUS*. Someone who wasn't afraid to jump on a moving train or climb atop a mountain peak to proclaim his love for me. It was hard to imagine that type of romance with any of these straitlaced, conservative-looking guys.

"No. No. Oh, God. No," the four of us repeated in unison as we skimmed through each page. Every now and then, one of us would point to a picture and say, "Oh, what about him?" or "He looks cute," but as soon as we'd click on his detailed bio, a quick glance at his profile would reveal that he was gluten-free *by choice*, or he had an affinity for parakeets, or he played the tambourine, and we would quickly write him off and move on to the next. After fourteen pages of no's, we eventually went back and modified our search criteria.

"I think you should adjust the age range up to thirty-five."

"And expand the mile radius from you."

"And consider checking 'normal' body types too, instead of just 'athletic' and 'muscular.'"

"And maybe you don't need someone *that* tall."

"Or someone *that* rich."

After some slight protesting on my end, we finally clicked SEARCH with more realistic expectations.

"Oh wait, what about this one?" Tania pointed to a thumbnail image near the bottom of the newly refreshed page. When she clicked it, a detailed profile for "Mahmoud" popped up on the screen. We all leaned in closer to get a better look at the full-sized image of him. I was surprised to admit, he wasn't too bad. He had short-cropped hair, light brown eyes, and a friendly smile that showed off his chin dimple. He had his arm around an older aunty, who I deduced by the facial resemblance was probably his mother. Tania clicked on the small arrow to the right, and the next image showed him leaning back with his arms outstretched—a classic Bollywood pose—in front of the Louvre Museum in Paris.

"He's kind of hot," Hannah swooned.

"And well traveled."

"And close to his mom."

"And did we mention hot?"

"Let's look at what he says in his profile," I said, wanting to make sure that his personality matched up with his looks. As I read through paragraph after paragraph describing his hobbies, ambitions, and what he hoped to find in a future partner, I could feel my heart flutter with every line. *He's an avid swimmer.* I didn't know how to swim, but I enjoyed lounging poolside, and *Finding Nemo* was my favorite Disney movie. *He loves to read.* That was definitely something we shared in common. Being an English teacher would finally work to my advantage! *He works at a successful consulting firm. He wants a cool, down-to-earth, independent girl who has a good balance of culture and religion.* Check. Check. Check. And check! It was as if he was describing me to a T. Each sentence was well-written, with correct grammar and punctuation. The more I read, the more hopeful I became. I kept searching for a catch, but when I couldn't find one, I finally turned to my friends and said, "I like him!"

Liv smiled and gave me a squeeze on my shoulder while Tania and Hannah typed up a quick message to send to him that included my phone number and email address.

"Do you think he'll call?" I asked anxiously. *Mahmoud.* I repeated the name in my head. It was such a great name. There was something exciting about the fact that my Mr. Perfect finally had a name.

"Of course he will!" Hannah exclaimed. "Didn't you see the gorgeous 'fair-complexioned' picture of you we posted? How could he resist?" She winked.

I stared nervously at the screen as they clicked SEND MESSAGE. *All I have to do now is wait*, I thought, leaning back against the couch. *Mahmoud.* I repeated the name again, playing with the syllables on my tongue. *Leila and Mahmoud.* It had a nice ring to it. I picked up my phone and switched the ringer on—eagerly awaiting a phone call from the dreamy, chin-dimpled man from behind the screen.

Mr. Catfish

It had been almost two weeks since Mahmoud first reached out to me, and the past twelve days had been an endless stream of emails and texts between the two of us.

Each morning, I awakened to a Good morning, beautiful text on my phone, and each night a Sweet dreams, Leila. Can't wait to talk to you tomorrow message arrived before I went to bed. Throughout the day, Mahmoud and I would talk about anything and everything—from the crusty tofu they sold at the salad bar in his office cafeteria, to the latest Atif Aslam song, to the annoying kid in my sixth-period class who decided to abbreviate the term *assonance* on his poetry quiz. The more we talked, the more often I thought about him as the days passed. He was funny and witty, and I loved how easily the words flowed between the two of us.

Even my mother noticed the significant improvement in my mood.

"How is the search going?" she asked me at breakfast one morning.

"Fine," I mumbled, grinning at the video of a grumpy cat that Mahmoud had just texted.

"Anyone in particular who you are talking with?" She glanced at my phone.

"Hm?" I looked up. "Oh, um, no. Just a friend," I stammered, taking a bite of my toast. Mahmoud was actually someone I was excited about, and I didn't need my mother ruining it by intervening. I stuffed the last of my breakfast into my mouth and got up to place the dishes in the sink. "I'm going to shower and get ready for work," I said quickly before my mother could ask me any more questions.

Ten minutes later, I walked back into the kitchen to see my mother talking to someone on *my* cell phone, which I had accidentally left behind.

"Yes, and what do your parents do? I see. I see. Please give me their number so I can give them a call." She scribbled the digits onto a Post-it note. I stood there watching her, horrified.

"*Ammi*, give me my phone," I hissed, trying to snatch it from her hand. She pulled away and lifted up her index finger.

"Yes, yes. Okay, then. It was very nice talking to you. And don't forget to email me your bio-data. Okay, I will be waiting." She pressed the red button and handed the phone to me.

"What are you doing?" I said in between clenched teeth.

"Your *friend* Mahmoud called while you were in the shower," she said casually. "Leila, it would be rude not to answer."

"Ammi!"

"Leila, I just had a very brief chat with him. All I wanted was to ask a couple questions—"

"You should've asked me first!" I broke in.

My mother looked at me with surprise. "Asked you first? Why? Are you not my daughter? Have I no right to know who you are talking to?"

"You promised if I went to the matchmaker, you would not interfere anymore—"

"*Beti*, I'm not interfering. But I need to know that the person you are talking to is the right person."

"Right person for who?" I cried, feeling frustrated. "You're not giving me a chance to do this on my own!"

"I am, *beti*, I just—"

"Just trust me, okay? Give me a chance to figure this out." I sighed, walking away. This was exactly what I was afraid of. I wanted to make sure Mahmoud was the right person for *me* before involving my parents. After what happened with Anwar, it was far too complicated to balance everyone's emotions.

SO sorry about that, I texted Mahmoud once I was alone.

No worries. Your mom seems . . . nice, he replied with a tongue sticking out.

I sent him an angry emoji face.

LOL.

I drew in a deep breath.

So, we've been talking for a while now. Maybe we should meet up soon? I typed. I held my breath, hoping he'd still want to meet after that conversation with my mother.

How's tomorrow night? he replied immediately.

Tomorrow night sounds perfect. I smiled. I was finally going to meet my cyberprince, and I could not have been more ready.

* * *

Friday evening, I arrived at Un Beso—a romantic Italian restaurant with twinkling lights and red-checked tablecloths. Although I had taken some extra time to curl my hair into long, loose waves and put on some red lipstick, I still managed to show up slightly earlier than planned. *This is finally going to happen*, I kept thinking as I nervously adjusted my red midi dress and crossed and uncrossed my legs for the fifteenth time.

Although I had never experienced love at first sight, all the Shah Rukh Khan and Kajol films I devoured over the years taught me it existed. This could be that defining moment for me. Like when Anjali saw Rahul for the first time after eight years apart in *Kuch Kuch Hota Hai.* Or when

Simran finally fell into Raj's arms as he pulled her onto a moving train in *Dilwale Dulhania Le Jayenge*. The thought of Mahmoud possibly being the King Khan of my real-life romance made me both exhilarated and nauseous at the same time. Lost in these thoughts, I didn't even notice Mahmoud enter the restaurant until after the hostess brought him to where I was seated.

"Here is your table, sir."

I looked up from my phone and all my hopes instantly plummeted.

"Hi, you must be Leila," he said as he sat down across from me. "Sorry, I'm a little late. I had to stop and get gas."

As I stared at him from the other side of the dimly lit table, I kept wondering if he had traveled here by time machine. It was the same face, but he somehow looked . . . different. He seemed older, more mature in person. He also seemed shorter . . . and chubbier. *Stop imagining things*, I told myself as I forced a smile and tried not to gawk at the sprinkle of gray peppered along his receding hairline.

"Wow, you're exactly how I imagined," Mahmoud said, returning the smile and taking off his blazer, which he hung neatly over the back of his chair.

If only I could say the same, I thought as I tried my best to act normal. Although we had never FaceTimed or Skyped or talked on webcam before, he had texted me almost a dozen photographs of himself over the course of two weeks.

Based on that exchange, I had felt fully prepared to meet him face-to-face. However, now that I was actually sitting across from Mahmoud, I could not wrap my mind around how *different* he looked. I was expecting him to look identical to the images that had been imprinted in my mind over the past twelve days, but instead, I found myself looking at the vintage version of those photographs. I couldn't help but feel caught off guard.

"Are you nervous?" Mahmoud asked as he grabbed a menu from the center of the table.

No, I'm freaked out by the complete stranger sitting in front of me! I thought as I slowly shook my head. *So what if he looks different?* I tried to reason with myself. *Apart from his appearance, the two of you still made a connection over this two-week period!* I tried to focus on all the things we had in common. *We both like to read. We both have a good balance of culture and religion. We both despise tofu in our salads. And how could I forget all the sweet and thoughtful text messages?* I tried to remind myself that we were *Leila and Mahmoud*, but something about the way he tapped his upper lip and grunted as he read through the menu filled me with overwhelming repugnance.

This wasn't the first time I had experienced Sudden Repulsion Syndrome. The first time I was hit with SRS was shortly after my dating debacle with Chad Edelstein. I was invited on a double date with Annie and her boyfriend, and the guy they had set me up with had shown up wearing slip-on boat shoes. In February. For whatever reason, the sight of his sockless feet in faux leather slippers caused me to feel an inexplicable sense of disgust, and the rest of the night was just a domino effect. From the way he leaned over to one side when he laughed to the shade of green on his sweater—the disgust was irrevocable. When he finally leaned across the table to reach for a plate of onion rings, every muscle in my body convulsed, and I had to run out of the restaurant before I spewed all over him. It had been years since I had dealt with such an acute case of SRS, but watching the crepey skin below Mahmoud's chin jiggle as he talked, I knew that no amount of memories over these past twelve days would salvage this relationship.

"What are you thinking?" Mahmoud's droopy eyes gazed directly into mine.

I was *really* thinking about how he should quit sending people photographs of himself from 1999, but I bit my tongue. "I'm thinking I'm just going to order something light. I'm not really that hungry," I finally said.

Mahmoud smiled. I noticed how his crow's feet became more accentuated with the lift of his mouth. "I hope you're not just saying that because you're nervous." He wagged his finger playfully, keeping his eyes on me. "I was serious when I told you that I like a girl who isn't afraid to eat." I shifted uncomfortably in my chair as flashbacks of our first text conversation came back to me.

As we waited for our food to arrive, I attempted to fill in the awkward silences with mundane chatter about the "pleasant weather" and the interior decor of the restaurant. Whether it was because I was still recovering from my initial shock at Mahmoud's appearance or just dealing with the symptoms of my SRS, it was obvious that the conversation between us did not flow as naturally in person as it did over texts. My discomfort was palpable, and I could tell Mahmoud was trying extra hard to impress me. When our dinner finally arrived, he shifted into a lengthy discussion about how incredibly busy he was at his corner office with his fancy-schmancy clients and the high-stakes project he was currently working on. I sat there with a forced smile on my face and nodded, pretending to be interested, even though all I really wanted to do was finish my bowl of minestrone and get the hell out of there.

When the check finally arrived, I exhaled with relief. I couldn't wait to get in the car and chew out Liv and the other girls for convincing me to give online dating a whirl. I should have known this was going to be a major fail with my luck. I was disappointed in myself for even getting my hopes up.

Mahmoud took out his phone and swiped up on the screen to open an app. He punched in a few numbers and then turned to me unabashedly. "Would you like me to calculate your portion of the tab?" he asked, reaching for his wallet.

I nearly choked on my water. Whatever happened to *#13: GENTLEMANLY* and *#25: CHIVALROUS*? I was not old-fashioned by any means, but I grew up in a household where I was taught that men always treated women with courtesy and respect. They opened doors. They carried groceries. They *paid the bill.* Especially when it was a first date at a restaurant that *they* insisted on. For the past twenty-four hours, Mahmoud had raved on and on about this "charming little Italian place" that he just knew I would *love*. Initially I was smitten by his confidence, but that was before he showed up looking more like an uncle than a potential husband, and then subjected me to forty-eight minutes of busy-bragging. And now Mr. Catfish—with his lucrative career and mahogany Wegner Swivel chair in his corner office—wanted me to split the tab with him?

"Are you sure you don't want me to just make it my treat?" I asked irritatedly as the small serving of soup violently threatened to push its way up my throat.

"Your treat?" His face lit up. "Are you sure?"

I looked at him, flabbergasted. I could feel my muscles convulsing, and I had to swallow the urge to scream from the top of my lungs. I wanted to grab twenty units of Botox and inject them into his face until he looked like the Mahmoud from the photographs. I wanted to print out all our past conversations, all the "good morning, beautiful" texts, shred them into a million pieces, and throw them at his wrinkly face. I wanted to do all these things, but instead, I pulled out my credit card and dropped it into the small black tray. If this was what it would take to get me out of this date, I figured it was a small price to pay.

"Thanks, Leila." He grinned, quickly stuffing his wallet back into his blazer pocket. "I'll tell you what. Next time, it'll be on me."

His words filled me with detestation. *Next time? There will never be a next time.* I cringed to myself as we walked out of the restaurant. Every cell of my body recoiled as Mahmoud placed his arm around my shoulder and leaned into me, laughing. "I think this went really well," he said, his leather-soled loafers flapping against the concrete. I turned and looked away in disgust as the image of my once-again-nameless Mr. Perfect floated farther into the distance.

Mr. Smoky

"Morning," I mumbled as I staggered into the kitchen the next day.

"Sleep well, *beti?*" my mother asked, glancing at the green numbers above the stove. It was 10:47. I rubbed my eyes and nodded, taking a seat on the counter stool.

"So," she said, placing two warm scallion pancakes on my plate next to a bowl of fresh Greek yogurt. "How did it go?"

"What?" I mumbled sleepily as I tore off a piece of flaky pancake and dipped it into the bowl.

"Your dinner? With your friend? *Mahmoud*." She turned the stove off and gave me her full attention.

"I don't know." I shrugged. "He was old."

"Old? *Beti*, he is not much older than *you*." She clucked her tongue. I ignored her comment and continued eating. "Besides, the bio-data he emailed said he was only twenty-eight."

"Twenty-eight going on forty," I muttered under my breath.

"Hm?"

"I don't know, *Ammi*. He just seemed older."

"Older is not so bad." My mother wiped her hands on the kitchen towel and rolled out another spiral of dough. "Your *abba* is seven years older than me."

I rolled my eyes. Just because my mother had married someone seven years older didn't mean I wanted to.

"What you think you want now, Leila, might not be what you want later in life. I used to think seven years was such a big distance, but now?" She smiled. "I am grateful. When I first married your *abba*, I was so young. I wasn't even eighteen years old! For the first couple months, I cried every day. I was so homesick. I wanted to go back and see my mother. I wanted to play with my siblings. I missed my home. But your father was so patient with me. He took care of me. He protected me. He watched over me like a precious piece of glass."

"Not everyone is like *Abba*, though," I said, still cringing over the fact that Mahmoud was okay with me "treating him" on the first date.

"Yes, *beti*, but remember, you are not getting any younger either, so it is important to keep an open mind. You never know how life will surprise you." She patted my hand. "Speaking of surprises, you won't believe who called me this morning," she said, placing the dough into the skillet.

"Amitabh Bachchan?"

She chuckled, shaking her head. "No, Leila, it was Seema aunty. Remember, the matchmaker?"

I groaned, stuffing another bite of warm, yogurt-covered pancake into my mouth. How could I forget Seema aunty? She was the worst professional matchmaker in the history of matchmaking. "Did she call to remind you that I was still not marriage material?"

"Of course you are marriage material!" My mother placed one more steaming pancake onto my plate and wiped her hands on her apron. "Why do you say this?"

"It's okay, *Ammi*. Maybe she was right. Maybe marriage isn't for everyone—"

"*Bas!*" She held up her hand. "Don't say these things, Leila. I don't want to hear it."

I sighed and looked down at my plate. I had felt so confident on the drive back from Seema aunty's office a few weeks ago. I felt so sure that I was going to find someone and prove to be matchable, but after last night's date with Mahmoud, I wondered how many more Uday Chopras I would have to date in order to find a Hrithik Roshan.

"Listen, Leila. Maybe for whatever reason you say, Mahmoud didn't turn out to be right. But you must keep trying," my mother said as she rolled another pancake with her pin.

"What difference does it make?" I propped my face against

my forearm. I had tried plenty over these past few weeks. And I had yet to find the perfect guy.

"The difference is, this time Seema aunty called because she thinks she might have found a match for you." She looked at me excitedly.

"No, thank you." I let out a scoff. "I'm not interested," I said, waving my hand.

"Don't you at least want to know about him, Leila?"

"Not really. And why are you even interested? I thought you hated Seema the matchmaker."

"Seema *aunty*," my mother corrected me. "And I never said I hated her." I looked at her, lifting my eyebrows. "Okay, Leila, it doesn't matter now. She has come through for us." She smiled once more and lifted my chin off my arm. "She found you an *engineer*."

"And?"

She looked at me with a confused look on her face. "*And*, she thinks you two might have a lot in common."

"Why, was he also placed in her file of rejects?"

"Stop it, Leila." My mother leaned over the counter and gently swatted me on the arm. "Here." She stuck her hands into her apron pocket, feeling around for something until she finally pulled out a yellow Post-it. "His name is Sajid, and this is his number. He already spoke with Seema aunty, and he's expecting your call."

"*Ammi!*" I cried. "What do you mean he's expecting my call?"

My mother raised both her hands and shrugged. "I'm just telling you what she told me. No pressure, Leila. Call if you want, or not."

She placed the number next to my plate and then returned to the stove while I sat there brooding quietly, trying not to make direct eye contact with the brightly colored sticky note glaring at me aggressively. *So this is supposedly my match? These ten digits scribbled hurriedly on a piece of paper?* I suddenly envied all the cute couples who had sweet, romantic stories of how they first met. "Both of us reached for the last copy of *Jane Eyre* at the bookstore, and he's been my Rochester ever since!" or "We locked eyes during 'La Macarena' at my sister's wedding and realized that this was much more than a one-hit wonder!"

What would my sweet first-encounter story be? "Oh, my mother got his number from a matchmaker, and since I was almost a month into my three-month deadline *and* I'd exhausted all my other options, I figured what the hell." I sighed. Leave it to South Asians to find a way to wipe out every smidgen of romance from the process. I stuffed the last of the pancake down my throat and placed the empty plate into the sink.

"Thanks for the food, *Ammi*," I said on my way out. "If

you need me, I'll be at the coffee shop," I called over my shoulder, leaving my ten-digit match on the counter untouched.

* * *

After spending hours inhaling espressos, grading papers, and making out a week's worth of lesson plans, I finally called it a day and returned home. My parents were in the living room watching a television show about child geniuses that was literally called *Child Genius*, so I walked back into my room unnoticed and shut the door behind me. The first thing I saw on my nightstand was the Post-it note beckoning me with its bright yellow hue. Of course, when my mother had said, "Call if you want, or not," she hadn't actually meant I had a choice.

I picked up the number and lay down on my bed, turning it over and over again, my fingers tracing the handwritten name scrawled in blue ink. *Sajid.* From the corner of my eye, I could see the calendar on the wall with three weeks' worth of X's crossed off.

I sighed and shut my eyes, trying to imagine what it would be like if I weren't Indian. If there were no time limit on my future, and I were free to pursue love however I wanted. Would I still be searching for the same thing? I thought about my forty-six-item list. The problem was not with *who*

I was searching for; the problem was with *how* I was searching for him. And the limited amount of time I'd been given to find him. Unfortunately, a life without this external time constraint was a freedom reserved for those who weren't wheat-complexioned. But since I was never *not* going to be Indian, I had no choice except to surrender to the fact that all my relationships were going to come with a healthy dose of marital pressure.

I thought back on the conversation with my mother that morning. When she first met my father, she had no idea that he would turn out to be her Mr. Perfect. She took a giant risk by moving halfway across the world with a stranger who was seven years older than her. But that risk eventually paid off. And now she was trying to make sure that it somehow paid off for me too—sooner rather than later.

I drew in a deep breath. Even if I weren't Indian and my mother were not in the picture, I would still want to find Mr. Perfect for myself. Maybe it didn't matter so much how I found him or even when, as long as I did.

I smoothed out my hair and picked up the Post-it note once more.

* * *

"Um, hello . . . Can I speak to Sajid?" I adjusted my sweatshirt and sat up.

"This is Sajid," said a deep, raspy voice on the other end.

"Hi, this is Leila. I got your number from Seema aunty."

"Oh, yeah. Hi," he said, coughing.

"Hi." I slapped my hand to my forehead. Why couldn't I say anything other than "Hi"? "So, how's it going?" I cleared my throat awkwardly. I couldn't remember the last time I had a phone conversation with someone other than my mom. *I should've just texted him.* At least I could've formed messages that contained more than a string of one-syllable words.

"Good, I'm good." he responded. I could hear some rustling in the background.

"Is this a bad time?"

"No, not at all. I'm just on my way to pick up some food."

"Oh, cool. So . . . um, you're an engineer, right?" I slapped my forehead again. I must've sounded like such a moron.

"Yeah." He coughed again. I could hear more rustling.

"Cool." I wanted to kick myself. Why had I let that obnoxiously bright Post-it note badger me into calling? This was exactly why no one talked on the phone anymore; it was physically painful.

"So, what do you do?" he asked after a few moments.

"I'm a teacher."

"By choice?"

"Just on the days I'm not handcuffed."

Sajid let out a deep, throaty laugh. "Handcuffed," he said, his laughter breaking into coughs. "You're funny."

"The teenagers at school would probably disagree. They *never* laugh at my jokes. But thanks." I smiled.

"Whoa! You work with teenagers. That's dank!"

"Dank?"

"That must be *mad* stressful."

"Uh, yeah. There are definitely days, but I suppose it's that way with most jobs."

"Definitely." There was a long pause. "So how do you relieve the stress?"

"Sleep, mostly. And being set up by matchmakers. Nothing releases tension better than placing your love life in the hands of a *rishta* aunty."

Sajid laughed again, this time loudly. "Yeah, *dude*. This whole matchmaking thing can be pret-*ty* stressful. You never really know who you're talking to." He giggled.

I smiled. So far, I was pleasantly surprised. Sajid seemed like a chill guy; a little quirky, perhaps, but as the conversation continued, I could feel my body start to relax a bit. "So what about you?" I asked. "Aside from being set up, how do you relieve stress on those long days?"

"I usually hit the gym after work. Burn off some built-up pressure."

"Nice," I said, my mind drifting as I pictured his broad, sweaty shoulders and oiled, chiseled chest. Granted, I had never actually met a *#46: SEXY* engineer before, but that didn't mean they didn't exist. Maybe Sajid was an anomaly. A hot brainiac who could code complex data with one hand while completing bicep curls with the other. As he talked about his workout regimen, I imagined his monster quads pounding out leg extensions like mathematical algorithms. My very own shirtless Salman with ripped acid-washed jeans and a bandanna headband. "*Oh Oh Jaane Jaana*!"

"What was that?" Sajid interrupted my thoughts.

"Nothing," I stammered, feeling the heat rise in my face.

He laughed again. "So yeah, I definitely try my best to stay in shape," he continued. I grinned and mentally checked off *#15: FIT*, *#23: MUSCULAR*, and *#42: ACTIVE* on my list. I knew there was a lot of hard work and sacrifice that went into getting a set of abs like Salman Khan's, and any man who was willing to put in that work had my attention.

"That's *really* great."

"I do what I can. Actually, can you hold on for a minute? I'm starving! I'm gonna order something."

"Okay, sure," I said over the rustling in the background. I could hear the crack of a speaker, and then it sounded like Sajid placed the phone facedown because his voice was muffled as he gave his order:

"Can I get two Doritos Locos Tacos, three Crunchwrap Supremes, one Quesarito with extra sour cream, and a large Mountain Dew."

The speaker crackled again. I heard Sajid cough, and then a few minutes later, he came back on.

"Sorry about that," he said.

"So, I'm guessing today is a cheat day?" I joked.

"Ohhh, yeah." He laughed. "I'm not as strict—food-wise—on the weekends," he said with a giggle. "So . . . what was I saying?"

"You were telling me about ways that you deal with stress."

"Riiiight. So, yeah, I work out a lot," he said, crunching down on something—probably one of his Doritos Locos Tacos. "And on *really* stressful days, when the gym just doesn't cut it"—he chewed loudly—"I'll typically hit the bong."

I dropped my phone into my lap.

"Hello? Leila? Hey, are you there?"

"I'm here. So you were saying, uh . . . you typically—um, what?"

"I chief some leaf. You know, blow some blunts? Blaze a joint? Marijuana?"

"Yeah, I know what marijuana is." I rolled my eyes. "So you . . . smoke weed?"

"Yeah," he said, giggling uncontrollably again. "But only on weekends. Or at night. Or when my buddy Travis comes over. It helps me unwind." He paused. "Like aromatherapy."

"Right."

"You should give it a try."

"Aromatherapy?"

He laughed. "You know, I know a guy if you're interested—"

I plopped my head against the pillow as Sajid rambled on about the quality of "hash" his dealer sold. The image of the *#46: SEXY* engineer floating in my mind had now been replaced by a beanie-wearing stoner with an oversize tie-dyed T-shirt looking for Froot Loops and corner market snacks. What would I, *nonsmoking, nondrinking Leila*, have in common with Mr. Midnight Toker?

"Look," I finally interrupted him, "I don't know what Seema aunty told you about me, but I'm not really a pot smoker."

"No worries, my dude! You don't have to smoke it. There are many ways to consume cannabis—"

"Yeah," I broke in. "Any of those ways, I'm not really interested." There was a long pause.

"Okay . . . yeah, cool," he said after a moment. "So . . . um . . ." He cleared his throat. "What kind of music do you listen to?"

We fumbled our way through another five minutes of conversation and then politely said goodbye. I grabbed the yellow Post-it from the nightstand, crumpled it into a ball, and tossed it across the room into the trash bin. It hit the purple wall and landed on the floor. Sajid, I'm sure, was a perfectly nice guy, but what did it say about me that a professional matchmaker thought I would have things in common with a pothead? Was this what Seema aunty thought I meant when I said "nontraditional"? Was she attempting to prove a point? Or did she really think this was what I wanted? I had officially hit a new low in this process. I was a third of the way into my deadline, and not even a fraction closer to finding love or romance than when I had started.

My phone buzzed next to me. I glanced at the message on the screen. It was Sajid.

Hey, it was really nice talking to you. Would it be alright if I asked you a favor? I picked up the phone.

Shoot, I replied.

Could you maybe not mention the cannabis thing to anyone? I wouldn't want it getting back around to my parents. LOL.

Of course he didn't. Sajid's parents would remain totally oblivious to the fact that their perfect engineer son was spending his nights dazed and confused, while I would have to make up yet another reason for why I was such a disappointment to my mother. I could already imagine the dreaded conversation:

Ammi: "Seema aunty just called, Leila. She wants to know how it went with Sajid."

Me: "It was okay. I'm not interested, though."

Ammi: "What do you mean, not interested?"

Me: "I don't know. We just have different . . . hobbies. It's not going to work."

Ammi: *Ya Allah!* Here we have found you an *engineer*, and you are saying it's not going to work? When are you going to stop being so picky, Leila?!"

I looked at the calendar and sighed. There were nine weeks left. *Nine weeks.* Either I could concede defeat now, or I could keep trying—this time on my own terms. No more matchmakers. No more interference from my mother. Just me doing everything I could to find my Mr. Perfect on my own. *What is it going to be, Leila?* I thought to myself.

The phone vibrated next to me. DUDE. Are we good? the message read, highlighted on the screen. I sighed, staring at the words. After a few reflective moments, I grabbed the phone and responded with a thumbs-up emoji.

Mr. Busybody

The next morning, I woke up earlier than expected to go for a jog. I needed to clear my head. I had approximately two months left before my deadline, and I desperately needed to figure out how to recalibrate my plans moving forward. As the brisk morning air brushed against my face, I thought about the one person who'd had the foresight to predict this situation years ago. I stopped at the end of the street to catch my breath and scrolled through my contacts, searching for her name. I hoped her insight would somehow offer me the guidance that I needed.

"Hello?" a familiar voice greeted me on the other end.

"Annie! Hey, it's Leila."

"Leila! What a surprise! Let me put you on hold for a second; I'm just finishing up a quick call."

As I waited for her to return, I stretched out my calves on the edge of the curb. Ever since I got caught up in all the marriage stuff, I felt stuck in this continuous cycle of disappointment. I had forgotten how good it felt to just be outdoors, away from all the distractions.

"Leila? You there?" Annie's voice broke through my thoughts.

"Let me guess, you were planning another adventurous getaway? Where to this time?" I asked. Although it had been a while since we last talked, we followed each other on social media, so I knew enough from Annie's posts to know that she led a pretty cool life as a freelance travel blogger.

"Palau. At the end of the month. I'm going to swim with the jellyfish."

"I don't even know where that is, but I would be open to trading lives," I offered.

Annie laughed. "How's teaching going?"

"I mean, the pay sucks. And I'm up to my ears in grading. But just the other day, one of my students told me how he aced the English portion of his ACTs because of my class." I grinned. "It's kind of cool to know they're learning something."

"You were always great with kids. Remember that orphanage visit you planned during our spring break in Cancún?"

"I think you were the only one who agreed to come with me! Everyone else just wanted to lie on the beach."

"Can you imagine? Wanting to relax on vacation. Ugh." Annie laughed. "So when are you going to teach abroad? I thought that was the plan?"

"I guess I've been preoccupied with some other stuff . . ." I trailed off.

"Do tell." I could imagine Annie leaning in closer to the phone.

I sighed. "My parents gave me a three-month deadline to find a husband. And I kind of agreed. And now I'm already almost a month in, and Mr. Perfect still hasn't shown up yet."

Annie remained quiet on the other end. I wondered what she was thinking. She probably thought I had lost my mind.

"Well." She finally let out a small whistle. "I see not much has changed," she said, a hint of disappointment in her voice. "Leila, when are you going to realize that Mr. Perfect doesn't exist?"

"In two months?" I joked.

"Leila." She sighed.

"In all seriousness, I have yet to meet even a decent guy these past couple months. Mr. Perfect is a *long* ways away."

"I never thought I would say this, but maybe you should go back to the serial-dating Leila from college," Annie suggested.

"But weren't you always advocating for long-term relationships?"

"You're attempting to do in two months what most people spend half their lives on, Leila. This is the rare exception when you can't just go on a few dates and expect to find the one. As much as I hate to say it, it's about probabilities. The more dates you go on, the greater your chances are of meeting this crazy deadline."

"I suppose I didn't think of it like that."

If this truly was a numbers game, then Annie was right: I was doing it wrong. Rather than going on one or two dates a week, I needed to amp it up.

As soon as I got home, I logged on to Muslims Meet—an app that brought together "single Muslims seeking a life partner the halal way," with an image of a winking goat—and went on a swiping spree. I even swiped on a few questionable guys, but if they happened to increase my odds of finding "the one," then I was willing to roll the dice.

That Tuesday, I kicked off my accelerated mission with an early dinner date with Imran, a hedge fund manager who had also swiped in my direction. Imran and I agreed to meet at a cafe downtown, and I was pleased to find that he had arrived before me. But as I walked up to the outdoor patio where he was seated, I noticed that he was engaged in what seemed to be an important business call.

"No, no, no. That was not what we discussed—" He gave me a slight wave and pulled out a chair. I sat down quietly, smoothing out my hair and waiting for him to finish. "We need to increase our capital expenditures—" he said loudly into the phone. He stood up and paced around the table. He was wearing a pale gray tailored suit paired with a crisp white button-down, and silver cuff links that gleamed each time they caught the afternoon light. I suddenly felt very underdressed in my striped maxi dress and open-toed sandals.

"Remember, it's all about the macro trends. Especially in the global market. We need to buy the best stocks in the trend, and ride out that flow until it compounds." I grabbed a menu from the table and tried to distract myself. *Do I want the grilled portobello burger or the ahi-tuna wrap?* I could barely think with how loudly Imran was talking.

"Yes. Yes. Yes. Tell Benson to keep an eye on those dividends, and we'll reconvene in an hour." He finally sat down, dropping his phone on the table and turning his attention toward me.

"So sorry," he apologized. "It's been one of those days. Work never ceases to—" Before he could finish, he was interrupted by his phone. He paused midsentence and glanced down at the screen. "I just have to . . . ," he said, holding up his index finger and accepting the call. "It'll just be real quick." He stood up. "I'll be back in a few min— Yes." He suddenly turned away. "Yes. Did you check with Benson to make sure there's not a liquidity issue?"

I excused myself to go to the ladies' room, and when I returned, there was a napkin on the table with a message:

ON CONFERENCE CALL. BRB.

I looked across the patio and saw Imran leaning across

the rails, holding his phone in the air and yelling into his earpiece. I grimaced. Imran was *that guy.* That habitual cell phone talker who had lengthy discussions on his phone in public, soaking in the conversational limelight while forcing everyone in his vicinity to listen in. I turned away and shrank into my chair. I couldn't believe I was on a date with *that guy.* The odds of this one being "the one" were highly unlikely.

Ten minutes later, Imran returned.

"Sorry about that. It's practically impossible to get a decent connection out here," he said, flustered.

"Yeah." I nodded. "How annoying."

Over dinnerw—despite his phone detonating every five minutes—I managed to learn that Imran had grown up in Chicago, was the youngest of four children, and played football in high school. He had created an account on Muslims Meet because according to his "ten-year plan," it was time for him to settle down.

"Where do you see yourself in ten years?" he asked after sending out an email.

"Ten years." I paused. "That's a good question." It occurred to me that I hadn't really planned out my future beyond the three-month deadline. I knew I wanted to find Mr. Perfect. By July. But then what? Marriage? Kids? Would I ever teach abroad? Would I go back to grad school? Would I live happily ever after? "I guess I don't know," I admitted.

Imran furrowed his brows, but just as he started to say something: *buzz.*

Whatever thought he had was completely forgotten the second he glanced at the screen. I sighed and mentally crossed *#9: ATTENTIVE* off my list. I couldn't imagine what it would be like to be in a relationship with Imran and his phone. There was no way I could compete with all that vibrating.

"Have you ever considered shutting that thing off?" I asked, taking a bite of my wrap.

"Huh?" He looked up.

"That." I pointed at the phone in his hand. "Have you ever thought about just turning it off?"

"Oh, this?" He held it up, the screen flashing with messages. He laughed dismissively and glanced back down, his eyes scanning the texts.

I pushed aside the half-eaten wrap on my plate and dabbed the edge of my mouth with the napkin. "Perhaps we should go." I motioned toward the exit.

"Uh, yeah, sure," he replied with his face still fixated on the screen, his fingers furiously clicking away.

The clicks continued as he paid for our meals, and they followed us all the way through the parking lot.

"So," I said when we reached my car, "Thanks for dinner. It was nice meeting you, Imran," I pulled open the door. "Oh, and tell Benson I said hi," I joked as I sat down inside.

Imran put his phone into his pants pocket and turned toward me. "What?"

"Never mind," I said, giving him a slight wave, hoping he would move aside so I could shut the door. But he remained in place.

"Say, Leila, I was wondering: would you like to have dinner again with me tomorrow evening?" I could hear the phone vibrating from inside his pants.

"Will your phone be joining us?" I asked, trying not to look directly at his pulsating groin.

"Oh," he said, brows stitched together. "Yes. Why?"

"No reason," I said, turning away. "I'll check my schedule and let you know." I could see his face drop.

We stared at each other silently for a moment, the buzzing in his pants increasing in intensity by the second. Finally, when he couldn't take it any longer, he pulled out the phone and looked at the screen.

"I'm sorry, would you mind—"

"Not at all," I said as he walked a few feet away and accepted the call.

I shut the door and waited until he was a few minutes into his conversation about "yields and interest" before I backed up and drove away. *One more down. An indefinite number to go.*

Ambushed

I texted Imran later that night to let him know that I was busy tomorrow evening—and every consecutive evening for the unforeseen future—and continued with my search in the hopes that my luck would eventually change.

Thursday afternoon, I had lunch with Salim, an Indian businessman who proceeded to end the date by bluntly asking me if I was ready to get married because he wasn't interested in "wasting time." As *#7: ROMANTIC* as his proposal was, I decided a second date was probably not in my best interest.

Thursday evening, I went to dinner with Imad, a recently divorced man who spent the majority of the night convincing me that he was ready to move on and find the one. Nevertheless, when his ex-wife called him in the middle of dessert to "check in" and the ringtone "Nobody Knows It but Me" by Babyface came blasting through his phone, I quickly realized that he was not as ready as he claimed.

Friday afternoon, I had coffee with Karan, an accountant/ magician who tried to impress me by making my credit card disappear. I would've been a lot more impressed had it not taken him another fifteen minutes to figure out how to get it back. Neither I nor the barista was very amused.

Friday night, I met up with Mo, a graphic designer who spent the evening reminding me of how his parents would not really "approve" of my career, as they preferred him to settle down with a doctor or a lawyer. When I asked him if that had anything to do with financial reasons, he looked offended. "Of course not. They obviously don't expect her to practice medicine or law after marriage. It'll be far too difficult with the children. They just want her to have the qualifications."

By the time the weekend rolled around, I had crossed *#2: HONEST, #18: EMOTIONALLY STABLE, #22: MATURE,* and *#30: SENSIBLE* off my mental list. I was thoroughly exhausted and my emotions were drained. I decided, for my own mental health, to take a couple of days off and resume my mission on Monday.

Sleeping in past noon and binge-watching old episodes of *Project Runway* was the perfect remedy. Just when I was beginning to feel slightly replenished, my mother barged into my room on Sunday morning and asked if I could drive her to her friend Yasmeen aunty's house for lunch.

"Why can't you drive there on your own?" I asked, yawning.

"I just wanted to spend some time with you, is that too much to ask?" my mother said, looking hurt. "Every day you are out, out, out. We don't even see you for dinner anymore."

I sighed. *Doesn't she realize that she is the one to blame for that?* I thought, pulling off the covers. Spending time with my mother was definitely not what the doctor prescribed, but I reluctantly agreed. After having a whole day to myself, I figured some fresh air might help get my mind off the Shakespearean tragedy my life had become.

On the drive to Yasmeen aunty's house, my mother attempted to cheer me up with her version of small talk.

"So, did you hear that Meena is engaged?" she began. I cringed. Meena was my first cousin on my mother's side. She was two years younger than me, and even though she lived in India, my mother had felt the need to share with me all of Meena's accomplishments over the past twenty-something years.

"*Meena was named captain of the badminton team at her school. Isn't that wonderful!*" my mother coincidentally mentioned a week after I told her I wanted to quit tennis my junior year of high school. "*Meena is studying engineering*," I learned after I announced to my parents that I was no longer considering law school but, instead, wanted to get my teaching credentials. Although I had never met Meena in person, I knew more about her than I frankly cared to through these snippets of information thrown my way. As a kid, I'd hated the mention of Meena's name because I knew whatever followed would be another reminder of how she had one-upped me for the millionth time. Therefore, it was no shock that she had also managed to get engaged—like the perfect Indian daughter—before me.

"Oh, that's nice," I said pretending to sound interested. I often wondered what it would feel like to be the Meena of my family. To just once do something that my mother would be proud of. But no matter how hard I tried, I always seemed to disappoint her. In my defense, things never quite worked in my favor. It seemed as though there was only room for one Meena in the universe, and the position was filled. I silently prayed that the barrage of lackluster dates from the past few weeks along with my impending deadline would not result in yet another major disappointment.

"Don't feel bad, Leila, *beti*. It will happen for you too," my mother consoled me, even though I had given her no indication of needing consolation. "Marriage is part of our tradition. Every girl dreams of one day being a wife. It is the most important job you will have—aside from being a mother." She looked at me and smiled. I bit my tongue and kept my eyes on the road. "You know, I think maybe you should spend more time with me in the kitchen," she offered. "I can help you with your cooking. A girl your age should know how to do more than just roll *chapatis*, don't you think?"

Once again, my mother did what she always did. She blamed my lack of domesticity for every one of my failures. As if cooking were the not-so-hidden answer to all of life's problems.

"I don't understand how cooking has anything to do with me not being engaged," I muttered, the frustration in my voice edging through.

"*Beti*, it has *everything* to do with you not being engaged. You know what they say: the way to a man's heart is cutting through his stomach."

"I don't think that's the phrase, *Ammi*. I think you've just described murder."

"Oh, you know what I mean, Leila." She playfully slapped my thigh. "The point is, you must make yourself more appealing as a wife. Learn to cook and watch how quickly you'll attract a husband. When I was your age I knew how to make all kinds of . . ." She continued on and on.

I sighed, looking glumly at the road ahead. Even though my mother was trying to be helpful in her own annoying way, she came from a different generation. She didn't understand that my views of marriage and gender roles differed from her own—which was exactly why I had refrained from sharing my answers with her at Seema aunty's office that day. In my opinion, there was more to being a wife than just cooking and cleaning. From my mother's perspective, that was the sole responsibility. While there was nothing wrong with her views, my vision of marriage was more American than Indian. I wanted someone who was not only my dance partner, but also my life partner. Someone who was my equal. Someone who challenged cultural expectations and didn't adhere to conventional gender roles. But how could I make her understand these things? How could I make her see that I desired more—more than what she had—without breaking her heart or causing her to go into hysterics? All her talk about cooking did was reinforce my belief that if cooking was the *only* way to a traditional Indian man's heart, then traditional definitely was not the type of man I wanted to attract.

* * *

"Come in! Come in!" Yasmeen aunty greeted us at the door. The spicy aroma of chai wafted pleasantly from inside.

My mother had insisted that I come in to say hello—even though *I* had insisted it wasn't necessary. I did not win that argument. Yasmeen aunty lived in this palatial home in Palos Verdes Estates with a circular driveway and tall, pristinely pruned hedges lined up like neat little soldiers around the edge of the yard. As we'd walked toward the door, my mother had turned to me and clucked her tongue in disapproval.

"You really shouldn't have worn that hoodie, Leila." She

shook her head. "Can you at least fix that hair on your head?" She reached over to push the hair out of my face. "Try and make yourself look somewhat presentable."

I dodged her reach and quickened my pace. *If I look like such a troll, why is she insisting that I come in? I haven't shampooed in two days; what does she expect my hair to look like?* I thought, trying to smooth out the frizz in the few seconds I had right after ringing the bell. When the door opened, I smiled sweetly. Now that we were in another person's presence, my mother would finally stop fussing over me.

As Yasmeen aunty led us through the marble-tiled foyer into the sitting room, I began salivating at the sight of pistachios, dates, fruits, tea biscuits, and other desserts piled on the coffee table. This seemed quite elaborate for a lunch—even for Yasmeen aunty—but who was I to object to extravagance? I beamed as she handed me a gold-rimmed plate.

"Help yourself, Leila," she said, smiling warmly. "You must be starving; look how thin you are!" She grabbed my waist.

I was suddenly glad I'd come in. Ignoring the daggers of death my mother kept shooting at me from the corners of her eyes, I quickly filled my plate with as many goodies as I could fit. Years of being dragged to social gatherings as a child had taught me it was poor etiquette to load up my plate at someone else's house. It was much more polite to take a small sampling of each item so as not to waste anything. But as soon as I popped a *laddu*, a ball-shaped sweet made entirely of butter, coconut, and sugar, into my mouth, all rules of etiquette flew out the window. I greedily stacked four more *laddus* onto the pile of sweets on my plate, paying absolutely no heed to my mother's embarrassed scowl. Besides, she was the one who'd insisted I come in. I was simply making the best of the situation.

I stuffed another ball of sugary heaven into my mouth and carried my plate of new friends into the living room. My mood lifted: I settled comfortably into the sofa next to my mother, chomping blissfully.

"*Beta*, come sit," Yasmeen aunty called out from the couch. Suddenly, a man a few years my senior walked into the room, nodding shyly at the three of us. "This is Zain, my eldest son. He is in town this week for a conference." Yasmeen aunty motioned him over. "*Beta*, why don't you come join us for lunch?" She cleared her throat and glanced at my mother with a suggestive smile.

The *laddu* suddenly hardened in my mouth. I had been ambushed: This whole thing was a setup! The fancy spread. All the desserts. How could I have so foolishly walked into their trap?

"Sure, *Ammi*," Zain said, taking a seat.

How could my mother do this? I glowered at her. She

was just sitting there casually eating a grape, pretending that she had nothing to do with this. This was a new level of betrayal even for her. I could feel the heat rising in my face. I turned toward the front door, calculating how long it would take to get from the couch to the car, but an escape was out of the question. It was too late. My anger festering, the only thing I could do was stay put and endure the impending humiliation.

I looked over at Zain to find him peering in my direction. He was seated on the opposite end of the couch, our mothers wedged in between us like an awkward tikka roll. *Is he in on this too?* He was dressed a lot nicer than I was, in pleated beige chinos and a light-blue polo shirt. I noticed that his hair had been neatly combed back and his face was freshly shaven. *Was I the only one who didn't know this was a date?* I pried my gaze away from his curious eyes and nervously adjusted the zipper on my hoodie, suddenly feeling very self-conscious.

"So, Zain, *beta*, I hear you are a chiropractor?" my mother began as she stirred a cube of sugar into her chai. She placed the spoon on the edge of the saucer and lifted her cup. "How long have you been practicing?"

"He's been working for seven years now at his own clinic in Houston," Yasmeen aunty responded, patting Zain on the knee. "We are very proud of him." She smiled as the steam from her teacup danced gracefully across her face.

"Very nice," my mother said, turning toward me. "Isn't that *nice*, Leila?" I nodded stiffly and forced a weak smile.

"Zain is thinking about opening up another clinic in Los Angeles, aren't you, *beta*?" Zain nodded, fiddling with his hands. "It will be *so* nice to have him nearby again," Yasmeen aunty exclaimed. Zain gave his mother a thin-lipped smile before glancing in my direction. I turned away.

"Oh, yes. That will be very nice," my mother responded, taking a sip. "You know, we are very proud of our Leila too," she continued after a moment. "She is an English professor."

"Teacher, *Ammi*," I muttered under my breath.

"Huh?" My mother looked at me, confused.

"I'm a teacher, *Ammi*; not a professor," I corrected her. My face flushed a deep crimson.

"Yes, yes, we know, Leila," she said impatiently. She turned back toward the other end of the couch, her back to me. I sank into the plush cushions and swallowed the last bite of *laddu*. It tasted like wet car keys as it passed down my throat.

"She molds the minds of the youth," my mother went on. "Shaping the next generation of thinkers. Our future is in her hands . . ." Every word out of her mouth made my skin crawl. *Why can't she just stop talking?* Indian mothers were known to exaggerate the accomplishments of their children, but this was next-level deception. Yes, I worked with teens, and at times it was honorable and offered small rewards. But the majority of my days were spent explaining why "YOLO" was not a universal theme, trying not to get caught in the cross fire of hormone-related drama, and convincing a bunch of apathetic fifteen-year-olds that writing was more than just texting. On most days, I was simply making sure their young brains weren't rotting rather than attempting to "mold" them.

"It's such wonderful work she does." My mother beamed with pride. I squeezed my eyes shut, hoping I could make the words stop. All of them. It took every cell in my body to force myself not to bolt out of the room.

Yasmeen aunty bobbled her head in agreement. "*Masha'Allah*. That is very admirable work, Leila. Isn't that wonderful, Zain?" Zain pressed his lips together and nodded. The corners of his mouth curled up in slight amusement. *Is it possible to die from sheer mortification?*

For the next hour, our mothers discussed our hobbies, likes, and dislikes while Zain and I sat there, completely mute. I eventually surrendered to the indignity of my situation and found comfort in the fact that I could at least remove myself, if not physically then emotionally, from the entire conversation. At one point, I even dozed off for a minute until my mother elbowed me in the gut. Luckily, I was able to quickly wipe away the drool trailing down the side of my mouth before Zain took notice from the other end of the couch. I could tell by the glum expression on his face that he too had grown bored. He sat there staring at his phone, reading what I imagined to be an article on the legal protocols for how to divorce your parents.

By the time lunch ended, I knew every detail of Zain's personal and professional life, even though we hadn't uttered a single word to each other. While we exchanged our goodbyes at the front door, our mothers exchanged our phone numbers without so much as asking our permission. It wasn't until we had reached the car that my mother finally turned to me excitedly and said, "That went well, Leila, don't you think?"

I glared at her, my mouth agape with incredulity. "*Ammi*, you set me up!"

"I did not do such a thing!" she said with a shocked expression.

"Pfft," I hissed, crossing my arms. "Whatever happened to you letting me find someone on my own?"

"Leila, *beti*, I just want what is best for you." My mother let out an exasperated sigh. "It is my duty as your mother to get you married. Can't you see? You need me, Leila. Otherwise, you're going to end up all alone, and I will have failed," she said with worry.

"I don't need you," I stated firmly as I unlocked the car. "I can do this on my own. In fact, I *am*, and it's only a matter of time until I find someone."

My mother sat in the passenger seat, and I slid in next to

her. "We shall see," she said, unconvinced, folding her hands into her lap.

While I waited for her to fasten her seat belt, I thought about how humiliating it was that my mother had dragged Yasmeen aunty into her little scheme. It was bad enough to be branded unfit for marriage by Seema the matchmaker; I didn't need another one of my mother's friends joining the "Single Leila" pity party. And the fact that the two of them had conspired to involve Zain—without so much as a courtesy warning—was infuriating. I had actually shown up with the word PINK splashed across my rear!

I squeezed my eyes shut. *He must've thought I was pathetic. A total loser.* The only reason I had agreed to this three-month deadline was so I could have some semblance of control over my life. But my mother and her shenanigans were preventing that from happening. I had less than eight weeks left of my own search to deal with. The last thing I needed was for my mother to add another layer of pressure to my situation by blaming me for not allowing her to carry out her "maternal duties." I pulled out of the driveway, tuning out my mother's yammering about how wonderfully the afternoon had gone. Instead, I readjusted the GPS to program the quickest possible route to get home. All I wanted was to crawl back into bed with the box of sweets Yasmeen aunty packed for us and erase all memories of this ambush date from my mind.

Speed Dating

"You should try speed dating!" Hannah exclaimed that Tuesday in Liv's apartment. I wondered if the *Millionaire Matchmaker* episode we were watching had gone straight to her head. "It'll be like going on twenty dates in sixty minutes. Imagine the odds!"

"I don't know," I said, unsure. "Isn't that . . . weird?"

"Says the woman with less than eight weeks left till her deadline," Hannah muttered.

"Leila, time is running out," Liv said seriously. "Weird or not, speed dating is efficient, and that's what matters at this point."

Clearly, Annie was not my only friend who believed in the theory of probabilities.

"I agree," Tania said, grabbing Liv's laptop. "Do you mind?" she asked as Liv gave her a nod of approval. "That Muslim matrimonial website we signed you up on is actually hosting a speed dating event next weekend," she said, bringing up the page. "And it's going to be here in Los Angeles. Look." She turned the laptop toward us so we were facing the screen. We leaned in closer.

"How did you even know about this?" I asked her.

"My cousin told me about it," she said. I glanced back at the screen, skimming through all the information presented on the flyer. Phrases like *Muslim professionals*, *like-minded individuals*, and *meet your other half and complete your deen* popped out at me. *That damn phrase again.* I rolled my eyes. Even if this would help with the numbers game, everything about this event screamed *super lame*. "You're not actually suggesting I go to this, are you?" I turned toward them.

"Why not?" Liv shrugged. "It does sound like a fast and practical way to meet someone. What's there to lose?"

"My dignity?" I exclaimed, but as I looked around at my friends' faces, I realized I wasn't convincing anyone. We all knew any trace of dignity had vanished the second I agreed to my parents' three-month deadline. I sighed dejectedly. "Fine. I'll do it. But one of you has to come with me."

"It says here it's a Muslim speed dating event," Hannah read aloud. "I'm not Muslim, so I'm out."

"Me too. Besides, I don't think Darian would approve of me speed dating other guys. Even if it was just for moral support." Liv smiled apologetically. With Hannah and Liv out of the running, there was only one option left. The three of us turned to Tania.

"I'm not going. No way." Tania shook her head adamantly.

"Why not? You're Muslim *and* you're single!" I stated the obvious.

"But *I'm* not looking!"

"But that doesn't mean you can't!"

"Leila, we both know I'm not exactly an ideal candidate for this."

"Why not? You're *Muslim.* You're *professional.* There's going to be all kinds of people there. How do you know you won't find a *like-minded individual*?" I said, pointing at the flyer.

Tania tugged at her hijab. All this dating talk seemed to make her uncomfortable, especially now that the focus had shifted to her.

"*You* were the one who suggested it," I said, grabbing her by the arm. "Just come with me."

"Leila—"

"Tania, *please*?" I pressed my palms together and pushed out my bottom lip. "I seriously can't imagine doing this with anyone but you."

"You should go, Tania," Liv encouraged her.

"You might even meet some hot guys there!" Hannah concurred.

Tania looked over at me.

"Hot Muslim guys—they could exist." I wiggled my brows playfully.

"Fine, I'll go," she relented as I jumped up and wrapped my arms around her neck.

"Thank you, thank you, thank you!" I cried out in excitement. I still wasn't too keen on the idea of speed dating, but maybe it would be fun. With Tania as my wingwoman, that was certainly looking to be more of a possibility.

* * *

"Are you sure this is it?" I asked as we stood outside the windowless exterior of an old warehouse in downtown L.A. The words THE LOT were spray-painted in graffiti across the side of the building.

"Yeah," Tania replied hesitantly. "I mean, this was the address listed on the flyer." Tania was wearing a pale pink hijab, a matching skirt paired with a sleek black blouse, and leather ankle boots. It was slightly more formal than my black fitted jumpsuit and short, suede, cropped jacket, but even I couldn't deny that Tania looked phenomenal. I suddenly felt slightly apprehensive as we walked through the roped entrance into the building. *Am I underdressed? Should I have worn something more traditional? What kind of men come to these events, and will any of them be husband material?*

The inside hallway was dimly lit with red lights casting shadows along the walls. We followed the sounds of clinking glasses into a large room with tall leather stools and tables lined along the exposed brick walls. There was an old-fashioned jukebox in the corner, and rows of bottles—of every shape and size—decorating the shelves behind a smooth dark countertop. We were in a bar.

"Why would they hold a Muslim speed dating event in a bar?" Tania yelled over the loud music, just as a tall blond man greeted us with a smile.

"You ladies must be here for the event," he said, gesturing toward the doors to his far right. "I'm Iain, by the way," he said, leading us through a sea of tipsy twentysomethings hanging around antique pool tables littered with shot glasses. Tania kept glancing back at me with a bewildered look. I shrugged. Everyone knew that Muslims didn't drink, so it made little to no sense for an Islamic matrimonial service to choose this particular venue for its event. *Perhaps they're trying something different*, I thought as Iain ushered us into a dim, lounge-like room toward the back of the building.

I looked at all the numbered tables lined up throughout the room. "Maybe the tablecloths are laced with bacon too," I whispered in Tania's ear as she suppressed a laugh. There were a sizable number of singles already there. The introverts were standing around awkwardly checking their phones. The extroverts had already begun mingling with drinks in hand. I wasn't great at math, but a quick sweep of the room made it clear the ratios were off. There were more women present than men.

Tania noticed it too. "We're still early," she said. "I'm sure more men will be arriving soon." I nodded, trying to ignore the knot of worry growing in the pit of my stomach. I glanced across the room, noticing a short, rotund aunty signaling us over. She greeted us with an amiable smile.

"*Salaams*! Welcome!" she exclaimed, waving her arms. She was wearing a traditional long-sleeved *salwar kameez* paired with a tightly wrapped hijab; her ultraconservative attire clashed with the sensual aesthetic of the room. The image was jarring. "Come, let's get you ladies signed up," she said in a heavy South Asian accent, leading us toward a long table lined with name tags and a stack of programs highlighting the schedule for the night. I grabbed a Sharpie and scribbled my name onto a white tag.

"Feel free to walk around and introduce yourselves," the aunty said, before waving over another group of singles. I noticed that most of the women in the room were wearing hijabs. *What if this event is geared toward more conservative Muslims?* I was dressed modestly, but I knew there were many Muslim men who preferred a spouse who was more outwardly conservative. Many of these men would consider a woman with an uncovered head to be a deal breaker. I hoped those men would not be in attendance tonight. I didn't need to have my options limited even more.

Tania and I studied the room and slowly inched our way

toward the extroverts, who seemed a bit friendlier. Unsure of what to do next, we lingered for a few minutes sipping the mocktails handed to us by another attractive blond bartender. Tania eventually finessed her way into conversation with a group of chatty professionals, while I walked back to the table with the name tags. I skimmed through the evening's program in order to mentally prepare myself for what was to come. There would be a short introduction by the event organizer (who I assumed was the cheerfully plump aunty), a round of icebreakers, and then the main event—the seven-minute speed dates. I took a few deep, cleansing breaths to calm my faltering nerves. My third exhale was interrupted by a sharp jab to my left rib.

"Look," Tania whispered, nodding her head toward the entrance we came in through. I turned my head in that direction, along with all the other eyes in the room, and saw what could only be described as a real-life Bollywood bombshell. She strutted in glamorously—fully aware of the attention directed at her—with perfectly kohl-lined eyes, high cheekbones, long black hair cascading down her back, and bright red lips to match the traditional red sari she wore—which of course accentuated her curves in all the right places.

She smiled and talked confidently with the aunty, who rushed to greet her, while the handful of men in the room scrambled to pick their jaws up off the ground. I leaned into

Tania, keeping my eyes on this exotic, magnificent creature. "Who is she?" I whispered.

"*She* is our competition," Tania said, nervously adjusting the edge of her scarf. A part of me was relieved to see another non-*hijabi* in the room, but having to go head-to-head with this perfectly contoured specimen didn't ease my confidence levels one bit. I smoothed my hair and leaned against the table, chewing my bottom lip anxiously. *If a woman like that is still single, there's no chance in hell for the rest of us.* I motioned to the bartender to bring me another mocktail.

In the next ten minutes, more attendees began to stream in, and the ratio of men to women—and *hijabis* to non-*hijabis*—gradually balanced out. When the room had reached maximum capacity, we began the icebreaker activities, which were carefully designed to get us moving around and talking to people in an effort to spark an initial interest. Although none of the men really grabbed my attention right off the bat, I reminded myself to remain optimistic. In the midst of all the chatter surrounding me, I even tried a few times to catch another glimpse of Ms. Bollywood Bombshell so I could make sure to situate myself as far away from her as possible. Although I had paid particular attention to my appearance while getting ready for tonight's event, the stress-eating from the past few weeks had finally caught up to me, adding a few extra pounds to my usually thin frame.

I felt attractive enough, but I knew my love handles could never compete with *her* voluptuous figure, so I felt it was best to steer clear. Fortunately, with so many bodies in the room, it was difficult to spot her—which was comforting, to say the least.

After a few minutes, the organizers began waving their hands to get everyone's attention. The chatter gradually faded to a quiet hush. The aunty handed each woman a pink index card while a formally dressed uncle passed out a blue card to each man. On the card, the names of each participant from the opposite gender were listed. Once everyone had a card, the aunty and uncle took turns dictating the ground rules for the main event:

There would be two women seated per table. (I made a silent prayer that I would not be seated at the same table as the red-lipsticked vixen). The men would rotate around the room every seven minutes until they'd had a chance to speak to every woman. After each "date," the participants would fill out *yes* or *no* next to their date's name on the index card. The organizers informed us that if we were on the fence about any of the candidates, it would be in our best interest to go with a *yes* because based on their past experience, "there's no harm in giving someone a second chance."

Tania looked over at me with a smirk, and I couldn't

help but think that my mother would've been very pleased by this philosophy. I rolled my eyes. What was it with South Asians and their emphasis on second—and third, and even fourth—chances? I usually knew whether it was a *yes* or a *hell no* within the first ten minutes. Very rarely did I find myself on the fence. While some may have considered this judgmental (my mother called it picky), I felt like it was more a sign of good intuition. It prevented me from wasting time, and since speed dating—as my friends had so aptly reminded me—was all about efficiency, I figured this intuitiveness would work to my advantage. The faster I sifted through all the frogs, the sooner I'd meet my prince.

At the conclusion of the speed dates, the aunty continued, the participants would submit their cards, and the organizers would review them to see if there were any two-way matches. If there were two yeses, they would contact the couple individually and provide them with each other's information so they could organize a second date at their own convenience.

Once the rules had been established, the women were asked to find a table and take a seat. I grabbed Tania's arm, and we quickly seated ourselves on the opposite side of the room from the Lady in the Red Sari. The men hovered anxiously in the center of the room waiting for the sound of the buzzer that would indicate the first "date." I rubbed my sweaty palms across my thighs.

"Are you ready?" I whispered to Tania.

"I think so," she said confidently, but her thin smile revealed that she was feeling equally nervous. I slowly exhaled, my eyes shifting toward the uncle with the buzzer. There was so much at stake. As reluctant as I was about speed dating, I really hoped this would work. I just needed to find *one* guy. Just one person with whom I clicked. I didn't want to get my hopes up, but with my deadline slowly creeping up, I was running out of time. I looked over at Tania, who was fiddling with the sleeve of her blouse. Even though she appeared calm, I could tell this was difficult for her too, but for different reasons. The probability of disappointment was high for both of us, but I was glad she had agreed to come along. This whole scenario would've been a lot more nerve-racking without a friend. I took in a final breath just as the uncle lowered his hand. The buzzer sounded; the dates had begun.

Speed Date #1

"Wow, you're really beautiful," Suitor #1 said as he pulled out the chair and sat down.

"Thanks," I replied with a smile.

"Yeah, I've been watching you."

"You've been . . . what?" I shifted uncomfortably in my chair.

"I've been watching you since I arrived. I hope I wasn't being too obvious."

"No . . . I mean, I didn't notice until you just told me."

"Yeah, sorry, it just came out." He let out a deep chortle. "I hope I'm not coming off as too much of a creeper," he continued, laughing.

"No, not too much."

"But really. How is a girl like you still single? Let me guess, you must be crazy, right?"

"I don't know, I guess that's for you to decide?" I pressed my lips together.

"Well, you can be crazy in certain areas that are good," he said, giving me a wink. "Do you know what I mean?" he teased.

I shook my head, confused. *Is he making a joke?*

He smiled and gave me another wink. "So," he said, leaning in, "tell me more about you."

"What would you like to know?"

"Anything and everything! Tell me something nobody knows about you."

"Isn't it a little too soon for deep, dark secrets?"

"We've gotta make the most of our time! I can start if you want."

"Okay . . ." I replied hesitantly, taking a sip of my water.

"Well, I'm a virgin . . ." he began. My eyes widened.

"But"—he leaned in closer—"I like that stuff a *lot*."

I sputtered out a cough. "What?" I exclaimed.

"I mean, I think about it all the time, probably because I've never done it." He laughed. *Are we really talking about his virginity? On a first date?* "Don't get me wrong, I want a girl who's conservative," he continued, "but who's also *really* into that stuff too, you know?"

"Yeah . . ." I said, looking over at Tania for help.

"So . . ." He grinned suggestively. "Your turn."

". . ."

BUZZ!

Speed Date #2

"Hi."

"Hi, nice to meet you—" Suitor #2 glanced down at his card. "Leila?"

"Yes, and you are . . ."

"*Doctor* Iqbal Bhatti."

"Right. *Doctor*," I said, trying not to roll my eyes. "So I'm not really sure how to do this, but I guess you can tell me a little about yourself?"

"Well, I'm just finishing up my second year of residency.

I'm adventurous. I like being outdoors, and I'm—I'm sorry . . . but wow, you're really hot!"

"Excuse me?"

"You're just . . . wow! You actually remind me of someone."

"Oh? Who's that?" I smiled, mentally going through all the Bollywood heroines I wouldn't mind being compared to.

"My sister, Najma. *That's* who you remind me of!"

"*Excuse* me?"

"Yeah, you two could literally pass for twins! Your facial features, your demeanor. It's crazy!" *Crazy creepy*, I thought. "Man, I wish I had a picture with me!"

"Oh, um, that's okay. So . . . are you and your sister pretty close?"

"Me and Najma? Nooo." He laughed. "She's my younger sister, so we don't have much in common, but she is *totally* hot!"

"Yeah, you mentioned that . . ."

BUZZ!

Speed Date #3

"So how weird is this?" Suitor #3 said, darting uneasy glances around the room.

"Yeah." I looked behind me, confused.

"No, I mean this is, like, *weird*!" He laughed nervously. "You know, I would never normally do this."

"Oh, speed dating? Yeah. Me neither. But now that we're here, tell me about yourself."

"My friend actually told me about this, so I thought I would check it out," he continued, seemingly distracted.

"Same. So tell me, what is—"

"You know, I always thought people who attended these things were *weird*."

"Really?" *Really?*

"I mean, the whole idea of speed dating is only for people who can't meet someone on their own, you know?"

"That's not . . . true." I frowned. I hadn't met anyone I connected with in real life. Did that make me weird?

"Oh, I mean, it's cool." He shrugged. "I'm not saying this applies to everyone, *obviously*." His eyes wandered to the left behind me. "I'm just saying it's a little weird, that's all."

"Maybe we should talk about something else—" I said as Suitor #3 ducked under the table. "What are you doing?" I asked as he bumped against my leg.

"Shhh," he hissed. "They'll see me."

"Who?" I whispered, turning around.

"I think I just saw someone I know." He shifted underneath the table, lifting up the legs. Tania looked over at me as the whole table tilted to the right. I pointed to my date and shrugged, perplexed. "Let's just keep talking," he called out, his voice muffled under the tablecloth. *Keep talking? With who? The empty seat across from me?*

"Can you just come back up?" I pulled my leg back as he accidentally brushed against it again.

"I don't want *them* to see me," he whispered. *Who the hell is "them"?* I quickly looked around once more for any sign of *them. Is it his boss? His ex-girlfriend? The FBI? This is ridiculous.*

"Look, can you please—"

"You know, I was just thinking," he interrupted, his head peeking out from under the corner. "If this actually works out between us, we shouldn't tell people how we met."

"We shouldn't?"

"No, let's just tell them we met at a coffee shop or something. That's less weird."

"Less weird," I said as he popped back underneath. "Sure."

BUZZ!

Speed Date #4

"So tell me, Leila, what are you looking for in a life partner?"

"Oh, I don't know. Someone who's smart."

"Yes!" Suitor #4 whispered under his breath.

"Funny," I said, pretending not to notice.

"Yes!" he whispered.

"Easy to talk to."

"Yes!"

"Adventurous."

"Yes!" I could sense the volume of excitement growing with each whisper until I finally couldn't take it anymore.

"I'm . . . I'm sorry, why do you keep doing that?"

"Doing what?" He looked at me, confused.

". . . Never mind."

BUZZ!

Speed Date #5

"Hello, hello!"

"Hello." I drew in a deep breath and smiled.

"How's your evening going so far?"

"So far, okay. Yours?"

"Much better now!" Suitor #5 flashed me a confident grin. "So, what do you think of—" His phone began to ring. He pulled it out and glanced at the screen. "I'm sorry, this is my mother calling. Do you mind if I . . . ?" He pointed to the phone.

"Not at all."

"Great, thanks!" He placed the phone to his ear. "*Salaam, Ammi!* No, I'm at the speed date now. Yes, in fact I'm sitting with someone now." He looked across the table and smiled. "No, no, she's very nice. Yes, she's *very* pretty, *masha'Allah,*" he said, blushing. "Yes, I think you would like her . . . I don't know, I was just about to ask her before you . . . Okay . . . Okay. Okay." He covered the phone with his hand and turned to me. "She wants to talk to you." He held out the phone. "Would you mind saying *'Salaam'* to her?"

". . ."

BUZZ!

Speed Date #6

"So is this not going as well as you thought?"

"Huh? What do you mean?" I asked.

"I mean, it doesn't really look like you're having a lot of fun."

"No, I am."

"I don't believe you!" Suitor #6 persisted.

"I'm having a great time. *Really*," I stated firmly.

"Let me see you smile then!"

"Excuse me?"

"Smile! It's the only way I'll believe that you're having any fun!"

"Or you can just believe me because I said so?" I said, trying to mask my irritation.

"I don't think I can do that, little lady."

I cringed. "And why's that?"

"Because of your face." I scrunched my brows together. "Yeah, your face. It just doesn't look like it's having much fun." *Did this guy just tell me I didn't have a fun face? How am I supposed to make my face look fun? Plaster confetti all over it?*

I pressed my lips together and forced a small smile.

"There it is!" He slammed his palm against the table. "*Now* let's have some fun!" He winked, grinning broadly.

BUZZ!

Speed Date #7

Suitor #7 sat down and barely said three words. Instead, he just stared at my breasts. I pulled the flaps of my jacket closer and tried to attempt a conversation.

"So, is this your first time dating . . . I mean, speed dating?"

"Hurrhhhh," he muttered unintelligibly.

I took a sip of my water, unsure what to do. I looked over at Tania, expecting her to give me a sign that this was going as disastrously for her as it was for me. But instead, she was deeply immersed in a conversation with a well-dressed, bearded man. He was leaning in toward her, and they were laughing as if they had just shared an intimate joke. Tania was shyly touching her face, and the man was gazing directly into her eyes. I sighed, looking back at my date, who had now focused his entire attention on my left boob. I glanced at my watch, waiting intently for the buzzer.

BUZZ!

Speed Date #8

I watched as the bearded man said goodbye to Tania and made his way over to my side of the table. "Hi," I said.

"Hi," he replied as he glanced over at Tania once more, watching her as she introduced herself to the next suitor.

"So, your name is?" I said impatiently.

"Zeeshan," he said, barely looking at me. He was so focused on Tania that he forgot to reciprocate the question.

"Well, I'm Leila, in case you were wondering." He made a low, inaudible sound, his gaze still distracted. After about a minute of silence, I finally broke my composure. "You really like her, don't you?"

"Who?" he asked, caught off guard as he turned to me for the first time. There was a look of sincerity in his dark brown eyes. I nodded my head to the right. "Oh, I mean . . ." He blushed and smiled bashfully.

"I don't blame you; she is pretty great."

He arched his eyebrows. "Do you know her?"

"Tania? Yeah, she's one of my best friends." I smiled as he glanced over at her again.

"Do you think she— I mean do you know if maybe . . . I don't know . . ." He trailed off nervously. I looked at Tania and noticed her peering at Zeeshan too.

"I have a feeling she might . . . *you know.*"

"Really?" He beamed and leaned back in his chair. "Cool."

BUZZ!

As Zeeshan got up to move to the next table, I motioned for Tania's attention and gave her a quick thumbs-up. She stared at me, confused, but then I pointed to Zeeshan and wiggled my brows up and down. Her face reddened as she smiled. I glimpsed at my watch once more. *Almost done*, I thought.

Speed Date #9

"Hey, so since we don't have much time, let me tell you about myself," Suitor #9 said before he even sat down. "I was in born in Kansas in 1982. Now, I know what you're thinking. *Kansas?* And before you say anything, let me just tell you that Kansas has a lot more to offer than just wheat and sunflowers! I went to this private day school in Atchison. Fun fact: it was the same school that Amelia Earhart attended until she was twelve—"

"That is interesting," I tried to break in. "But since we've only got seven minutes, maybe you can skip the early years and tell me more about—"

"So when I was fourteen, my family moved to Fort Dodge, Iowa. Now, if you thought Kansas was an interesting place for a little brown boy like myself, wait until you hear about Iowa—"

"Actually, we could probably skip your teenage years as well—"

"My sophomore year, I joined the Math Olympiads, and boy was that a trip! During our first competition, Jonathan De Russo . . ."

I glanced at the clock. For the next three minutes, Suitor #9 continued to talk nonstop—his words hitting me like a bullet train. He told me about his first crush, his delayed puberty, his sex-addicted roommate in college. With the minutes ticking down, I eventually exploded.

"Are you even the slightest bit interested in anything I have to say?"

"I'm so sorry!" he said, taken aback. It was the first second of silence we had gotten since the moment he sat down. "Of course, you're right! I'm so sorry! I really am!"

"It's okay." I relaxed a bit. I hadn't meant to be so blunt, but since he seemed genuinely sorry, I decided to let it slide. "Well," I began as Suitor #9 pulled out a pad of paper and a pen from the inside pocket of his blazer. "I teach high school English. I'm an only child, and I've lived in L.A. my whole life." I noticed him jotting down notes. I tried to continue as normal, but my curiosity finally got the best of me. "What are you doing?" I asked, pointing to his pad.

"Oh." Suitor #9 looked up, smiling sheepishly. "I'm just writing down all the things I want to tell you when it's my turn to talk again."

I placed my head in my hands and silently prayed for the night to be over. This was not at all what I'd had in mind.

BUZZ!

Speed Date #10

"Last but not least." Suitor #10 smiled, taking a seat. "So what does a pretty girl like you do?"

"I'm a teacher. What about you?"

"I'm an engineer," he said, still smiling. "Original, I know."

I laughed. "Where do you work?"

"I'm actually in between jobs right now."

I lifted my brows.

"It's a long story," he said, waving his hand. "But my work visa expired recently, so I'm not able to work per se."

"Oh. I see."

"That's kind of why I'm here."

"In L.A.?"

"No, at this speed dating event." He leaned in. "I need to find a solution, quick." He laughed nervously.

"Oh," I said, taking a sip of my water. I had heard about "status seekers" from Tania before. How these men often made the rounds, searching for women who would help them live out their American dreams in exchange for money or jewelry or companionship. Unfortunately for Suitor #10, I was not interested in a business transaction. I was looking for a husband. A husband who found *me* more attractive than my blue passport.

As Suitor #10 spent the next few minutes attempting to pitch me a sale, my mind began to drift. Two months ago, I was spending my weekends hiking and shopping and hanging out with my friends. Now I was sitting here at this lame event trying to remember the last time I had had any fun. Another Saturday totally wasted. From a distance, I could hear the sound of the final buzzer.

"Well, it was very nice meeting you, Leila. I'm glad they saved you for last."

"Ditto." I smiled back politely. "You were definitely the perfect way to end this night," I muttered under my breath as I got up.

As Mr. Status Seeker walked away, I picked up my index card and wrote a giant *NOPE* across the top. Then I drew a dark vertical line through each guy's name, and handed it to the aunty, who was making her way past each table with an eager smile. I waited for Tania to finish so we could walk out together.

The night was cool as we stepped outside. A safe distance from the building, I finally turned toward Tania expressing my frustration. "Oh my goodness. Could that have gone any worse? I mean, are there *no* normal guys in this city anymore?"

Tania remained silent. She was staring straight ahead with a small smile across her face.

"*Helloooo.* Are you even listening to me?" I snapped my fingers in front of her.

"Yeah!" she exclaimed, finally making eye contact. "I don't know." She shrugged. "I guess I just didn't think they were that bad."

"Not that bad?! Seriously?" I asked, confounded. She had this weird, dazed look in her eyes. "What is with you?"

"*Nothing*," she said defensively, still smiling.

"Are you thinking about that guy with the beard?"

"Zeeshan," she said, her smile spreading into a grin. I hit her on the arm. She flushed a deep pink and turned away.

As Tania gushed about how quickly she and Zeeshan had hit it off and how she hoped he had selected *yes* for her too because she really wanted to see him again, I checked my phone to see two missed calls from my mother. My heart felt heavy with disappointment. I knew she was going to ask me about my night as soon as I got home, and I really wished I had better news.

I looked over at Tania. I hadn't seen her this excited about a guy . . . *ever.* After everything she had been through in her past, she was more deserving of finding love than anyone, and I was glad she had made that connection. But her excitement just highlighted the fact that I had yet to feel the same way. Not once in this entire process had I felt the giddiness that she was experiencing now. *That's what love is supposed to feel like, right?* I knew that the more dates I went on, the greater my chances would be of finding the one I was meant to be with. But as I listened to Tania recount every detail from her seven minutes with Zeeshan on the drive home, I was starting to wonder if a real connection was ever going to happen for me.

Summer Lovin'

School was finally out for the summer. After saying goodbye to the last of my students, I settled at my desk, grading papers and submitting final grades. Halfway through my third stack of essays, I heard a knock on my classroom door. "Come in," I called out from behind a pile of papers. It was Tania.

She greeted me cheerily as she walked in carrying two iced tea lattes.

"Hey! I thought we were meeting at the Twisted Olive?" I said, glancing at the clock hanging above the door. My friends and I were going out tonight to celebrate the end of the school year, but also—and more importantly—to discuss the major problem we were facing (and by *we* I meant *me*). We were a month and a half into my three-month window, and I had yet to find a decent prospect. Time was slipping by, and we needed to come up with a solution. Fast.

"Happy last day of school!" Tania raised a celebratory cup and placed it on my desk, the condensation from the ice creating a circular ring on the wooden surface. "I just thought you could use a break," she said, pulling up a chair next to me.

"Great!" I pushed my laptop in her direction. "I was just thinking about getting a cat. What do you think of this one?" I asked, clicking on a picture of an orange tabby from the local shelter. "I'm wondering, does this face scream 'cat lady' or whisper it, because you know how I prefer subtlety," I said, taking a sip of my drink.

"Stop." She rolled her eyes and jabbed me with her elbow.

"Ouch!"

She laughed, elbowing me again. Her usually reserved disposition was much more sprightly these days.

"So what's new with you, Ms. Sunshine?"

Tania shrugged. "Nothing." She said with a playful smile.

"How are things with you and Zeeshan?"

"They're good," she said, her cheeks turning the same hue as the roses on her blouse. "We went out for dinner again last night."

"*And?*" I leaned in, prying inquisitively. From what I had heard, the two of them had either met or spoken to each other every day since the speed dating event last weekend. It sounded like things were getting serious fairly quickly.

"And, he's great." She beamed.

"Tania!" I cried. "This is so exciting! Do you think he might be . . . *you know*? The one?"

"I mean, it's too soon to tell but—I *really* like him." She sighed.

"That's great news . . . *right*?"

"It's just we haven't exactly had *the talk* yet."

"Ohhhh." I leaned back in my chair.

We both knew how judgmental the South Asian community was. Particularly toward divorced women. Once a woman had that stigma attached to her, regardless of the circumstances, it was almost impossible to change people's opinions of her, especially as a prospect for marriage. As tough as it was for me to find a husband at the "ripe" age of twenty-six, I knew that Tania's situation was even tougher because of her past.

"Maybe you shouldn't say anything yet," I finally said. "It's only been a week. Get to know him a little more, and when you feel comfortable, then you should let him know. If he's as great as you say he is, it might not even be a problem."

"You think?" She bit her bottom lip. I could tell she really wanted to believe me, but the tone of her voice indicated that she wasn't quite convinced. "You know, I actually came here for another reason. I wanted to talk to you about something before we met up with Hannah and Liv."

"Oh?" I looked at her quizzically. "Did you rob a bank? Are you looking for an alibi? Do you need to flee the country?

Because with everything going on around here, I might not be opposed to it."

She shook her head. "Leila, I wanted to talk to you about your situation."

My situation?

I pushed the laptop aside to let her know that she had my full attention.

"I think it's good that you're putting yourself out there and have been open to speed dating events and dating online. I know this is hard." She gave me a sympathetic smile. "Believe me, I know. But sometimes I feel like you might be making things harder for yourself."

I looked at her, confused.

"I think you need to consider investing more time in people. First dates are rarely great. You know this better than anyone. But it takes more than one meeting to *really* get to know a person." As she continued, my mind reeled through all the one-date disasters I had experienced over the past six weeks. Was she talking about those guys? I had a difficult time believing I might've written any of them off too soon.

"There's no harm in giving someone a second chance, Leila," she said. Suddenly, the plump aunty from the speed dating event was sitting in the corner sharing *chum chums* with Seema the matchmaker and my mother—the three of them nodding in unison.

This was my future we were talking about. This was the person I could potentially spend the rest of my life with. While there was no harm in second chances, the right guy wouldn't need a second chance to prove he was right for me. It would be obvious from the get-go. Of this I was convinced.

"Tania, you were at that event last weekend. Aside from the *one* normal guy you met, do you honestly think any of those speed dates were worth a second chance?"

"They weren't *all* bad—"

"What about Mr. Bollywood?"

"Omar? The guy Hannah set you up with?" She shrugged.

"Mr. *BAM BAM BAM*?" I emphasized to jog her memory. "You're telling me *that* guy wasn't as obnoxious as a self-checkout machine at the grocery store?"

"Leila." She sighed. "He liked to sing. What's the big deal?"

"The big deal?!" I stared at her, feeling frustrated. Why was she trying to minimize this? "You know what, forget Omar. What about Imran, Sajid, Mahmoud, and all the other ones?!" I cried in defense. "Do you really think I missed an opportunity with any of them?" I waited as she thought for a moment.

"Assuming they were *really* as bad as you described them . . ." She hesitated.

"Are you saying I exaggerated how awful those dates were?"

"No . . . Leila . . ." She trailed off. "Leila, I get that you're under a lot of pressure—"

"I've got *six weeks* to find a husband. Not a date for prom, Tania. I'm looking for a *husband*! Yeah, I'm under a lot of pressure," I said with a sneer. Why was she acting like the idea of marriage was no big deal? If anyone understood the magnitude of this situation, it should've been her.

"I'm just suggesting—for *your* sake—to perhaps reconsider your approach moving forward."

What approach did she think would help me be more successful at this? I had agreed to go on blind dates, online dates, speed dates. I had gone to a professional matchmaker and even suffered through an ambush date! After all my efforts, I still had to endure taunts from my parents about "not trying hard enough." And as if that weren't bad enough, I had to watch my mother's face crumple each time she asked me about another failed date. I really didn't need my friends to start criticizing me too.

"I just think it might help to relax a bit."

"Easy for you to say. You've already found someone," I muttered scornfully.

Tania turned a deep red.

"Look, Leila. I know what it's like to be tossed aside at first glance," she said, her voice slightly quivering. "But no one is perfect. Everyone you meet is going to have flaws or something about them you may not like."

I looked down at my hands and sighed. I didn't want flaws. I wanted the quintessential, human embodiment of those seven napkins.

"Choosing to focus only on a person's flaws rather than all the other things they may have to offer is only going to hinder you in this process."

I slumped back in my chair, allowing her words to sink in. My mind drifted back to all the men I had rejected from the matrimonial sites without so much as meeting them because they had used a dangling modifier, or liked pineapple on their pizza, or mentioned "collecting stuff" multiple times in their bios. I still felt justified in most of those dismissals . . . but perhaps there may have been *some* instances when I reacted too hastily.

"It might help to ease up on some of your expectations, Leila. That's all I wanted to tell you."

I sat there for a moment ruminating over her advice. I wondered if anyone had ever told Rani Mukerji's character to "not be so hasty" when she dressed up as a man to impress her sexy yet serious cricket coach in *Dil Bole Hadippa!* Or if they had asked Aishwarya Rai's character to be "more realistic" when she spent decades pining after a childhood crush despite his family's disapproval in *Devdas.* I sighed again, taking a sip of my drink.

As much as I wanted my real-life love story to mirror the fictionalized romances I saw in the movies, maybe it was time to come to terms with the fact that these tantalizing fantasies were nothing more than just that. Fantasies. *What if I did invest more time in people? What if I gave myself more than an hour to get to know someone?* Maybe Tania had a point. I was starting to come to terms with the fact that Mr. Perfect probably didn't exist, but that didn't mean I couldn't find someone great.

Suddenly, my phone vibrated, jolting me from my thoughts. Before I could check to see who it was, Tania grabbed the phone off my desk.

"Who's Zain?" She searched my face for a reaction as she held up my phone.

"Zain?" The single syllable floated in the air for a few seconds before registering in my mind. Suddenly my mother, Yasmeen aunty, the plate of *laddus*—all of it came rushing back. "Give me that!" I reached for my phone.

She swiveled back in her chair, just out of my reach. "He enjoyed meeting you the other day," she read the text message aloud, her voice emphasizing each intonation. "He wants to see you again—minus the supervision this time." Tania raised an eyebrow. She cleared her throat when I refused to say anything. "Um. Mind telling me what this is about?"

I squirmed in my seat. "Nothing," I groaned, rotating her chair forward with my leg and snatching the phone from her hand. "It was just a date that my mom arranged. I didn't even know about it." I rolled my eyes, trying to ignore the pounding in my chest.

I looked at the screen and reread the text messages. I couldn't believe Yasmeen aunty's son was texting me. He had barely said two words to me that entire afternoon. I couldn't really blame him, though. The whole setup by our mothers was utterly humiliating. I left that afternoon hoping to never be within a five-mile radius of him—or his mother—again. But maybe this was what Tania was talking about. *Did I dismiss him too soon? What if this is my opportunity to give someone a second chance?*

As I tried to reason with myself, little voices of doubt kept creeping into the back of my mind: *Why is he reaching out to me? Is it possible that he likes me? Even after the awkwardness of our first meeting? Or is he being forced to text me by our mothers?* I tried to push these questions out of my head, but a tiny part of me couldn't help but feel slightly skeptical.

"I'm not really sure what I should say." I looked at Tania sheepishly.

"Here, give me that." She took the phone from my hands. "Based on the great advice I've just given you, you're going to message him back saying, 'Yes, of course I'd love to see you again, Zain,'" she read out each word slowly as she typed. "'Let me know when you're free.'" She tapped her finger on the screen. "*Aaaand* send." She held out her hand in my direction—the phone sitting neatly in the cup of her palm—with a smug look on her face.

I grabbed the phone and desperately clicked on my messages. My heart sank as soon as I saw the blue bubble. "You put a winky face at the end!"

"Yeah, so?" She shrugged.

"Oh my God!" I covered my face in shame. "Tania! Only desperate girls use the winky face emoji!" I grumbled through my hands.

"Leila, relax." Tania tried to calm me. "Haven't we had this discussion before? You *are* desperate."

I shot her a dirty look through my fingers.

She laughed. "Don't overthink everything." She pulled my hands from my face. "You have six weeks left till your deadline. Forget all your expectations and just go with it."

I glanced down at my vibrating phone.

Great! How's tomorrow night? the message read.

I stared at it. My first date with Zain had not exactly been romantic by Bollywood standards, but my repulsion to that afternoon had more to do with my mother than with him. Although I'd had my doubts as to whether he had been involved with the ambush in some way, maybe a second try would still be worth it—as long as he wasn't being coerced by his mother this time. Also, the likelihood of a second date going any worse than the first was staggeringly low, and with my deadline looming, I knew I couldn't afford to lose out on another potential prospect. My heart palpitating like a magnitude five earthquake, I finally picked up the phone and started typing.

Sounds great! I texted back. I looked at Tania nervously. She gave me a reassuring grin, and the little tabby smiled at both of us from behind the illuminated screen, reminding me that there might be a small glimmer of hope just yet.

Take Two

I walked into the lounge area of the Blue Dolphin. The smooth, soulful sound of jazz greeted me from the small stage at the front of the room. I crisscrossed my way between cocktail tables covered with liquor-filled glasses and steeped in intimate conversations, scanning the room for Zain. *Seriously, what is with Muslims and dating in bars?* I adjusted my blouse nervously and smoothed out my ankle-length pencil skirt. I had taken extra care to look my best, since the last time we had met, I'd been sporting a hoodie and drool.

There were plush sofas lined up along the back wall separated by thin curtains giving an illusion of privacy. The air was thick with a smoky quality, and the lights were dimmed, with the exception of a single spotlight focused on a sexy singer onstage—a slender, mocha-skinned woman with curly hair and a sultry voice nuzzling up against the microphone as if she were a slinky cat on the prowl. A saxophone player and a pianist played in the background, but all eyes were drawn to the singer. I watched her curiously, trying to memorize her subtle movements in hopes that her coolness would somehow transfer onto me. I was so entranced by her performance that I didn't even realize that Zain had arrived until I felt a hand on my shoulder.

"Hey." He smiled, still touching my shoulder.

"Hey." I returned the smile, tucking a strand of loose, wavy hair behind my ear.

"You made it."

"I did."

His hand softly glided down my arm to my elbow. "I saved us a seat," he said, leading me toward the back wall. He drew aside one of the semi-sheer curtains and gestured me in. There was no one in there. *I guess he meant what he said about not wanting any supervision.* I took a seat on the couch and adjusted the pillows behind me. Zain sat down next to me. We both glanced at each other and then quickly looked away, laughing nervously.

Within moments, a cocktail waitress appeared. "Would you like something to drink?" she asked.

"An Arnold Palmer would be nice."

Zain turned to me with surprise. "You don't drink?"

"No," I replied, surprised by his surprise. "Do you?"

"I don't," he said, still smiling. This time I was taken by

surprise. In my past experiences, it was rare to find a Muslim American man who didn't drink, at least socially. While my abstinence to alcohol was partially for religious reasons and partially a personal choice, it was refreshing to know we shared this in common, even though I didn't yet know Zain's reasons for not drinking. What if he was more religiously conservative than I was? Which might end up being a turnoff . . . Or what if he swung farther to the left and was a recovering alcoholic who was laying off the booze for some kind of twelve-step program? Despite my desire to find out more, I resisted the urge to judge prematurely and simply returned his smile.

"How about we make it two Arnold Palmers," he told the waitress, and waited until she left before facing me again. "I had a feeling there was more to you than your love of *laddus*."

"I had no idea that was a setup, by the way." I touched my face nervously with the tips of my fingers. I could feel my cheeks getting hot.

"Neither did I." He grinned. "But I think that was the point."

I was relieved to know he hadn't been involved with the ambush. It made him seem more likable. More trustworthy. The waitress came in with our drinks, and Zain politely thanked her.

"So what made you reach out to me after all of that?" I stirred my drink with the thin red straw and took a sip. "One afternoon of torture wasn't enough for you?"

"Well, to be honest, I felt bad."

"Oh?" I asked, trying to push aside my disappointment. *He felt bad?* I *knew* he'd only contacted me out of pity. I tried to play it cool, but I could feel the heat rising in my face once again.

"I felt bad," he repeated, taking a sip, "that we didn't get a proper chance to meet each other the first time around, so I wanted to do it right." He gazed directly into my eyes, and I blinked, looking away. It was the first time I noticed how attractive he was. He had warm brown eyes that half squinted each time he laughed. His short hair curled neatly at the nape of his neck, and there was a small black mole right above his upper lip that disappeared whenever he smiled. "You're definitely someone I'd like to spend more time getting to know."

"Really?" I squeaked, then suddenly looked down, embarrassed about coming across as too eager.

"Really." He smiled. My skin tingled as I felt his eyes on me. I liked that I didn't need to compete with his phone, or an ex-lover, or his passion for singing to get his attention. I had it all, and there was something exhilarating about that.

"I do feel like there's something missing, though," he said.

I looked around the enclosed room, the sounds from the other side of the curtain filling the small space. "Our mothers?" He chuckled and moved in closer on the cushion next to me. The top of his knee bumped against my leg, and for a brief second, the room felt electric.

"I was thinking food." He grinned, motioning toward the waitress, who had come back inside.

After we had given our orders, I asked Zain about the new clinic he was opening in Los Angeles. He shrugged and said, "You don't really want to talk about that, do you? Why don't you tell me more about all the young minds you mold?"

I smiled and began telling him about teaching—how I stumbled into it accidentally and ended up falling in love with the idea of somehow making a difference. I talked about my friends; my family; my life. I was drawn to his sense of ease. His humble mannerisms. He was confident but not arrogant. Affectionate without trying too hard. On past dates, conversations had felt loaded, fraught with nerves, but talking to Zain was comfortable. Easy.

"So what kind of movies do you like?"

"Action, thrillers. Oh, and my all-time favorite movie is *Star Trek: First Contact*!" he said, excitedly.

"*Star Trek*!" I feigned shock. "I had no idea you were such a nerd."

Zain pretended to look hurt. I giggled.

"You know, normally this would be the point where we

would go our separate ways, but I'm trying this new thing out where I actually give people a chance."

"Oh?" He raised an eyebrow. "I feel so lucky."

"Also, I'm really hungry, and the food hasn't arrived yet."

Zain laughed. "You know what I like about you, Leila?" He leaned in as if to tell me a secret. I took in the smell of his skin—clean and sharp, like the cool air right after it rained.

"What?"

"I like that you make me laugh," he said, his eyes creasing at the edges.

The heat from Zain's body closed in the gap between us, and everything stood motionless as our eyes locked for a few still moments. My heart pumping in my ears, I felt like I was under a spell. *Is he thinking of kissing me?* I thought as he reached out and gently tucked a strand of hair behind my ear. His fingers lightly caressed the outline of my chin, the soft touch lingering even after he drew his hand away. Zain playfully leaned his shoulder into mine, and I turned away. We both laughed just as the waitress walked in with our food.

We spent the next couple of hours in the privacy of our curtained enclave enjoying each other's company. We swapped embarrassing childhood memories—like when his mother dressed him up in a gold sequined shirt and had him perform "*Tu Cheez Badi Hai Mast Mast*" onstage at his school talent show. Or when he found out that the marshmallows in his favorite Lucky Charms cereal were not *halal* and he locked himself in his room and cried for half a day.

Through the night, I had to keep reminding myself to play it cool because the last thing I wanted was to end up disappointed. But every time I heard the sound of his laugh, or felt his body close to mine or his fingers press against my knee, I felt fireworks inside. I was engrossed by his presence. I wanted to know everything about him. Even when he was sharing the most mundane details about his work, I found myself captivated, hanging on his every word. I liked Zain. I liked who he was. I liked how he made me feel, how I could be entirely myself around him.

At the end of the night, Zain walked me back to my car, and just as I was about to turn away, he pulled me in close, embracing me with a tight, lingering hug. I could feel myself melt into his arms, the sound of our hearts synchronizing into one steady beat. As I mentally went down the list of all the traits I could remember, I couldn't believe how easily I was able to check them all off: *#2: HONEST*—check. *#4: SENSE OF HUMOR*—check. *#8: SUCCESSFUL*—check. *#10: NORMAL*—check. *#17: CHARMING*—check. *#46: SEXY*—check, and on and on. Never had someone come so close to everything on that list. He might not have been Mr. Perfect, but he was pretty damn close.

When I finally got home, I tiptoed into my parents' bedroom. By the sounds of the snores, I could tell they were both fast asleep. I went over to the right side of the bed, where my mother lay passed out, and kissed her softly on the cheek, careful not to wake her. Despite all her crazy antics, I was glad she hadn't given up her matchmaking schemes entirely. Maybe she did know what she was doing. And maybe . . . just maybe . . . I needed her after all.

Ghosted

It had been exactly two days, nineteen hours, and twenty-nine minutes since the last time I had heard from Zain. Not that I was counting. I wish I could say that I spent the time casually going about my day, totally cool and confident with how the date went. But in reality, I spent every waking minute dissecting the entire night in my head, replaying every single minute, picking it apart to the bones. I checked my phone obsessively while simultaneously hating the fact that I had allowed myself to become so invested after just one date. A million insecurities clawed at the back of my mind, preventing me from thinking clearly: *Why hasn't he called yet? Will he ask me out again? What if he isn't interested? What if I wasn't pretty enough? Maybe it was just a pity date after all.* By the time Tuesday rolled around, I was a total mess.

"So he hasn't texted or called you since Saturday?" Liv asked.

I nodded and buried my head in my knees. "What do you

think it means?" I asked, my words smothered behind my sweatshirt.

"Maybe he's following the three-day rule," Hannah offered. "You know, when a guy waits three days before asking to see you again, so he doesn't appear desperate."

"No one follows that rule anymore." I looked up at Tania and Liv. "Right? That rule no longer applies, *right*?" My voice rose with uncertainty.

"I suppose it depends on how interested the guy is," Liv said. "I've had guys call or text back the very next day. Sometimes even the same night."

I buried my head once again. There was a hollow pit forming in the base of my stomach.

"I just don't understand what happened." I squeezed the corners of my eyes. "That night seemed so . . . perfect. He kept leaning in close to me. We practically laughed the whole time. He even held my hand as he walked me to my car—and not just a flimsy hand-hold but like this." I interlocked my fingers to show them. I could still feel the warmth of his fingers as they wrapped around mine. I swallowed the lump that was rising in my throat. "I just . . . I . . . I really like him."

The room was quiet, none of us knowing what to say.

After a few moments, Tania broke the silence. "Okay, let's break this down. What did he say to you after he walked you to your car?"

I scanned my mind, trying to remember as clearly as I could. "We hugged, and he said good night? I think?" I had spent so much time replaying the dinner portion of the date that the last part of the night seemed hazy now.

"But did he say he's looking forward to seeing you again? Or that he'll call you? Or . . . something?"

I shook my head. "I can't remember."

"He lives in Houston, right? How long was he in town for?"

"I think only a week. Do you think he might have flown back and that's why he didn't call?" I perked up at the possibility. What if I was overreacting? It had only been two days. Maybe everything was fine.

"Possibly. But . . ." Tania trailed off.

"What?"

Tania looked over at Liv and Hannah, and then back at me. "It's not like they don't have phones in Houston." She sat down next to me. "He still could've texted you or something to let you know he had a nice time."

My heart dropped again.

"If the date went as well as you say, Leila, why don't *you* just text him?" Hannah looked around at our faces. "There's no rule against that, is there?"

The room went silent again.

"I disagree," Tania stated firmly. "I think if there's interest, it's the guy's job to initiate."

"Says who?" Hannah pushed.

"No one . . . it's just kind of understood," Tania said. I nodded, letting her know that I agreed. I had gone out with enough *desis* over the past couple of months to know that men were always the ones to initiate a second date. I think it had something to do with the thrill of the chase. Whenever women did the pursuing, it ended in heartbreak. Take Naina Kapoor in *Kabhi Khushi Kabhie Gham* or Veronica Malaney in *Cocktail*—the last thing I wanted was to share their fate.

"I just don't think it's that big of a deal," Hannah said.

"I do." Tania shrugged.

"I'm kind of with Hannah," Liv said. "What if he's just really timid?"

"Or what if he's unsure of how *you* felt about the date, so he's just playing it safe?" Hannah asked.

"Do you really think?" I suddenly felt perplexed. I thought I'd made it clear to Zain that I really liked him. I laughed at all of his jokes—even the one about the imam in a bar. I could no longer remember the punch line, but I was pretty sure it wasn't that funny. I listened attentively to stories about his patients at the clinic; I pretended not to be horrified when he admitted he was a Trekkie. I "accidentally" touched his arm multiple times throughout the night. I was nothing short of obvious in the way I flirted with him . . . unless, *maybe I wasn't? Maybe I should have made more eye contact? Or sat closer to him?* I suddenly began second-guessing my every move. Every detail from that night was now painted with streaks of doubt.

"Most guys aren't that good at picking up on subtle cues. Maybe you felt like you were making your feelings clear, but he still had no idea," Hannah explained.

"Maybe . . ." I wondered aloud.

"*And* technically, he did initiate the second date," Hannah continued.

"He did?"

"Yeah. Wasn't the first date the one your moms set up?"

She was right! I'd completely forgotten about the ambush.

"What's the rule on third dates?" Liv asked, turning toward Tania.

"I . . . I don't know," Tania said slowly. "I don't go on many third dates."

"What about with Zeeshan?"

"He's always initiated all our dates," she said quietly, turning a deep pink.

"If only Zain were the same way." I dropped my head in my hands. "What do I do?"

"Text him!" Hannah exclaimed.

"It couldn't hurt." Liv nodded in agreement. I looked at Tania. She shrugged but didn't protest. Maybe that meant she wasn't totally opposed to the idea. Maybe it wasn't that big a deal. I had just spent the last two days agonizing over why

Zain hadn't texted me. My patience and emotions were wearing thin. And why should I be the one doing all the waiting? I was a modern, independent, twenty-first-century woman who didn't even want a traditional husband! Why was I adhering to traditional rules by sitting around in the hopes that Zain would make the next move? And, he *technically* did initiate the second date, as Hannah pointed out. Maybe the ball *was* in my court.

"Grab my purse," I finally said, my mind made up. All these rules were silly. I had wasted days wondering and doubting and guessing when I could've just texted him. Women initiated dates all the time. Maybe not in Bollywood films, but in real life, it was no big deal. *If Zain is the type of man who's uncomfortable with a woman texting him first, then maybe he isn't the nontraditional husband I'm looking for after all*, I thought, biting my lip.

"Have you thought about what you're going to say?" Hannah asked, handing me my purse.

While rummaging through the contents at the bottom of my bag, I tried to compose the perfect message. *Should I be forthright? Should I be coy? Should I be breezy and casual?* My palms were sweating and I hadn't even started texting yet. I finally fished out my phone and held it in front of me like a ticking bomb. "I can't think of what to say!" I exclaimed desperately.

"Want me to do it?" Tania offered. I jerked back the phone.

"No thanks. In case you forgot, that was how I got into this mess in the first place!" I stared at the screen until my heartbeat steadied, and then finally clicked on Zain's name and began typing—my fingers shaking as they hovered over the screen.

"'Hey, you! Had a great time the other night . . .'" I read aloud.

"Tell him you want to see him again!"

"Oh, and ask him when he's available."

"Is that too aggressive?"

"Maybe you should just wait another day before texting him?"

"Tania, she's already waited three days!"

"But how do we know he's not going to—"

"How about this?" I interrupted, impatient. "'Hey, you! Had a great time the other night. Looking forward to seeing you again. Let me know when you're free.'" I held up my phone so they could see the message.

"Flirty yet casual."

"But still direct."

"Maybe too direct?"

"No, not at all. It's perfect," Liv said, giving me a thumbs-up.

"Should I put an exclamation mark at the end?" I asked.

"No, that's definitely too eager," Tania said, shaking her head.

"Didn't you put a winky face in the last message?" I said, annoyed.

"I think the exclamation shows that she's bubbly and excited."

"A bit *too* excited."

"I think she should."

"But she's already got one exclamation mark in there!"

"I didn't know there were also rules against punctuation!"

We finally settled on a smiley face—which was just as friendly without being as high risk. I checked the message and then double-checked once more before finally clicking SEND, and then the four of us waited. Almost instantly, the "read time" showed up below my message.

"He read it!" I shrieked. We all crowded around the screen anxiously waiting for the three dots to appear that would indicate his reply. A few minutes passed. Then ten. After about fifteen minutes, I started to feel the lump reemerging in my throat. *Why hasn't he replied? He's obviously seen my message. It even said he read it . . . What could be his reason? Did he not have a good time? Does he not want to see me again?* This was not a scenario I had expected. I blinked back hot tears of disappointment as I tried to figure out what his nonreply could mean.

"Maybe he just clicked on your message accidentally but didn't really read it?"

"Maybe he's in the middle of something and can't respond right now?"

"Maybe he needs more time to come up with a witty, well-crafted response?"

"Maybe he dropped his phone?"

"Or maybe his phone got stolen just as he was about to text you back!"

After about twelve additional *maybe*s, Hannah, Liv, and Tania came to the conclusion that Zain would most likely text me later. Not most likely, but most *certainly*. He would most certainly text me later, they reassured me. I really hoped they were right.

* * *

After I got home that night, I checked my phone about a thousand times, rereading my text and overanalyzing every single word. *I never should have put in that smiley face! It was too juvenile. I should've just used the extra exclamation mark. Why did I let them talk me out of it?* In the back of my mind, I knew I was being irrational. But when I still didn't hear anything the following day, or the day after, I conference-called my friends, hoping they could offer me some insight.

"I can't believe he still hasn't responded!" Hannah exclaimed.

Liv, however, was not nearly as shocked.

"I hate to be the one to say it, Leila. But you just got ghosted," she said gently.

Ghosted? I let her words sink in. Could it be? Was Zain—thoughtful, funny, sweet Zain—really the type of guy who would just disappear like that? Was he really the type of guy to fall off the face of the earth without so much as a simple explanation?

"It's a shitty thing to do," she continued sympathetically. "But we've all been there, Leila. You've probably even done it yourself."

I would never be that insensitive! I reflected back on all the one-meeting dates I had been on over the past few weeks. I was always forthright when I was not interested in a second date. There were only a few instances, especially if the guy was persistent, when I would take longer to respond to texts—or I would respond less frequently—until communication eventually ceased. But I justified this strategy by telling myself that this was a far kinder way to reject a person. Besides, who wanted to hear all the reasons *why* a person didn't like them? Sometimes it was just easier to not say anything . . .

"So is this Zain's way of . . . rejecting me?" I held my breath, dreading their response. Even just hearing myself say the R-word caused my insides to ache.

"We don't really know what it means because he hasn't

given you an explanation," Tania said. I suddenly realized that all those unanswered texts—which I'd perceived to be a form of kindness—were just another level of ghosting. Now that I was on the receiving end, I finally understood how cruel it was for me to withhold that closure from those men, just as cruel as it was for Zain to withhold it from me.

"Maybe he's not rejecting you. Maybe it's just bad timing. Or maybe he really did get his phone stolen! It could be anything," Hannah said slowly. I knew she was trying to remain optimistic, but her excuses provided me with little solace.

"Whatever it is, Leila, I think you just have to be okay with the fact that you may never know the exact reason." Tania sighed.

I squeezed my eyes shut, swallowing the pain as the truth sank in: I had been ghosted. I had been rejected. No reason given would lessen the hurt surrounding this fact.

"Maybe I've been guilty of ghosting in the past too," I said in a thin, shaky voice. "It's just usually when you ghost a person, it's because you know there's absolutely no chance of it working out between the two of you. But with Zain," I continued, trying not cry, "I don't know . . . it was different."

"It was for you, Leila," Liv said softly.

"No, not just for me," I said, the sting of her words puncturing my shattered heart. I was aware of how crazy I sounded, but I needed to make them understand. To make *me* understand. "He liked me! Zain, he . . . I could tell he—" My voice cracked.

"But how do you know?"

I muted the phone as tears pushed against the rims of my eyes. *There was something there. The way he looked at me. The way he leaned into my shoulder. The way he hugged me goodbye . . . he held me so close . . . clinging on longer than expected. Where did it go wrong?*

"I'm so sorry, Leila," Liv said.

"Yeah, Leila, it'll be okay," Hannah added.

"So, do you . . . do you think I'll ever hear from him again?" I finally asked, weakly.

"Maybe not," Tania said. I drew in a deep breath. The thought of never hearing from Zain again, let alone seeing him, crushed me. It felt like all of my hopes had been snatched from me, and I couldn't bear the thought. "Leila, whether you hear from him or not, *you* have to be ready to move on."

"She's right," Liv said. "You can't waste any more of your time and energy on Zain when you only have a few more weeks before your deadline is up."

I knew my friends were trying to keep me focused on the bigger picture, but the last thing I wanted to think about was the stupid deadline. I was heartbroken. I had finally met someone I liked. Someone I could see myself falling in love with. But my Bollywood fairy tale had ended before it even started, and I had no idea why. *The least Zain could have done was give me a simple reason for why he didn't see it working out between us. Why wouldn't he at the very least give me that? Was I that insignificant to him that he doesn't even think I'm worth an explanation?*

After hanging up the phone, I sat there for hours, imagining all the beautiful, thin, fair-skinned girls who were probably throwing themselves at Zain in Houston. With each agonizing thought, my insecurities chewed away at me, bit by bit. *Of course he's not interested in you. You're not his type. You're not even in the same league as him. He can definitely do better.*

This was the first time in the entire process that I, Leila Abid, had been rejected, and it finally dawned on me that this was a two-way street. All this time I had focused solely on finding *my* Mr. Perfect. It hadn't even occurred to me that Mr. Perfect would have to think *I* was Ms. Perfect in order for this to actually end the way I had hoped. Looking at the calendar on my wall marking down the days until my deadline, I finally broke down and cried for the first time since I had started this search seven weeks ago. I cried for the possibility of what could have been. I cried for the disappointments that would inevitably follow, and for the growing realization that this might not be something I could pull off after all.

Family Dinner

"Everything okay, Leila?" my mother asked me at the breakfast table the next morning.

"I'm fine," I said, pushing my eggs from one end of the plate to the other. I had no idea if my mother knew that I had seen Zain again, but I didn't want to risk giving her more access to my life than she already had.

"You haven't eaten anything. Can I make you something else?"

"No. No, *Ammi*, I'm fine, I'm just a little tired," I said, getting up.

"You can always talk to me if something is wrong," my mother said softly.

I nodded and walked back into my room. I knew she could sense I was upset, but she was the last person I wanted to talk to about Zain. If I so much as mentioned his name, she would immediately call Yasmeen aunty, and I couldn't deal with any more humiliation. If my mother had never forced me to go to that lunch, I never would have met him, and I never would have gotten my heart broken. I knew it was unfair to hold her solely responsible for what happened between the two of us, but I couldn't help but feel that she shared at least some portion of the blame.

In an attempt to protect my fragile emotions, I decided to avoid my mother for the next week and tried everything I could to get over Zain on my own. I even pushed myself to go on a few more dates—and some second and third dates; however, my self-esteem had been so rattled, I just couldn't think clearly. Zain remained in the back of my mind like an unwanted guest.

When I used to go out, I was mainly concerned with how much I would like my date. Now, I was petrified that *he* wouldn't like *me*. These feelings of self-doubt consumed me entirely, and I resented Zain for that. Each time I met a potential suitor, I felt like I had to try extra hard to come off as smart and witty because I desperately needed validation. I needed to prove somehow that Zain had made a mistake. But even when a date would express interest, I instantly assumed there was something wrong: if I wasn't good enough for Zain, then anyone who did think I was good enough must be substandard. I knew my thinking made no sense, but nothing made sense anymore. My life had been reduced to mere contradictions. I hated Zain, but I also secretly wished he would call me so everything could go back to the way it was that night at the jazz club. With each day that passed, though, the silence on his end eventually started causing me to hate myself. I hated that I felt so powerless over the situation. I hated how crappy I felt all the time. But most of all, I hated that I had allowed myself to yearn for the one guy I couldn't have.

* * *

"Would you like more *biryani*?" my mother asked at the dinner table Sunday evening. My date had just called to cancel because of a work emergency, and I was relieved at the opportunity to just spend a mellow night in. My father nodded as she heaped a generous helping onto his plate.

"So, Leila, *beti*, what have you been up to?" My father turned toward me. I looked down and spooned a lump of rice into my mouth.

"Nothing much, *Abba*. Same old," I mumbled with my mouth full. My mother glanced at me from across the table.

"And how is your search coming along?" he asked.

"It's coming." I shoved another spoonful in. I could tell my father wanted more details, but I had nothing more to share. Anything I said would launch them into an hour-long tirade about all the things I was doing wrong. I didn't have it in me to hear those same criticisms. Not now. So I remained silent.

After a few uncomfortable moments, my mother changed the topic, much to my relief.

"Leila, I was telling your father about Meena's engagement. Her wedding is less than two weeks away, you know." I nodded. As much as I hated hearing about Meena's upcoming nuptials, I was grateful that they at least shifted the focus off of me. "I was actually thinking of attending. What do you think?"

"That's great," I said, with as much fake interest as I could muster.

"But there is only one problem. Your father cannot accompany me."

"*Jaan.* You know I have to work."

"I know. I know."

"You will have to go without me. Besides, I would rather save up my vacation days for our own *beti*'s wedding." He winked at me. I looked away and slumped back into my chair.

"Actually, I was hoping our *beti* would come with me this time."

"Me?"

"Yes, Leila. What do you say?"

I was not interested in attending Meena's wedding at all. It was bad enough having to hear about it from eight thousand miles away. Why would I want to experience it up close and personal?

"Can't you just ask one of your friends to come?" I offered. Considering the ever-growing list of aunties my mother knew, I was sure she could convince one of them to come along. Of all the skills she possessed, her strongest by far was persuasion.

"Nonsense, Leila. Why don't you just come?"

"Leila, you are also off from school right now," my father added. "It will be the perfect summer vacation!" I scrunched my face. Spending time with my mother hardly sounded like a vacation. "I think it is a great idea," my father said, his spoon waving in the air.

"Leila, please come," my mother urged. "Everyone will be so excited to see you. *Especially* Meena."

As if that makes a difference. I had made up my mind years ago that I didn't care for her, so why should I suddenly care that she would be excited to see me? The last thing I wanted was to be around someone who was arrogant and smug and proved to be better than me in every way possible. That sounded miserable. And I had enough misery to deal with without her help.

I pursed my lips together. "Can I think about it?" My parents looked at each other and finally nodded. But the truth was, even if I did somehow forget all the Meena comparisons over the years, the fact that she had now "beaten" me in the marriage race was just too much. There was nothing to think about. I wasn't going.

* * *

After dinner, I lay in bed staring at the ceiling and thinking of an excuse for why I could not accompany my mother to Meena's wedding. The simple fact that I didn't want to would not be enough. It had to be a strong enough reason that neither of my parents could object. Like a serious case of aviophobia. Or mono. Or pregnancy—but not quite as drastic. As I went over the different scenarios in my mind, I heard a soft knock on my bedroom door. I sat up as the door cracked open. It was my father.

My heart began to race. *My mother must have sent him to talk with me*, I thought, panicking. *Is he going to try to convince me once more to go to India? I don't even have a good excuse yet!* Feeling flustered, I tried to steady the emotions rising inside.

"Leila, *beti*? Can I come in?" I nodded, crossing my ankles and resting the tip of my chin on my knees. He walked across the room and took a seat next to me, pushing aside the comforter. Neither of us said a word. The only sound was the ticking of the clock above my bed. I waited quietly for my father to say something, anxiously wondering what it was that he wanted.

After a few silent moments, he finally turned toward me. "Tell me," he said gently. "Are you okay, *beti*?"

I wasn't sure if it was the simplicity of the question or the concern with which he asked, but my eyes suddenly moistened. Not once in the past seven weeks had I—or anyone else, for that matter—stopped to check if I was okay. The truth was, I wasn't. Everything was *not* okay. After what had happened with Zain, my life felt like it had scattered into pieces and all I wanted, in that one moment, was for someone to fix it.

When I was a kid, I would always run to my father whenever I had a problem. When I accidentally killed my goldfish in third grade because I filled its bowl with hot water instead of cold, my father was the one who helped me flush Fluffy down the toilet. When I fell behind in AP Geometry freshman year of high school, my father sat with me for hours each night teaching me his Indian shortcuts until I finally understood every problem in the book. When I failed my driver's test the first time around, he spent the entire weekend in the empty lots behind the South Street Mall showing me how to parallel park. And even after that, when I rammed our minivan into an adjacent vehicle while attempting to park at the post office, he climbed into the driver's seat and took the blame for it so I wouldn't have my learner's permit revoked.

I consistently relied on my father for his comfort and generosity, but as I'd grown older, I'd come to him less frequently because I felt like I had the capacity to figure things out on my own. For the first time in a long while, however, I realized I was in over my head. If only my father could fix my broken heart, my dejected self-esteem, my sense of hopelessness, my uncertainty in love. I had no idea how he would do it, but I just needed to hear that everything was going to be okay.

My father placed his arm around my shoulder and held me as I cried into his shirt. "I know it has been tough on you these last couple months, Leila," he began. "I know your *ammi* can be a little . . . pushy." I lifted my head off his shoulder and looked at him with teary eyes.

"A little?" I said, with a cracked voice. "*Abba*, she made me go see a matchmaker!"

"*Ya Allah!*" He covered his face with his hand. "I told her to forget that matchmaker! She is of no use to us. Setting you up with that *faltu* boy!" He shook his head.

"Sajid? How did you know about him?"

"*Beti*, I called and spoke with him before you did. Crazy boy kept giggling like a madman!"

"But he never even mentioned that he talked to you . . ."

"*Arey*, he was so medicated on who knows what that he probably didn't even remember."

I let out a small laugh. "You could've at least warned me, *Abba*!" I said, wiping my eyes.

"I trust you, Leila. I know you will make the right choice," he said. I looked down, wishing in that moment that I shared my father's belief in me. "You know, *beti*, your mother just wants what is best for you."

I shook my head. "*Abba*, how can she expect me to find someone in such a short amount of time? It's just . . . it's just not possible." I dropped my face into my palms.

My father sat there quietly while I continued to cry. After a few minutes, he got up, went into the bathroom, and brought back a box of tissues. As I wiped my face, he cleared his throat and began talking.

"Did I ever tell you the story of how your mother and I met, Leila?" I took in a choppy breath and shook my head. "Ahhh." He cleared his throat and smiled. "When I was twenty-four years old, I found out I had been accepted into a master's program at UCLA. I had only four weeks before I was supposed to leave, and your *dada* and *dadi*'s one request was for me to be married before I left."

"Wh-why did they want you to be married so young?" I said, sniveling.

"It was not too young in those days, Leila. They were worried about my being so far away. They wanted to make sure that someone would be there to take care of me." He looked at me, patting my knee. "You know, in the weeks leading to my departure, they showed me pictures of four different girls." He held up his hand. "But I refused every single one," he stated proudly.

"H-how come?"

"One was too tall. One too thin. Another had a large nose." He folded each finger one by one, and laughed. "To be honest, Leila, I didn't know what I was looking for. That is until they showed me your mother's picture." He smiled at the memory. "She had a *very* nice nose."

"You picked *Ammi* because she had a nice nose?" As he sat there shrugging and smiling bashfully, I thought about how much time and thought I put into even the most routine things. Just this morning, it took me twenty minutes to decide which sweatpants I was going to wear. And looking now at the gray fleece with the stain at the knee, I was sure I had made the wrong choice. How could my father base the most important decision of his life solely on who had the better nose? *What about personality? And life views? And compatibility? Aren't these just as important when it comes to selecting a spouse as the size of their nose?*

"Once I made my choice, her parents invited my family to their home that very weekend. We sat on opposite couches, but we were so shy that we barely looked at each other." He chuckled as he reflected on the memory. "But I could tell by how she served us chai that she was a nice, simple girl. Two days later, we had our *nikkah*, and the following week, we were on a plane to America to start our new life together."

I couldn't believe that was all it took for my parents to get married. Five pictures and four bad noses, and now here they were, about to celebrate their thirtieth wedding anniversary. A part of me couldn't help but feel a tiny bit jealous at how simple it had all been for them. But I also knew that

that strategy would never work for me. I had more complicated wants. A laundry list of expectations. No matter how badly I wanted my Bollywood ending, I knew it would take much more than a nice nose for me to fall in love.

"The first step is always the hardest, Leila. Your mother and I were practically strangers when we married, but we took the time to learn about each other."

"But what if there's not enough time to learn everything?"

"Leila, you cannot know *everything*. Your mother and I are still learning about each other. After thirty years! Just the other day, she told me she doesn't like the way I chew my food. I didn't even know that!"

"But that's what scares me, *Abba*. What if I discover something I don't like? And by then it's too late!"

"Leila, *beti*, the truth is you can never fully know a person. No matter how much time you spend with them. In fact, the more time you spend with someone, the more wrongs you discover. That is why so many people just continue to date but never marry."

"But not everyone is lucky enough to find what you and *Ammi* have." I sighed. "The risks are just too high to jump into a marriage blindfolded. What if I choose the wrong person? Or I don't fall in love? Or I suddenly realize we're not compatible?" I rambled off all my worst fears until my father finally stopped me.

"You cannot worry yourself with these things, Leila.

Once you marry, every day you will discover something new about each other. Some things good, some things not so good, but that is the fun of marriage." My father bobbled his head.

Fun? That sounds frightening.

"It worked for your mother and me because we allowed love to take its course," he continued. "You have to step aside and trust that love will happen, Leila. Over time, you will learn to make adjustments and come to respect each other. And soon, that respect will turn to like and then eventually it will turn to love. This kind of compromise cannot happen before marriage. It cannot happen overnight. It slowly grows over time and becomes stronger, and that is why it lasts."

He patted my knee and gently lifted my chin. "Leila, if you want to be truly happy, you must realize that there is no such thing as love before marriage. *True* love exists only *after* marriage. Simple as that." He snapped his fingers, smiling.

I said nothing, just sat there quietly, absorbing his advice. If there was no such thing as love before marriage, then what about all the movies I had watched growing up? What about all the fairy tales I had read? What about all the feelings I had felt for Zain? Who knew if what I experienced with Zain was *true love*—as my father called it—but it was the closest I had gotten to . . . *something*. I had spent my entire life wishing for *pyaar, prem, ishq, mohabbat*—the kind of love that was instantaneous; that didn't require time or compromise or adjustments to blossom; that just was—and now my father was saying that *that* didn't exist? Or at least not in the context that I had always envisioned. I blinked back the tears and looked away. Maybe this type of love didn't exist for him and my mother, but I refused to believe that it wouldn't for me. It *had* to . . . otherwise what was even the point?

Departure

"What are you going to do?" Tania and Liv looked at me curiously. Hannah was out of town at a conference, so it was just the three of us at our Tuesday night ritual.

"I've decided I'm going to go," I said.

"What made you change your mind?" Liv asked.

"I couldn't get pregnant in time."

"What?!"

"Never mind." The truth was I couldn't come up with a strong enough excuse for why I couldn't go to Meena's wedding. At least nothing that would convince my mother, so I decided to just surrender.

"But you have less than a month left!" Liv reminded me. "What about the deadline?"

Deadline. It sounded so final, so uncompromising. I could see the concern in both my friends' eyes. "The deadline is still there," I stated matter-of-factly. "But either I stay here and continue going on terrible, dead-end dates, or I try to focus on the silver lining."

"Which *is*?" Tania asked doubtfully.

"It's an opportunity to go someplace new. Someplace far."

"You're not still thinking about Zain, are you?"

"No!" I said, trying to sound convincing. But that was a lie. I *had* been thinking about Zain and that night I fell for him on our second first date. I still experienced a pang of sadness each time I thought about the excitement I'd felt. The hope . . . the possibility of that evening turning into something more. It had all seemed so real—so tangible—but as the weeks passed with still no word from him, I knew that whatever I once believed we shared had already dissolved. I no longer clung to the expectation of receiving an explanation for what had happened. Instead, I managed to find some semblance of closure in the lack of closure I received.

"Forget Zain," I said with more conviction. "I just think it's time for me to move on. And what better place to find a Bollywood romance than the land of Bollywood itself?"

"So . . . you're going to keep looking for a husband?"

"In *India*?"

"My three months aren't up yet. Why should I stop now?" I said, my tone waxed with emotion. Liv and Tania looked at each other with uncertainty.

"I guess we just thought you preferred someone American-born," Tania finally said.

"Well, I also *preferred* a chiropractor from Houston, but you can't always have what you want. Right?"

"Leila—" Tania said, carefully studying my face.

"*What?*" My voice cracked.

"It's okay if you need to take a break from all this. You don't have to go. I'm sure your mother will under—"

"*No*, she won't," I said flatly. "Besides, my ticket is already booked. I leave in two days."

"You're sure about this?" she asked hesitantly. I nodded.

"When was the last time you visited?" Liv asked.

"A long time ago. When I was just a baby," I replied.

I was too young to remember that visit, but I had heard countless stories from my parents growing up. Stories about the one-eyed *chacha* who would wave his cane in the air and yell at all the kids from atop his balcony; the juicy *kala khattas* that melted with each bite, leaving sticky trails down the sides of their arms; the delicious *golgappas* served on paper plates by leathery-skinned vendors at every street corner; the rows of colorful, hand-stitched *mojaris* hanging from the open-air bazaars. I always dreamed of visiting again one day as an adult—when I would be old enough to experience those memories on my own. But as curious as I was to see where my parents grew up, and the place where they married, these were not the circumstances I had hoped it would be under.

"So whose wedding are you attending?" Liv wanted to know.

"My cousin Meena." I winced at the thought. There was no way to find the silver lining in that.

"Indian weddings are *so* intense," Tania remarked.

"How long do the ceremonies last?" Liv asked.

"At minimum, three days. First you have the *mehendi*, then the *nikkah*, followed by a wedding reception," Tania explained. "And then the *valima* . . ."

I had refrained from asking my mother any questions about Meena's wedding because, frankly, I didn't care enough to know. But based on Bollywood movies and albums I had seen of my own parents' wedding and the handful of Indian weddings I had been forced to attend growing up, Tania was accurate in her assessment.

"Are you going to wear a sari?"

"Is there going to be dancing?"

"Will the groom ride up on an elephant?"

"Are you going to get your henna done?"

"Do you think there will be a lot of single guys at the wedding?"

"Liv, there's *always* a lot of single guys at weddings."

As Liv and Tania continued their discussion, my mind floated back to that morning, when I'd announced to my mother that I would accompany her on the trip. She'd wrapped me in her arms and held me in a tight embrace.

"We can take notes for your own wedding someday," she'd whispered in my ear. My father, who was seated across from me at the kitchen table, tilted his head and flashed me a hopeful smile.

Thinking back on it now, my thoughts lingered on her last word. *Someday.* A part of me still hoped for that someday. A part of me wondered when that day would come, and another part questioned *if* it would come at all. But I knew in order for *someday* to be a possibility, I needed to get out of Los Angeles, away from this vicious cycle I had been trapped in. Perhaps going to India would not just appease my parents, but would also help me gain some perspective. Maybe India—a place that felt so familiar yet distant at the same time—would give me the clarity I desperately craved and the *someday* I so hopelessly desired.

Motherland

Sixteen hours. For the past sixteen hours, I had been wedged in between my mother and a wiry, bearded Caucasian man who was wearing open-toed sandals, a bright orange bandanna, and a tie-dyed T-shirt with the word NAMASTE written across the chest. As soon as I saw him place a yoga mat in the overhead compartment, I knew right then it was going to be a long flight. Luckily for me, Mr. Yogi passed out fairly quickly, after only forty minutes of mind-numbing conversation about his "spiritual journey of self-discovery." While he dreamed blissfully about his *Eat, Pray, Love* fantasies on my left, my mother was reclined comfortably on the other side of me, snoring like a chainsaw.

The plane was dark, and the majority of the passengers were fast asleep. Although I was utterly exhausted—given that I had been awake for almost twenty-four hours—my mind would not turn off. *I was going to India.*

I wondered what it would feel like to finally set foot in my parents' homeland. For the first time in my life—that I could remember—I was going to be in a country where everyone looked like me. Where my long black hair, dark features, and wheat-colored skin were not considered "exotic" but just normal. A place where Bollywood romances were born, and the supply of South Asian men was abundant.

I shifted in my seat, pressing the small circular button attached to the armrest—the only thing separating me from Mr. Yogi to my left. I closed my eyes as the emotional twang of violins and keyboards sounded through the cheap plastic headphones. The classic film *Veer-Zaara* was playing on the small screen, and for the next three hours, I was entirely immersed in the melodramatic story of two star-crossed lovers separated by the politics of post-Partition. When the movie reached its final scene, when Veer and Zaara finally see each other again after twenty-two years apart, I could feel the waterworks coming.

Up ahead, the flight attendant was making her way down the aisle checking in on all the passengers who were still awake. *Oh, man, pull yourself together, Leila!* I told myself. *You've seen this movie a hundred times. No one cries at such a cliché ending.* But as the on-screen couple walked toward each other in slow motion with scenes from their past fading in and out and the sweet voice of Lata Mangeshkar singing "*Tere Liye*" in the background—I couldn't control myself. I started blubbering like a baby.

"Are you okay, miss?" The flight attendant appeared suddenly with a concerned look.

"Yes," I said, quickly switching the channel to a *Family Guy* episode. "There's just something in my eye," I lied, giving her a teary smile.

I waited until she moved on to the next passenger before turning off the screen. I leaned against the seat, still moved by the love shown in the movie. Veer and Zaara's relationship was able to endure the most challenging of obstacles—political conflict, false imprisonment, even old age—but their love still managed to find its way. Yet my relationship with Zain had fizzled out over an unanswered text. I sighed.

I had started out in this process with such certainty that I would find a husband within the allotted time. I had convinced myself that all I had to do was find Mr. Perfect and the rest would be easy. How greatly I had been mistaken. I thought I had found him in Zain. But finding him wasn't enough; it wasn't my guaranteed ticket to a happily ever after. If it were, we would be in each other's arms at this very moment as the lyrics of "*Tere Liye*" played in the background. Maybe Zain wasn't as perfect as I thought . . .

As drowsiness suddenly began to descend upon me, my thoughts drifted back to the movie. Zaara never expected to fall in love with Veer. He was Indian. She was Pakistani. He was the total opposite of everything she thought she wanted.

She was already engaged to someone else. But, despite their circumstances, they ended up together. After twenty-two years. They trusted love to take its course. The same way my parents did . . .

* * *

I wasn't sure for how long I had dozed off, but when I opened my eyes next, all the lights in the cabin were turned on and the seat belt logo above my head was lit.

"Ladies and gentlemen, as we start our descent, please make sure your seat belt is securely fastened and all carry-on luggage is stowed in the overhead bins or underneath the seat in front of you."

Mr. Yogi was fully awake and chomping down on a snack he pulled out from his fair-trade hemp bag. It appeared to be a seaweed and tuna sandwich. *You have got to be kidding me*, I thought, scrunching my face.

As he chattered away about "activating his chakra," I leaned over my mother—who was still fast asleep—and lifted the white plastic screen from the tiny window to the right, careful not to wake her. As my eyes adjusted to the bright rays of sunlight, I looked out over the dissipating clouds below. I could make out the immense skyline lying beneath a thick layer of gray smog. My heart skipped a beat. *So this is Mumbai, my parents' homeland. The City of Dreams. The epicenter of Bollywood. The setting of the most iconic love stories to ever grace the screen.* I looked once more at the nearing landscape below and felt the rapid pounding of my heart as the plane continued to drop in altitude. My mother finally stirred awake.

"Are we already here?" she asked groggily, wiping the sleep from her eyes. *Yeah, twenty-one hours, two layovers, and eight thousand miles across the world, and we're "already" here.* I nodded and leaned back.

"*Ladies and gentlemen, please make sure your seat backs and trays are in their full upright position. Cabin crew, please take your seats for landing.*" I closed my eyes as we prepared for touch-down.

"Can you believe we're *finally* here!" Mr. Yogi turned toward me excitedly. "*Namaste*, India!" he shouted just as the wheels hit the ground with a rocking jolt. I gave him a small smile and held my breath, trying not to inhale the foul stench of tuna wafting in my direction. We had arrived in the motherland. I guess there was no turning back now.

Family Reunion

Bright lights. Loud voices. Hordes of unfamiliar faces passed by as I timidly pushed my way through the crowded entrance of the Chhatrapati Shivaji Maharaj International Airport. Shielding my eyes with the back of my hand, I glanced apprehensively across the sea of people. Then I saw them. All of them. It was hard to miss them as they were all standing together, smiling and waving their arms furiously. My mother's sister, Jamila aunty; her family; *and* extended relatives had all shown up at the airport to receive us. Within seconds, I was surrounded by aunties and uncles and cousins—most of whom I had never met before in my life but looked vaguely familiar from the photographs mailed to us over the years. There was lots of pinching and hugging and exclamations of *masha'Allah!* The younger children were huddled around our luggage, talking excitedly as they tried to guess what presents we had brought from *Amreeka.* Aside from a small bag of Hershey's chocolates, I wasn't sure how thrilled they would be with our offerings: bulk-sized bags of almonds and pistachios and pounds of cheese blocks my mother had insisted we pack.

As we waited for the rest of our suitcases to make their way around the revolving carousel, I glanced around wondering which of the faces belonged to Meena. Meena, the girl who had beaten me at every turn in life. The daughter my mother had always wanted. The Regina George of my existence.

"Where's Meena?" I finally asked Ahmed—who I had deciphered was Meena's younger brother from the bits of conversation occurring around me. The wiry patch of facial hair growing at the bottom of his chin allowed me to deduce he must've been about sixteen years old.

"She's at home," he said, quickly taking the large suitcase from my mother's hand as she waited for the next round. Sixteen-year-old boys in America were not nearly as well-mannered, and I could tell she was impressed by his chivalry and respect.

"She is thrilled you and aunty have come all this way for the wedding." He turned to me and grinned. "She's really looking forward to meeting you, Leila!" I returned the smile, not quite sure how to respond.

Once we finally got the last of our bags, I followed my mother and the rest of the clan as we exited the airport. The moment we stepped outside, I instantly felt like all of my senses were being assaulted at once. My parents had always described the crowds and chaos of Mumbai, but it was something else to actually experience it. The cars and motorbikes whizzed past us on the busy streets ahead. Rickshaw drivers shouted across the concrete barriers, urging us to take a ride, salivating greedily at the prospect of ripping off foreigners. I squinted and tried not to make eye contact with the swarms of drivers fighting for our attention. I was modestly dressed in jeans and a track jacket, but I still felt slightly self-conscious. All of the women in the family—young and old—were dressed in dark-colored *abayas* and long-sleeved *salwar kameezes.* As a single stream of perspiration dripped down my back, I wondered how they were all not melting in their layered attire. I looked over at my mother, who was wiping her face with the edge of her *dupatta*, and I was glad I wasn't the only one experiencing hot flashes.

The air was sticky, and the smells of smoke, sweat, and exhaust fumes permeated our noses as we made our way toward the side parking lot, where we were introduced to Sahil, the family driver. He was standing in front of a red four-door Maruti Suzuki with a metal basket attached to the roof, smoking a cigarette—which he immediately tossed to the ground when he saw us approaching. As I watched him hoist my and my mother's belongings into the basket, I could not help but wonder if the weight of our suitcases was equivalent to that of the entire car.

The other family members motioned toward the rickshaw drivers, and within seconds, there were three drivers lined up in front of us. "*Kahan ja rahe ho?*" the drivers asked, and the aunties noisily rattled off the directions. Despite their conservative dress, the female relatives were the ones who seemed to take charge, while the male relatives just waited around. Ahmed took the front seat of the Maruti, while Jamila aunty squeezed into the back seat with me and my mother. Feeling the tires sink into the asphalt as I sat down next to the window, I nervously clutched the small messenger bag in my lap and said a quick prayer as we slowly edged our way onto the road, the three brightly colored rickshaws following closely behind us.

The drive to my mother's family home was nauseating. The car kept weaving in and out of lanes. Cars were honking, people were shouting. I couldn't figure out why they even had lanes on the roads when clearly no one bothered to stay in them. I gripped the side handlebar on the door, knuckles white, and glanced over at my mother to see if she was aware of all the traffic rules being violated by the second. But she was fully preoccupied with Jamila aunty as the two of them talked loudly and excitedly over the noise of the busy streets around us. The two sisters were only a few years apart and strikingly similar in terms of facial features, talking styles, and personality. My mother and Jamila aunty had remained close over the years; they had written letters back in the day, which eventually turned into emails, and they spoke regularly on the phone, keeping each other posted on the recent goings-on in their lives—hence the constant Meena updates. Finally together for the first time in over two decades, they were completely unfazed by the commotion around us, focusing solely on each other, making up for lost time.

As Sahil squeezed past a truck and a motorcycle with an entire family on it—a turbaned man in the front, a sari-clad woman seated behind him holding an infant, and two small children wedged in between—I clenched my eyes shut, praying we would not claim one of the small children as a casualty. My bad driving skills back home were a joke compared to these drivers. I kept my eyes shut and continued reciting a prayer. I came to the conclusion that a drive through Mumbai was all it took to make someone religious.

Suddenly the Maruti jerked to an abrupt stop. I opened my eyes, silently hoping that we had safely reached our destination without any mangled children, but much to my disappointment, we instead found ourselves in the middle of heavy gridlock. "What is happening, Sahil?" Jamila aunty leaned forward and asked from the back seat.

"I don't know, madam. Let me take a look." Sahil opened the driver's-side door and stood up on the edge of the seat, peering over the rows of honking cars in front of us. He shaded his eyes with the back of his arm. After a few moments, he sat back in the car, wiping the sweat from his brow, and calmly said, "It is a cow, madam. It has stopped in the middle of the road."

"Oh, I see," she said without reaction.

"Did he just say a *cow*?" I asked, looking over at my mother.

My mother nodded. "Yes, Leila, a cow." Her tone was so matter-of-fact that I actually felt ridiculous for attempting to push for any more information. A cow had stopped traffic. Of course. This was India. This made perfect sense.

"So how long will it be?" Jamila aunty asked impatiently.

"Hopefully not long, madam. We are just waiting for it to cross."

As she leaned back in the seat, she and my mother continued chatting away. "Oh, Jamila! How I've missed this place! Isn't this just wonderful, Leila?" my mother asked, turning toward me, her face beaming with pride.

I smiled as Ahmed glanced back at me.

"Ahmed, why don't you go out and guide the cow," Jamila aunty finally urged.

"*Ammi*. Can't we just wait for the cow to move on its own?" he asked. But his mother simply raised her eyebrow, and Ahmed quickly got out and shut the door behind him. We waited for him. With the car turned off now, little beads of sweat had formed on all of our faces, but I seemed to be the only one bothered by the heat. Well, me and Sahil, who I noticed kept wiping his face with the handkerchief he carried in his back pocket.

"*Ammi*." I nudged my mother, licking the sweat from my top lip. "*Ammi*, I'm dying." I nudged her again.

"Oh, Leila, you are not dying." My mother laughed, shaking her head. "These Americans have so little tolerance for discomfort," she said to Jamila aunty. We had been in India for less than an hour and all of a sudden I was the American, the outsider. Since when was a hundred degrees slightly uncomfortable? I slouched back in my seat; the heat, the cows, my mother—the combination of it all was almost unbearable.

Sahil turned the car on for a moment to lower all the windows, and I placed my head against the seat, hoping that Ahmed would find a way to get the cow to the other side of the street soon. From behind shut eyes, I could hear little voices amid all the honking. I looked out the open window and saw three barefoot children running up to each car asking for change, but most of the passengers shooed them away. Their soiled faces and torn clothes gnawed at my curiosity. I had never seen children in such poor condition before—aside from the ones in the Save the Children commercials back home.

Suddenly, the little girl came running up to my window. I looked over at my mother, but she and Jamila aunty were so immersed in their conversation that they didn't even take notice. I lifted my head from the seat and quickly opened my messenger bag. I finally pulled out some crumpled dollar bills and two Tootsie Rolls and placed them in the little girl's palms. She smiled a crooked smile, kissed the top of my hand, and went running toward the other two kids, probably her siblings.

In that time, Ahmed finally returned and informed us that the cow had safely made it across. I breathed a sigh of relief as the engine roared to life and a gust of hot air blew from the vents above. While traffic continued to pick up pace slowly, I sat in the back seat staring at the top of my hand where the little girl had kissed it.

Meena

After we'd been stuck in the car for over an hour, Sahil finally stopped in front of a tall stuccoed building. "We have arrived," he announced as he put the car into park. I got out, stretching my cramped legs, and looked up. There were floors of windows along the exterior of the building and yards of colorful fabric were flowing from clotheslines hanging along the open-air balconies. Sahil, Ahmed, and the uncles took turns unloading our luggage from the basket above, while the younger cousins chased each other in the courtyard. As the aunties paid the rickshaw drivers, Jamila aunty led my mother and me toward the main entrance of the building.

"This place looks so different from how I remember," my mother said, touching the newly painted exterior as we stepped inside. This was the home my mother had grown up in—where she and Jamila aunty held *carom* competitions and flew brightly colored handmade kites from the terrace.

It was the home where my father first saw my mother; the place he picked her up from before they departed for America. It had been more than twenty-five years since my mother had last seen her childhood home, and she looked around curiously, taking in all the details. Jamila aunty explained how the building had been renovated a few years back, but the one thing they left untouched was the rickety old elevator.

"Ah, yes, *this* I remember." My mother laughed as she pulled back the crisscrossed door of rusted iron and stepped inside.

"Remember that time me, you, and Vishali from the third floor got stuck in here?" she said to Jamila aunty, laughing. There was a giant gap between the elevator and the lobby floor where I was standing, and staring into it reminded me of a deep black abyss. Seeing all the levers and ropes exposed above the wooden box made me very nervous.

"We refused to ride this thing for months afterwards!" Jamila aunty replied, shaking her head and stepping inside. "Come, Leila." She motioned me in. "There's just enough room for you without risking another jam, *insha'Allah.*" She and my mother laughed.

I warily stepped over the gap and stood next to my mother, holding my breath as the entire box swayed gently. My mother pulled the door closed and pressed the wooden button, smiling nostalgically. I pushed the hair back from my sweaty forehead and swatted away mosquitoes. With no air-conditioning and barely enough room for the three of us to stand vertically, I tried not to think about the probability of an elevator jam.

We made our way to the top floor and walked down the narrow corridor to a flat at the end of the hall. I could hear lots of shuffling and movement on the other side, and as soon as we buzzed the bell, the door swung open to another frenzy of hugs and introductions. I tried my best to hang in the back. I wasn't sure how much more pinching and squeezing my face could handle.

For the next ten minutes, we were introduced to *potas* and *potis*, *bhaiyas* and *bhabhis*, *chachas* and *chachis*. Even the *padosis* from every floor in the building had come by to greet us. I stood there amid a sea of people, smiling as politely as I could, trying to respond to their questions in broken Urdu.

"*Arey*, we all speak English here!" one of the *chachas* teased as I stumbled over my words, and the whole room broke into laughter. I flushed a deep red.

"Oh, and this here is Meena," Jamila aunty interrupted, pulling forward the arm of a thin, fresh-faced girl and bringing her forward.

"*As'salaamu Alaikum*, aunty," Meena said shyly, looking at my mother. She had fair skin, long black hair that was loosely braided to the side, and slight dimples that deepened as she smiled. She was wearing a bright pink *salwar kameez* and her *dupatta* was wrapped lightly around her head. I crammed my hands into the pockets of my track jacket. *Of course she's prettier than her photographs*, I thought miserably. I shrank back toward the door.

"*Walaikum As'salaam*." My mother pulled her close and kissed her on both cheeks. "And *Mubarak, beti*!" Meena blushed and smiled. "We are so happy we could be here to attend your *shaadi*!"

"I'm so glad you came all this way, aunty," Meena said, her voice soft and gentle. She looked around quietly. "And where is Leila?"

My mother glanced back and spotted me a few feet behind her, still swatting at the mosquitoes. She took my hand and pulled me to the front. "Here she is."

"Hi," I said, lifting my hand in a small, awkward wave. I had my hair matted in a messy bun, beads of perspiration across my forehead, and a tangled messenger bag wrapped around my waist—for every ounce of grace that was Meena, I was an ounce of hot mess. *If I had known we would be meeting half of Mumbai upon our arrival, I would've dressed up more.*

"Hi!" Meena replied, a hint of excitement rising in her voice.

"Meena, *beti*, let's get Leila and her mother something to eat," Jamila aunty suggested. "They've had a very long flight, and they must be very hungry!"

Within seconds, Meena and a gaggle of aunties began buzzing around as they cleared the dining table and disappeared into the kitchen to prepare dinner for all the guests. My mother made herself busy by helping out wherever she could, and the sound of chatter filled every corner of the flat. All the men in the family sat in the drawing room cheering loudly at a cricket game while the women could be heard laughing and talking in the kitchen. I wasn't used to such distinctly separated spaces for men and women. Being deficient both domestically and socially in a room full of strangers made me uncomfortable to enter either space, so I lingered around awkwardly trying not to get in the way.

I found a secluded seat on the window ledge between the living and dining rooms—away from all the noise—and tried to make myself invisible. Every now and then, an aunty would appear from the kitchen and offer me spicy *pakoras*, warm, flaky samosas, or steaming masala chai. I accepted all of it, eating quietly as I observed the commotion around me from a distance. Each time Meena would come out with a tray of something to place on the dining table, she would glance over at me and smile. I looked away, busying myself with my plates of food so I wouldn't have to converse with her, but I could still feel her watching me. *What is her problem?* I wondered, wiping my hands on my jeans. *Hasn't she ever seen an American girl eat before?*

Once all the food was set out, the uncles filled their plates before heading back into the living room while the aunties gathered around the dining table. The conversations darted back and forth between the food and stories from years ago, before my mother married. Since my mother was the only one in her family to move abroad, there was a lot of curiosity surrounding her life in *Amreeka* and all the things they had heard over the years.

I heard you can find Shan masala at the local grocery stores, is this true, Nida? Is it true that women also attend the masjid *for* Jummah namaz*? Do they really teach sex education to children in elementary school?*

My mother lived for this sort of attention, and she had no problem exaggerating mundane experiences—like discovering *halal* lamb at Costco or streaming her favorite Hindi serials on Netflix—for their entertainment.

"So when are you planning on getting Leila married?" one of the aunties asked after my mother finished a story about the "staggering rate of teenage pregnancy." It was only a matter of time before the discussion shifted toward my unmarried status. And unfortunately for me, everyone had an opinion.

"Nida," Fawiza aunty said, turning toward my mother, "Leila is much too old to not be settled already. You know, marriage is half her *deen*!"

And here we go again.

"That is what I keep telling her, but she won't listen." My mother shook her head, scowling in my direction.

"Leila, it is time for you to get married," Jamila aunty called out to me matter-of-factly. "I know many young boys who would be a good match if you are interested." I sipped my chai silently. My marriage clock was ticking on Indian time now, and Indian time was even more aggressive than I was used to.

"You know Masoud's boy?" Shazia aunty said to my mother. "He just returned from completing his studies in London."

"What about putting an ad in the *Indian Express*? You know, something simple like 'Seeking an alliance for educated, fair, U.S.-born daughter.'" Jamila aunty looked at me and smiled. "Don't mention her age and just watch. Leila will be the hot commodity!" She snapped her fingers. I looked away, trying to mask my humiliation.

"Yes, the Haider family down the hall found their daughter a very nice boy in the matrimonial section, even though she was nearly *twenty-five*," Asima aunty said in hushed tones.

Suddenly Rashid uncle entered the dining room, clearing his throat loudly. All the women went quiet. He looked around sternly at each of the faces around the table, and then slowly turned to me. I gulped.

"What about Bilal? You know the Abdallas' boy? He's a CPA accountant," he finally said, bobbling his head.

"Very good suggestion!" Jamila aunty chimed in. "He would be an excellent match for Leila."

Was this seriously what my life had come to?

"He's a very nice boy, but his hair is slightly thinning," Rashid uncle said, reaching across the table for more *pakoras*.

That's his pitch? Thank goodness Rashid uncle is a physician and not a salesman.

As the conversations about my marriage continued, I stared out the window, feeling helpless. Meena, watching carefully from the table, slowly got up and took a seat on the ledge next to me. Below, people rode past on bicycles. A group of boys were playing with an old soccer ball in the front courtyard. A *pani puri* vendor had set up a cart across the street and was doling out plates of the tasty snack to customers walking by. Meena looked at me and smiled. "So how do you like it here?" she finally asked.

As I heard my mother break into a monologue of all the prospects she had found for me and how I had refused each one, I rolled my eyes. "The only thing anyone cares about is whether I ate and when I'm getting married. So I guess it's not much different from home," I replied. Meena smiled and turned back toward the window.

"So, what is America like?"

"It's okay, I guess."

"Is it really as clean as it looks in the movies?"

"I suppose it's cleaner than here."

"California must be *so* glamorous," she said wistfully. "Have you visited Hollywood?"

"Yeah, it's like a twenty-minute drive from my house."

I refrained from telling her that Hollywood was full of homeless people and crackheads. I also left out the details of how unglamorous my life back home was. She was getting married. Perfect, pretty Meena. The only thing I had was her unrealistic fantasy of America.

"Would you like something more to eat, Leila?" Jamila aunty suddenly called out. I shook my head, looking at all the empty small plates stacked on the ledge next to me. *If I don't start pacing myself, I'll be grossly obese by the end of the week*, I thought, glancing down at my belly. And I knew that my mother would be the first to remind me that overweight and single did not make a good combination.

"I'm actually feeling a bit tired. Would it be all right if I lie down for a bit?"

"Of course, *beti*. Meena will take you. You two will be sharing a room."

Great.

I followed Meena down the hallway to the other side of the flat, the chatter from the front rooms becoming fainter. At the end of the hall, she flipped on the switch, and as the fluorescent lights flickered, a small bedroom came into view.

The walls were painted in faux Venetian plaster, and there was a large bed in the center of the room with a luxurious gauze canopy and hand-embroidered throw pillows. Two mahogany armoires stood elegantly at the top corners of the bed. The room looked straight out of a Pier 1 catalog—but authentic. It was vastly different from the traditionally bland decor in the other rooms.

"Whoa," I muttered, unable to hide my awe. "Your room is beautiful," I said, touching the tiny wooden ornaments lined across the shelves.

"Thank you," Meena replied, taking a seat on the bed.

I gazed up at the elaborately painted ceiling. "I'm surprised you went into engineering instead of design. You clearly missed your calling," I said, enviously wondering if there was anything she *couldn't* do.

"My parents preferred engineering," she said quietly.

I continued looking around the room, stepping past a row of large shopping bags to take a glimpse at the single photograph on the nightstand. It was a framed picture of Meena and a handsome man sitting next to each other on a couch. She was wearing a pale pink *lehenga choli*, and he was wearing a white *kurta* suit. They were smiling into the camera as he placed a ring on her finger.

"So this must be the lucky guy." I pointed to the photo.

She nodded, blushing, as she leaned against the headboard.

In the few hours I had known her, Meena had only asked

questions about me. She had yet to say anything about her wedding. Not that it mattered, but it was so unlike American brides. When my friend Harper got engaged her senior year of college, she talked about her upcoming nuptials ad nauseam. And although that was almost five years ago, she continued to post wedding photos online even to this day. While I still didn't really care much for Meena or her wedding, a part of me was eager to know more about the handsome man in the photograph. Where did they meet? What was he like? Was he as perfect as she was?

"How did you and your fiancé meet?" I finally asked, plopping down on the bed.

"Our fathers work at the same office."

"Have you known each other for a while?" I pried curiously.

"We only met three times."

I raised my eyebrows.

"His father showed him a photograph of me and that's how it began." She smiled.

This was oddly reminiscent of my father's story about his choosing my mother. *What is it with Indian people and picking a spouse from a single photograph? Aren't they aware of Instagram filters and Photoshop and catfishers?* Meena must have also been a subscriber to the whole "love after marriage" theory.

"How did you know he was the one after only *three* meetings?"

"This is a very common saying in America, no? *The one.*" She held out both hands as she emphasized each word dramatically. She turned to me, her dimples deepening. "Haroon is a nice boy. Both our families approve. That makes him *the one.*"

It seemed like too simple a criterion to explain such a huge decision. I still couldn't wrap my mind around it.

"You know, Leila, marriage is different for us Indian girls," Meena explained. "I've never lived away from home or traveled abroad. We don't have the same privileges as you do in America."

Privileges? What privileges did I have that she didn't? In fact, she was much more accomplished in every aspect of her life than I ever could be.

"I always admired you, Leila."

"Me?" I scrunched my face.

"You are so independent. And confident. I loved hearing all the stories of your life." She laughed. "I still remember when my mother told me you quit playing tennis. I was on my way to a badminton match, and I remember sitting there thinking you were so brave."

Brave? That wasn't exactly the word I remembered being used when I broke the news to my parents. *Uncommitted*, *hasty*, and *unfocused* all popped up, but never *brave*.

"I wanted to quit badminton for years, but every time I would muster the courage to tell my parents, I would get scared. I always wished I could be more like you."

Pretty, perfect Meena wanted to be more like me? I couldn't believe it.

"I'm so happy you're here, Leila. I always knew we would be friends."

I gave her a small smile. I wondered if she would feel the same way if she knew of all the unsavory things I had thought about her over the past two decades.

"Haroon is actually a very nice boy. He might not be the boy of my choosing, but I am excited to marry him." She looked at me with her large brown eyes. "In just a few days, I will be moving out of my father's house!" Her voice rose with excitement. "I will finally live my own life, not just a life that is pleasing to my parents."

I nodded, suddenly feeling extremely guilty. I had spent so much time disliking Meena because of how perfect her life seemed, but I understood now that it was her parents' life, not her own. I thought about my four years away at college; my spring break getaways and spontaneous road trips with my girlfriends. I thought about my job, how I was able to choose a career of my liking even though my parents would have preferred that I finish law school. I thought about how marriage was a choice for me—something I desired, but in no way my only option. I had never considered any of these things to be privileges; I just took them for granted. But I suddenly realized that not everyone was so fortunate to be given these same choices.

"You know, Hollywood is not *really* that glamorous," I said, turning toward her.

"What?"

"Hollywood. It's pretty grimy, in fact. Not at all like what you see in the movies." Meena gave me a look of surprise. "And even on the rare occasion that you run into a celebrity, it's not always what you imagine. One time, I was at the Grove, and I saw Mario Lopez doing a live interview—"

"Mario Lopez?"

"You know, A. C. Slater? *Saved by the Bell?*"

Meena stared at me blankly.

"He's just this guy who used to be famous in the nineties but is not so relevant anymore. Anyways, he's known for being this super handsome actor who never ages, but in real life, he was wearing about two tons of makeup on his face, so of course he looked young!"

"Makeup? Even the men?" Meena covered her mouth and giggled. I broke into a grin.

"And let me tell you about this one time I had this run-in with this homeless woman, but it turned out to be Jared Leto . . ."

* * *

That night as I lay in bed next to Meena, I thought about everything she had shared with me. For her, marriage was a ticket to freedom. A chance at independence—something that was not accessible to her as a single woman. What was the purpose of marriage for me? My father married because it offered him a companion, someone who would care for him in a foreign land where he had no one else. My mother married because it gave her the opportunity to live abroad, a destiny not given to anyone else in her family. *What will a husband offer to me? Besides simply appeasing my parents or living out a Bollywood fantasy, how will marriage enhance my life in a way that being single can't?* I had independence, opportunities, companionship, people who cared for me. Yet I had focused all my energy these last few months on finding a spouse. As I lay there enclosed beneath a cocoon of mosquito netting, I found myself questioning what my ultimate purpose was. Was it marriage itself? Or was there something greater?

Seeing Double

"*Oye! Thoda is taraf!*"

"*Yahaan par?*"

Dhak! Dhak!

"*Thoda us taraf . . . bas! Ab frame bilkul sahi lag rahi hai!*"

I rubbed my eyes and turned over. The sound of voices hammering outside my door had stirred me awake. The other half of the bed was neatly made—sheets smoothed, pillows propped. Meena was not there. I pulled back the thin gauze of mosquito netting and wrapped a robe around myself. Yawning, I walked down the darkened hallway toward the commotion. *What time is it? And where is everyone?*

I peeked into the kitchen before stepping into the living room—the source of all the noise. The room was teeming with almost a dozen people—none of whom I recognized from last night—all working meticulously on every square inch of space. There were short, potbellied uncles holding clipboards and shouting instructions. There were sari-clad aunties bustling around as they arranged elaborate bouquets and adorned the windows and door frames with colorful garlands made of carnations, roses, and marigolds.

I walked through the room, taking in all the sights and smells. The sweet scent of gardenias lingered in the air, mixed with an aromatic incense. All the sofas had been pushed against the walls, leaving a large open space in the center of the room in front of an impressive makeshift stage. Along the other three walls were scattered dozens of pillows and cushions, silk and embroidered. The stage was embellished with yards of bright silky fabrics that draped elegantly over two chairs with beautiful designs hand-carved into the wooden frames. A big gold-sequined heart was centered behind the chairs. The words MEENA + HAROON were spelled out in blooming crimson roses. I held my breath, taking in the vibrancy of the decor—the yellows and reds and purples and teals. The colors were loud yet understated. Over-the-top, yet classy. *It was beautiful.* It was exactly how I imagined a traditional Indian *mehendi* ceremony to look. It was exactly how I'd dreamed my own Bollywood-themed wedding would look . . .

Absorbed in every detail, I turned the corner and bumped nose first into a tall figure walking straight toward me.

"Oomf!" I said, staggering backward in surprise.

"Oh!" the figure said, looking into my face. It was the man from Meena's photograph. In person, he was about six feet tall with chestnut-colored skin and a single dimple that punctuated his left cheek as he pursed his lips together. "Did I hurt you?" he asked, lines of concern appearing between his light brown eyes.

I shook my head, patting my nose.

"*As'salaamu Alaikum.*" He smiled; the indent in his cheek deepened. "I was looking for Meena?" Directly behind him was the giant heart hanging from the stage.

So this is Haroon. I tilted my head to get a good look at him. I was impressed. He might not have been the boy of Meena's choosing, but her parents had come through for her, at least in the looks department.

"That makes two of us," I said, smoothing the tangle of hair from my face and trying not to get distracted by his striking good looks. After my talk with Meena last night, any negative feelings I once had for her had dissolved. I was surprised by her willingness to open up to me about her reasons for marrying. I couldn't believe how gravely I had misunderstood her all of these years. And now, as someone whom she trusted as a friend, I suddenly felt this big-sisterly responsibility to make sure the sacrifices she was making would be worth it.

"I've heard so much about you."

The look in his eyes switched from concern to confusion.

"I'm Leila, Meena's cousin." I held out my hand and he shook it slowly. "Meena is a great girl. And as someone who once felt very differently about her, trust me when I say you got yourself a good one."

"Oh. Yeah . . . Meena's great, *masha'Allah*—"

"And I know you guys are doing the whole arranged marriage thing, but you should know that Meena has so much more to offer than just being a stay-at-home housewife who cooks and cleans all day."

He crumpled his brows.

"She's smart. And strong-willed. I mean, she'll probably still cook for you because, you know, she's Indian—but what I mean is, that's not *all* she can do."

"I see. Um . . ."

"I know you two have only met three times—which is still in-*freaking*-sane to me—but did you know she has a talent for design?"

"Huh?"

"Interior design."

"Oh . . . I—"

"You should see her room. I mean, obviously after you're married—not now because her parents would probably *flip*—" I laughed nervously. In my head, I knew I sounded as crazy as I looked with my disheveled hair and polka-dotted pajama bottoms, but it was too late. The words kept coming. I couldn't stop. "Design is Meena's passion, and she needs someone who's going to support her in that dream."

"I—I think that's great. I'll make sure to—"

"But just saying it is not enough," I interrupted. "You have to show her you support her. Like give her a whole house to decorate, not just a bedroom. You know what I mean?"

"Uh . . ."

"She needs someone who's going to stand beside her, not on top of her."

He scratched his head.

"Basically, Haroon, what I mean to say is you're a good-looking guy—I mean, you were cute and all in the photo, but in real life, *whoa*! You're even better than I anticipated—"

He tilted his head and gave me a sideways smile.

"—but a relationship is more than just charmingly good looks. You need to be more than that. You have to be the type of husband who is deserving of a girl like Meena." I drew in a deep breath before I continued. "Anyways, that's all I wanted to say. Congratulations again." I smiled.

He stood silent for a moment as if processing everything I had just said. He finally opened his mouth, but before he could respond, Jamila aunty walked into the room.

"*Beta!*" she exclaimed with her arms outstretched. She walked over and gave him a warm embrace.

"*As'salaamu Alaikum*, aunty," he said, still scratching his head.

"And Leila, you are finally up?" she said, glancing at the clock. It was 9:32. Much earlier than I normally woke up during the summer. I was pleased with myself. "I see that the two of you have already met." She smiled at us. "Leila, this is Hisham, Haroon's twin brother."

Hisham? His twin bro—

"I'm sorry . . . *what?*" I stammered, confused.

Hisham looked at me with an amused smile.

"Hisham has just stopped by to pick up a few things for the *mehendi* ceremony tonight."

I wrapped my robe around me tightly, suddenly feeling very aware of the fact that I was in my pajamas. *This isn't Haroon?* My cheeks burned with humiliation. *Why didn't he stop me? How could he just let me go on and on like that, yammering away about Meena?*

"Yes, aunty *ji*, I was just here to pick up Haroon's outfit and to find out what time his party should arrive."

I stood there awkwardly while the two of them discussed details. *Did I really tell him that I thought he was even better-looking than I anticipated?* I glanced at the hallway, wondering how quickly I could make myself disappear.

"And Meena? Is she around? Haroon wanted me to give her this." He pulled out a blue velvet box. "It is a small gift for her to wear for the ceremony tonight."

"Leila's mother has taken her to the beauty parlor to get ready," Jamila aunty said. "But Leila, *beti*, why don't you hold on to it and you can give it to her when she returns."

"Huh?" I said, my eyes still glued to the hallway.

Hisham smiled and placed the small box in my hand. “Thank you, Leila,” he said with a twinkle in his eye.

“Come both of you into the kitchen with me,” Jamila aunty said suddenly. “Leila, have you eaten anything? Of course not,” she continued before I had a chance to reply. “You have just woken up! Hisham, tell me, what would you like me to prepare for *nashta*?”

“No, no, aunty, I must get back,” Hisham said. “There is still plenty to do for tonight.” Jamila aunty’s face dropped, but after a little back-and-forth, she finally gave in.

“Leila,” Hisham said, turning toward me. “It was a pleasure meeting you.” He nodded his head forward. “I will be sure to convey your . . . *advice* . . . to Haroon.” He smiled mischievously and gave a slight wave as he walked toward the door. I stood there feeling utterly mortified.

As soon as he had gone, Jamila aunty shifted her attention back to me. “Come, Leila, let us eat something,” she said, walking quickly. “Do you like *halwa puri*? It goes very well with chai.” She bobbled her head.

I stood there clutching the small box tightly in my hands. The velvet exterior was soft and smooth. *I can’t believe Haroon has a brother. Not just any brother—but a twin brother . . . a ridiculously good-looking twin brother.* I scratched my head, wondering how Meena had managed to forget to mention that tiny detail.

“Leila? *Beti*, are you coming?” Jamila aunty called from

the hallway. I placed the box in my pocket and followed her into the kitchen.

* * *

"And then I said something like, 'She needs someone to be next to her, not on top of her!'"

Meena threw her hands over her face and laughed loudly. As soon as she had gotten home, I'd pulled her into her bedroom so I could share with her my humiliating faux pas. For the past twenty minutes, I had relayed every embarrassing thing I had said to the man I'd assumed was Meena's soon-to-be husband as she held her sides and wiped the tears from her eyes.

"And now, I'm going to see him again at your *mehendi* tonight and—" I pressed my face against a pillow and groaned. "Have I just made a total fool of myself?"

"Not at all." Meena smiled reassuringly. "Hisham has a good sense of humor, from what I've heard from Haroon. He probably got a big laugh from it."

"I'm sure he did," I said, shaking my head.

"So, you really told him you thought he was good-looking?"

"*Charmingly* good-looking, I think was my exact phrase," I corrected her as we both broke into giggles.

"You know," she said, suddenly composing herself. "I could ask *Ammi* to talk to your *ammi* about Hish—"

"Absolutely not," I interrupted her, waving my hand. I could only imagine the level of humiliation I'd have to endure if my mother took up her matchmaking nonsense in the land of arranged marriages. "I made the mistake of falling for a charmingly good-looking guy once. Let me tell you, it did not end well."

"Maybe your search for 'the one' brought you to India for a reason," she said, her eyes gleaming.

"The only reason I'm in India is to celebrate you and your wedding. And speaking of weddings, I have something for you." I pulled out the small blue box from the nightstand. "Hisham came by to give this to you. It's from Haroon."

Meena took the box and gently lifted the top. Inside was a beautiful gold *tikka* with small diamond accents and a teardrop topaz stone glistening in the center. We both leaned in to take a closer look.

"It's beautiful," I said, watching as she lifted out the piece from the box and held it against her forehead. We walked over to the mirror so we could admire it together.

"You know, eight weeks ago, I didn't even know Haroon. And now I am going to be his wife," Meena said softly, glancing at my reflection. "Never underestimate kismet, Leila. It is a very powerful thing."

Mehendi Nights

I smiled politely as I attempted to make my way through a crowd of strangers. Every inch of space in the flat was occupied with guests of both the bride and the groom, and the sheer number of bodies made it difficult to breathe—let alone move—without bumping into someone.

The *mehendi* ceremony, hosted by the bride's family, was the first big event to kick off the three-day wedding festivities and was typically followed by a *sangeet*, *nikkah*, and reception. In my parents' generation, *mehendi* ceremonies would have been attended only by women; however, Meena and Haroon's families decided to combine the *mehendi* with the *sangeet*, making it a joint affair so that everyone could come together in the celebrations and bless the soon-to-be-wed couple.

The elders in the room were seated near the front of the stage, soberly *wah-wah*-ing to traditional *qawwali* and *ghazal* songs, while the youngsters were gathered in gender-segregated groups along the back walls, obsessively grooming themselves while sneaking flirtatious glances at members of the opposite sex.

I glanced around the room, feeling slightly disappointed. We were two hours into the *mehendi* ceremony, and there was still no sign of Hisham. After my talk with Meena earlier, I'd started thinking about what she had said about kismet. Maybe there was such a thing as fate. Or chance encounters. It happened for Meena and Haroon. It happened for my parents. Maybe it was what happened this morning with Hisham. Embarrassing as that run-in was, maybe we were destined to meet.

A part of me was still digesting my thoughts from the night before. I wondered what the greater purpose of marriage was for me; my reasons for wanting to marry. However, the thought of my deadline remained at the forefront of my mind. Hisham was cute, and I would be crazy to not explore an opportunity that was right in front of me. My heart fluttered as I thought about his smile. With less than a month before my parents' anniversary, this could very well be my last true shot at . . . something. American-born *desi* men wife-shopped abroad all the time—perhaps it was time I did the same.

Near the stage, I noticed Asima aunty clapping and swinging back and forth unrhythmically to the music. I quickly inched my way in her direction.

"*Salaams*, aunty," I shouted when I reached her, slightly out of breath.

"*Walaikum As'salaam*, Leila *beti*!" She turned around, giving me an enthusiastic smile. "Are you enjoying the ceremony?" she shouted back.

"I am." I nodded.

"Good, good, because you are next in line, Leila." She wagged a finger at me. "Soon, we will be dancing at your *mehendi* party!" she said, still swaying awkwardly.

I gave her a tight-lipped smile. Asima aunty was the fifteenth person this evening to tell me I was *next in line*. The only time I was glad to hear it was when I was at the buffet.

"What time does the groom's party arrive?"

"I'm sorry?" She pointed at her ear and shook her head.

"The groom's party," I repeated loudly. "When do they arrive?"

"Not until the very end . . . *tafri abhi shuroo ho rahi hai*!" She bobbled her head, giving me a teasing wink.

I sighed, looking down at my watch. For all I knew, this party could go through the night, and frankly, I doubted if my patience—or my hairstyle—would last that long. The last time I saw Hisham, I had funky morning breath and an unkempt ponytail. This time around, I'd decided I would step it up, so I was wearing a green *banarasi* sari and red lipstick, and had styled my long hair into tight, sleek curls in an effort to come across as a modern-day Sridevi. But as I patted the sweat from my forehead with the edge of my *dupatta*, I was afraid I was looking more like a modern-day poodle than an iconic eighties heroine. Sadly, even the strongest hair spray was no match for Mumbai humidity.

Asima aunty turned back to the music, and I distracted myself by readjusting the *pallu* on my shoulder. While my outfit would have been perfectly appropriate for a wedding function in L.A., I couldn't help but feel grossly under-dressed as I took in the extravagance surrounding me. All of the women—young and old—were decked out in their most lavish attire: glittery saris, silky hijabs, and enough gold jewelry to buy a small island. I remembered hearing once that Indian housewives held eleven percent of the world's gold, and it seemed about half of that reserve was currently dancing around in Meena's living room.

I looked up at the stage to see Meena seated perfectly still in the center, smiling shyly at each guest as dark green henna was carefully applied to her delicate hands and feet. Although I had only attended a handful of *desi* weddings over the years, I was always enchanted by the vibrancy and beauty of a traditional Indian bride. Meena was no exception. She was wearing a bright yellow *lehenga choli* with heavy silver embroidery throughout the front. Her thick hair was braided along the side with jasmine and roses weaved into it, and the golden *tikka* framed the crown of her head. Her quiet beauty rose above all the pomp and glitter and emanated through each and every corner, captivating all eyes in the room with her simple radiance. She was the prettiest bride-to-be I had ever seen.

Meena's eyes suddenly met mine and she nodded at the empty seat beside her. I stepped over the platform and made my way next to her. Before sitting down, I carefully adjusted the bottom of my sari, the jingling of my glass bangles barely audible as the music from the speakers thumped behind us.

"How are you doing?" I leaned in and whispered into her ear.

She looked at me with both her arms outstretched and shrugged. Her thin arms were covered with intricate patterns of lotus buds, peacocks, and flowers spiraling delicately along the curves of her forearms, adorning every inch of skin all the way up to her elbows. I laughed, wondering how she managed to stay so composed with everything going on around her.

While we waited for Meena's arms to dry, the henna aunty hunched over and carefully applied the dark green paste to Meena's feet using a paper cone with a fine tip at the end. We watched as the aunty expertly drew in each pattern, adjusting her designs to follow the shape of Meena's foot. Her hands were steady, yet quick with each movement.

"What is the significance of all these designs?" I asked.

"Lotus signifies beauty and femininity," the aunty explained. "And these spirals," she said, drawing delicate vines that curved up and around Meena's ankles, "these are for longevity."

"And the flower buds?"

"The start of new life."

I looked at Meena and smiled.

"The meaning is not just in the design," the aunty continued, "but also in the color of the *mehendi*. The darker the color, the deeper the love between the couple."

"Shall we take a look?" I whispered to Meena. She nodded, her eyes sparkling with anticipation.

Both of us watched with bated breath as I scraped a tiny section beneath Meena's wrist with my fingernail. The dried, hardened paste flaked off, leaving dark red stains across the skin beneath.

"Ohh, it's beautiful!" we exclaimed at the same time.

"*Waah*." The aunty smiled and tilted her head. "It looks like the new couple will be very happy, *insha'Allah*."

"*Insha'Allah*," I repeated, grinning widely.

"Okay, one final touch." The aunty picked up a fresh cone. "What is the groom's name?"

Meena's cheeks flushed a deep red. "Haroon," she said quietly.

"What is that for?" I asked, watching curiously as the

aunty drew out each letter of Haroon's name within the different motifs on Meena's arm.

"This is a game for the newlyweds." The aunty smiled as she finished up the final *N*, which she squeezed in between the mango-shaped design near Meena's wrist. "The groom searches for each letter of his name in the designs drawn on his new bride on the night of their wedding." She gently lifted Meena's chin and looked into her blushing face. "And the bride is not allowed to give any clues as he searches, even if it takes him all night!"

"Oh, how scandalous!" I blurted, and the three of us broke into giggles.

As I watched Meena's face redden, my mind drifted back to my father's theory about love after marriage. This was how it all started. These were two strangers who had never kissed, hugged, held hands, or even been alone in the same room together, yet this small game would force them to shed their inhibitions and share their first intimate moments. It was *crazy*. But as I looked into Meena's excited face, I couldn't help but smile. Underneath all the craziness, there was an innocence and sweetness to this first physical interaction that even I couldn't deny.

An Unexpected Hero

"The groom's party has arrived!" Jamila aunty shouted over the music. I held my breath as the entire room erupted in cheers.

A small crowd gathered near the doors. While everyone tried to catch a glimpse of the groom, I was hoping to catch sight of someone else. From atop the shoulders of his entourage, Haroon entered ceremoniously through the garlanded entrance smiling and waving nervously as each guest stepped aside to create a path. His grin widened when he locked eyes with Meena waiting for him on the stage. She dropped her eyes to her hands and smiled shyly.

Haroon was wearing a golden brocade *sherwani* with silver embellishments around the collar, and traditional *khussas* on his feet. His *dupatta* was draped across his shoulders with one side looped casually around his neck. Behind him was Hisham, looking dashing in a white cotton *kameez* with his face freshly shaven and his hair slicked back.

My heart skipped a beat.

As the procession danced their way to the stage, Haroon's entourage lowered him to the ground so he could make his way up the platform. He walked onto the stage and sat down next to Meena just as the cameras started flashing. Guests slowly began taking turns coming up to the stage to give their blessings to the blushing bride and groom while live performers entertained the crowd with the singing of *nasheeds* and traditional songs. Excitement buzzed throughout the room.

I stood on my tiptoes trying to catch another glimpse of Hisham. However, I quickly lost sight of him as the sea of new guests swallowed him up. *Did he see me? Will he try to say hello?* I walked past the buffet tables continuing to scan the room but instead caught sight of myself in the mirror hanging above one of the serving stations. I gasped.

"Crap!" I muttered as I frantically dabbed drops of sweat from my face. My T-zone was glistening from the humidity in the room, and my tight curls had loosened, hanging flatly down my shoulders like limp noodles. I dipped my hair forward and scrunched out the waves in a desperate attempt to revive them. Then I pulled out a tube of lipstick from my small clutch and applied it generously. I was determined to make a better impression than the one I had made this morning. As I blotted my lips on a piece of tissue paper, I suddenly felt someone grab my arm and pull me into the adjacent hallway.

"Leila! Where have you been?"

It was my mother.

I didn't have the heart to tell her that I had been intentionally avoiding her all night.

"I have been looking everywhere for you! Come. *Jaldi*. I have someone I want you to meet." She hurriedly led me toward the kitchen, where a short, stout, mustachioed man who looked to be in his early thirties awaited us. He was smiling eagerly at me. "Leila, this is Asad." My mother beamed. "He is a friend of Haroon's. I just met Asad's mother, Zainab aunty, and she is lovely!" Asad looked at me approvingly.

"Can I see you in the hallway for a second?" I hissed into my mother's ear. She gave me a quizzical look, but I walked out quickly and waited until she appeared a minute later.

"*Ya Allah*, Leila! What is it?" she asked, impatiently. "Asad is waiting for you. He will think you are being rude!"

"*Ammi*," I said, trying to steady my frustration. "What are *you* doing?"

"Nothing. I just thought I would introduce you to Asad. He is a very nice—"

"*Ammi!*" I interrupted her. "We are supposed to be celebrating Meena and Haroon! Not looking for a spouse for me!"

"Leila," my mother said, an expression of calm washing over her face. "*Beti*, this is what weddings are for!" She smiled at me piteously, as if I had failed to understand something so obvious. "Weddings are the best place to meet a spouse. Did you know that Fatimah aunty, the heavyset one with the brightly colored fingernails, pointed you out to Ruksana aunty, the lady who is wearing high heels with the stylish hijab . . . high heels . . . can you imagine such high heels on a woman her age?" She clucked her tongue judgmentally. "Anyways, Ruksana aunty found Jamila aunty and Jamila aunty is the one who told me that Asad was asking about you. So, Jamila aunty introduced me to Asad's mother, Zainab aunty, and it was she who personally asked me to conduct an intro between you two!"

I squeezed my eyes shut, trying to make sense of all her words.

She patted my arm. "Leila, any girl in your position would be lucky to catch the eye of a handsome boy like Asad." I rolled my eyes. "If we are diligent," she continued, ignoring my disinterest, "your engagement will be *pakka* by the end of the week, *insha'Allah*!" She bobbled her head.

She was crazy if she thought I would agree to an engagement with Mr. Mustache in there. "*Ammi,* I'm not interes—"

"Just *talk* to him, *beti*." She pushed me toward the kitchen. "At least give him a chance!"

I sighed, hanging my head in defeat. "One conversation and *that's it*. I'm serious," I said firmly. She nodded quickly and led me back in. Asad was anxiously pressing his hands together and pacing back and forth.

"Hi."

"Oh, hello." He shoved his hand forward and smiled so widely that his mustache curled up at the corners. I lightly placed my hand into his, and he shook it vigorously. "So, I hear your good name is Leila?"

I scrunched my brows. "What did you hear my bad name was?"

My mother coughed loudly and gave me a look. Asad pulled out a chair at the small table and motioned toward it. "Shall we?"

I sat down as he took a seat across from me, his eyes piercing through me intently from the other side of the table. I cleared my throat and looked away. My mother quickly excused herself and stepped outside, leaving the two of us staring at each other awkwardly.

"So I hear you are Meena's cousin?"

I nodded.

"I suppose good looks run in the family." He winked. I pressed my lips together and forced a small smile.

"And how do you know the groom?" I asked.

"Oh, Haroon and I go way back to our college days."

"So you must know his brother as well?"

"Hisham? Oh, yes." He nodded. "The three of us were excellent friends." I suddenly perked up. Finally, a conversation I was interested in.

"What was Hisham like in college? Did he play any sports?"

"I . . . I'm not sure. But I used to play some squash back

in the day. I have very strong arms, you see." He pulled up his sleeve and flexed his forearm.

"Was he a good student?" I ignored him, trying not to focus on the veins popping out from his elbows. "Do you know what he studied?"

He shrugged. "I'm not sure. But I was a top student in computer science." He gave me a self-satisfied grin.

"Cool. So, um, would you say Hisham was popular? Did he have a lot of friends?"

"I suppose?"

I sighed. *Is he going to give me any information at all?* I leaned back in my chair, feeling impatient.

"Haroon, Hisham, and I used to do a lot of *masti* back in the day," he continued. "We were like the three . . ." He snapped his fingers, trying to recall the end of his sentence.

"Stooges?"

"Musketeers!" He pointed his finger at me and laughed. "Sense of humor; I like it!"

I grimaced.

"So, your cousin and my college friend . . . quite the coincidence, no?"

"I guess . . ."

"*Rishtas* can form from anywhere, Leila. I just want you to know that when it comes to marriage, I am very open-minded."

"Uh-huh," I said, glancing at my watch, trying to figure

out how we could speed this thing along. If he wasn't going to give me any details about Hisham, I was ready to get back to the party.

"You will come to find that I am looking for a very equal relationship."

Come to find? This is a one-conversation deal. The only thing I need to find is a way out of here.

"I will allow my wife to work; I do not expect her to be a housewife. Unless, of course, that is what she wants."

"Really? You'll *allow* her that?"

"Yes. I will also permit her to dress how she likes. I am not too conservative, you see."

Giving a grown woman permission to dress herself. How liberal! I thought.

"She will also be granted leave to visit with her friends and family as she likes. I think it is important for her to have a social life." He pulled the tip of his mustache and twirled it upward.

"How generous of you to *grant* her these things."

"I am not like most Indian men, Leila," he went on, not catching my tone. "In fact, I am very Westernized. I like English movies and songs. I don't even eat very spicy foods."

"That's a shame, because I love spicy foods."

"Oh, me too," he quickly changed his tune. "I am willing to adjust my tastes to whatever my wife likes."

How agreeable.

As Asad carried on about how atypical he was, I was reminded of all the qualities that turned me off about conservatively traditional men. Men like Asad were oblivious to their sexist, controlling, and chauvinistic tendencies. They touted their open-mindedness with contradictory statements of "permissions" and "allowances." Needless to say, I was not impressed.

As much as I wanted to leave, my mother kept popping in every five minutes pretending to "look for something" and walking out with a pleased smile. I couldn't believe this was how my night was going to end. I propped my elbow on the table, leaned my head against the inside of my hand, and wondered what Hisham was doing at this very moment. Was he busy with the festivities? Was he looking for me too? What if he was talking to someone else? I needed to get back out there.

"Listen," I finally interrupted, just as Asad began describing his favorite scene from the movie *Titanic* in excruciating detail. "As much as I've enjoyed—"

The door suddenly swung open, and I swallowed the rest of my sentence, expecting it to be my mother again. However, when I glanced up, it was Hisham.

"Hey," he said, stopping in his tracks, looking at the two of us. "Do you two . . . know each other?"

Asad smiled and twirled his mustache. "Hey, *dood*," he said in such a heavy accent that my body automatically recoiled.

"We are getting to know each other." He gave Hisham an obnoxious wink.

Hisham stared at us for a few silent moments as I stared at the floor. This was hardly the second impression I was hoping for. Hisham poured himself a cup of chai from the carafe and walked back toward the door. As he held the cup in his left hand, he lifted his free hand to his eye, giving us a quick salute. He then pushed his shoulder against the door and disappeared just as Asad launched into another "fascinating" tidbit about himself.

I exhaled slowly and slouched into my chair, staring at the clock. What was I supposed to do now? Should I go after him? Try to talk to him? Even kismet couldn't help me recover from this. *So much for fate.*

Suddenly Hisham poked his head back in. "Oh, by the way, Leila, your mother is looking for you."

This night officially blew. My mother had just been in the kitchen no less than five minutes ago. Whatever she wanted now could not be good. "Okay." I quickly excused myself while my head reeled with frustration. *I've already wasted thirty minutes of my time talking to Asad. And now the one guy I want to talk to is under the impression that Mr. Mustache and I are an item. And to top it all off, my mother is looking for me.* As I dragged my feet into the hallway, preparing myself for the worst, Hisham quickly jerked my arm and pulled me into the dining room.

"Is my mother in here?" I asked, looking around, panicked.

"No. I just . . ." Hisham's eyes flickered playfully. "I just had a feeling you were in need of some help." I knitted my brows, my brain still working to catch up with what he was saying.

"Wait, so my mother's *not* looking for me?" I asked, a little disoriented, as I was still expecting her to jump out from one of the corners.

"You're welcome?" He smiled. It finally dawned on me that he had just saved me. I leaned against the wall, letting out a deep sigh, and grinned.

"My hero."

He laughed.

"No, really, between this and what happened this morning, you deserve some sort of badge."

"If it helps, what happened this morning was not a first for me." He shrugged.

"By the way, that, in there." I pointed toward the kitchen. "My mom totally cornered me into that conversation. It's actually pretty embarrassing—"

"No need to explain," he cut me off. "We're at an Indian wedding. It's expected."

"So I hear."

"Besides, I'm sure Asad isn't the only one chasing after you tonight."

I blushed.

"I mean . . . um . . ." he stammered nervously. "What I mean is there are a lot of *rishta* aunties circling around. You should beware."

I laughed, feeling the heat rise in my face. "*Rishta* aunties are pretty bad, but they're not the only aunties to avoid at these types of functions."

"Oh?"

"Yeah, there are also the career-focused aunties. The ones who ask you a million questions about your studies and profession. '*What do you mean you studied English? Aren't you from America?*'" I mimicked.

Hisham laughed.

"And the judgmental aunties. The ones who have an opinion about *everything,* from the food, to the decor, to the appropriateness of your outfit! And don't forget the lay-it-on-thick aunties. The ones constantly bragging about their kids. '*My daughter just won the Nobel Prize AND got engaged in the same week!*'"

"Those are the worst!" Hisham shook his head. "What about the pushers? The ones who aggressively force you to eat even after you tell them you're full?"

"Those aunties I don't mind so much," I teased.

Hisham grinned. "You're right. There are far more evil aunties to worry about."

"So anyways, what do we do about—" I rolled up the corners of my imaginary mustache.

"Oh, Asad? He'll be fine. He's probably YouTubing scenes from *Titanic* on his phone right now."

I covered my mouth, giggling.

"Now that you're free, though—" He grabbed my hand. "Come, you have to see this," he said, leading me toward the living room. We pushed our way through the crowd until we secured a spot near the front of the stage. We watched, along with the other guests, as Haroon's mother dipped her hands into a clay pot and rubbed yellow *haldi* all over Meena's face and neck. Next, Jamila aunty dipped her hand into the pot and rubbed the yellow paste over Haroon's face, neck, hands, and feet.

Although I had witnessed this part of the *haldi* ceremony at previous weddings, this was the first time I felt inclined to know more about the deeper significance behind the tradition. "What is the purpose of using turmeric?" I asked Hisham.

"It's meant to ward off the evil eye and leave the bride and groom glowing on their wedding day," Hisham whispered into my ear. I smiled as Meena and Haroon glanced shyly at one another and carefully placed a garland around each other's neck.

"And the garlands?"

"It's a symbol of their intention to marry one another."

We watched as Ahmed, Meena's brother, joined his mother onstage, followed by all the other cousins and siblings in the family. Members from Haroon's family also went up. Meena and Haroon took turns applying the yellow paste on each of their relatives, one by one—with Jamila aunty occasionally checking Meena's *mehendi* beneath the clear plastic glove she wore as protection.

I spotted my mother standing on the other side of the room, looking directly at me. She kept motioning her head to the stage, trying to communicate with me. From where I was standing, it looked like she was either telling me to go onstage . . . or she had developed a strange crick in her neck. I pretended not to see her.

"What's happening now?" I asked as a crowd began forming around the couple.

"Oh, it's just a silly custom," Hisham said. "Supposedly, whoever gets touched by the sacred paste will soon find a good, attractive partner. At least that's what the tradition says."

"Is it true?"

"Why, are you interested?"

I shrugged. While my feelings about marriage were still slightly mixed, I'd be lying if I said a teensy part of me wasn't intrigued by this "silly custom."

"I mean . . . I suppose it wouldn't hurt to try." I smiled sheepishly as he let out an amused laugh. I blushed, suddenly realizing how ridiculous I sounded.

"I suppose it wouldn't." He smiled and gently pushed me toward the stage.

"Are you coming?" I asked, looking back at him. He waved his hand to indicate that I was on my own. However, he gave me a thumbs-up, encouraging me to keep going as I hesitantly made my way through the crowd.

As I neared the stage, I spotted my mother, who nodded at me with approval. As much as I hated satisfying her wishes, it was too late to turn back now. I knew she was probably hoping my going up there might mean good news for me and Asad, but Asad was not the one for me. Of that I was certain.

When Meena saw me approach her, she removed the plastic glove from her hand and dipped the tip of her *mehendi*-covered finger directly into the pot—despite Jamila aunty's anxious looks. She brought my face close to hers and rubbed her finger gently across my cheek; the paste was refreshingly cool against my skin.

"May this bring you 'the one' you are looking for, Leila." She smiled as her eyes drifted toward Hisham and then back to me. I drew in a deep breath and thought about everything I had gone through over these past few months. Every disappointment, every disaster, every heartbreak flashed through my mind like a tragic movie reel. From the corner of my eye, I could see Hisham watching me from the crowd with a slight smile across his face.

I turned to Meena with a hopeful heart. "*Insha'Allah*," I whispered softly. "*Insha'Allah*."

Guilt Trip

Bright rays of sunlight greeted me from the dining room as I stumbled in groggily. The *mehendi* festivities had continued late into the night and well into the early morning. By the time my head finally hit the pillow, the *fajr adhan* was sounding off in the distance. I was hardly able to squeeze in a few winks of sleep in between all the giddiness I felt from the second half of my night.

After the *haldi* ceremony, I spent the rest of the night with Hisham. From our insightful discussions about traditions and customs, to consuming bowls of *rasmalai*, to dodging *rishta* aunties, my mother, and Asad, there was something about Hisham that was different from the guys back home. He was funny and sharp-witted, yet at the same time cultivated and courteous. It was the first time I found myself attracted to someone Indian-born, and the more we talked, the more I found myself drawn to his endearing mix of traditional and modern values. As I nibbled on a cake rusk, silently lost in these thoughts, my mother suddenly emerged from her room.

"Good morning, Leila *beti*," she said sleepily, sitting down next to me at the dining table. The celebrations must have also taken a toll on her because it was a rare occurrence for her to sleep past sunrise. She squinted her eyes as she glanced at the clock hanging above the sofa. "Why are you up so early?" she asked, yawning.

"I was thinking of going out for a bit," I said, handing my mother a cup of chai.

"Oh?" she said, raising a brow and taking a sip.

"I wanted to buy a new outfit for the wedding tomorrow," I explained. After I had witnessed the sheer extravagance in the room last night, I realized the outfits I had brought with me would not cut it. I needed to step up my game. "I was thinking of maybe asking Meena to come with me."

"No, no, no." My mother shook her head. "The bride must not step out of the house after the *mehendi* ceremony. It is *maayun*. Don't worry, Leila, I will come with you."

"No," I said quickly. "That's not necessary; I can just go on my own."

"Nonsense, Leila," she said, getting up. "Let me quickly change, and I will arrange for the driver." I watched her hurry into the other room as I sat there confounded by how quickly my relaxing plans for the day had just unraveled.

Ten minutes later, we were seated in the back of the

Maruti Suzuki with Sahil behind the wheel, the poor guy wiping drops of sweat from his forehead and nodding repeatedly as he tried to keep up with my mother's complicated instructions: "We want to go to Santacruz West, but drop us off near the Tirupati Shopping Center across from Sai Baba so we can browse through all of the shops along the street . . ."

I leaned my head against the window. The last time I had gone dress shopping with my mother was my high school graduation, and that excursion had ended in tears. Not happy ones. I had a feeling this was going to be a long day.

"We should look for a nice *lehenga choli* or a stylish sari for you, Leila. Something fashionable that all the young girls are wearing these days," my mother babbled excitedly. "And no more of these dark, gloomy colors. We should get you something light and bright. By the way, how did things go with Asad last night? He seems like a very nice boy, no?"

Only my mother could expertly maneuver an innocent conversation about outfits to a loaded question about *rishtas* in the same breath. She didn't even use an indicator before she swerved. I was blindsided.

"It went okay, I guess." I shrugged.

"He is a good boy, Leila." She patted my knee. "I really hope that you will give him a chance."

"I did, *Ammi*," I said, my tone slightly aggravated. "In case you forgot, I spent a good deal of time talking to him last night." *Or rather listening to him talk about himself*, I thought, but held my tongue.

"That is very good, Leila. The more the two of you talk, the better. And the good news is, you will see him again at the reception tomorrow. It will give you time to get to know each other even more."

"Great," I said with as much forced enthusiasm as I could muster. My mother smiled weakly and then looked out the window. After a few moments, she cleared her throat.

"You know, Leila, sometimes I wonder if things would be different if you had grown up here." She hesitated for a minute. "I just look at all these girls—even younger than you—and they are all happily married and settled. I just wish that for you too."

I remained silent.

"I just want you to be happy, Leila." She turned to me with tired eyes.

"But I am happy, *Ammi*." I tried again to reassure her as convincingly as I could.

"Yes, yes, I know," she said with a sigh. I hated how she always made me feel so guilty. I wanted to be happy too, but how could I tell her that my happiness was not defined in the same way hers was? She was convinced that my getting married would bring me happiness, but truth be told, these last few months had been utterly miserable for me. In retrospect, I realized I had been much happier before this process started—before she had gotten involved and tried to "help" me.

"It's very difficult, *beti*," she continued. "You don't understand how hard it is when everybody keeps asking me why you are still unmarried. What am I supposed to say?"

"Why is it anybody else's business?" I blurted angrily. "I mean, who cares if I'm not married! Why does everyone keep bringing it up? They should be more concerned about Meena's marriage, not what's going on in my life!" I slumped back against the seat, my heart raging inside my chest.

"Because that is not how it works, Leila," my mother replied calmly. "*Beti*, once you pass a certain age, people start wondering . . ." She trailed off.

"Wondering *what*?"

"Wondering if something . . . is wrong." She looked at me. "I just don't want people to think I've failed as your mother." Her face looked so small and fatigued.

"I'm trying, *Ammi*. I am. I don't know what else you want me to do."

"Just try harder, Leila. Please, do it for me and your father. That is all we ask."

I looked away, fuming. Why was it so hard for my mother to see that I had been trying? That I was *still* trying? My reason for marrying was not the same as hers. Or my father's. Or the same as Meena's. I was still trying my best to find a way to please them and satisfy their expectations; however, nothing I did, it seemed, would ever be enough. Somehow, my mother never missed an opportunity to remind me of what a disappointment I was. Or how I was causing her to fail. Only she could find a way to somehow make this about her. I squeezed my eyes shut, feeling the hot tears pushing against my lids. We hadn't even started shopping yet, and it was like high school graduation all over again. At least some things never changed.

Sari Not Sorry

SEASONS. The slanting red letters in front of the store summoned us from across the street.

"There." My mother pointed. "That is where we must go." I slung my messenger bag across my shoulders and quickly followed her into the busy street—trying not to get leveled by a rickshaw. As we neared the entrance, I stopped to admire the breathtaking window displaying dozens of mannequins dressed in the most beautiful Indian outfits I had ever seen. Every dress looked like it had just stepped out of a scene from *Bajirao Mastani*.

"Come, Leila." My mother pulled me inside. "Those are all bridal dresses. They will be of no use for you. You need something more suitable."

"Right," I muttered, wondering if there was a specific selection of dresses for unmarried spinsters that she would be more approving of. As we stepped through the heavy glass doors, we were greeted by the same level of magnificence on the interior—rows and rows of racks filled with vibrant, heavily embroidered silks and chiffons. There were floor-to-ceiling compartments brimming with glittery saris, and tall showcases along the back walls full of accessories and shoes to match any dress in the store. For a brief moment, I forgot all about my mother and drew in a deep breath. It was every girl's Bollywood dream.

A prissy-faced young saleswoman stepped out from behind one of the counters and walked toward my mother. "Hello, madam, how can I help you?" she said in a heavily affected British accent. She was dressed in a slim black pantsuit and her hair was wound tightly in a topknot, lending a bewildered expression to her heavily made-up face.

"Yes, my daughter is looking for a wedding outfit to wear."

"Your wedding, miss?" The saleswoman turned toward me.

"No, no, no," my mother interjected before I could respond. "She is just a guest, *not* the bride."

"I see," the saleswoman replied haughtily, looking me over with pity.

"You know what, I'll just take a look around myself." I quickly turned away as my mother continued yammering to the saleswoman about the different styles she felt were "appropriate" for my body type.

I moved to the back corner of the shop, making sure I was

clearly out of sight. Once I felt safely invisible again, I began looking through the racks, pulling out anything that caught my eye. There was a gorgeous burgundy *lehenga choli* with gold and ruby crystals scattered throughout the tulle bottom; I picked out a sleeveless *salwar kameez* with an elegant high neck, floral designs, and small silver buttons lined delicately down the back; I spotted a navy blue *anarkali* with a long-sleeved form-fitting bodice covered in golden sequins. I kept pulling and piling dresses over my left arm until it felt like it would collapse under the weight. If I was ever to have a Bollywood moment, it was happening right then—that is, until I turned the corner and bumped straight into my mother. Both her arms were also hidden beneath multiple layers of dresses, as were those of the judgmental saleswoman, who was trailing closely behind her.

"Leila, *beti*, I have found all these beautiful dresses for you. Why don't you go in the dressing room and start trying them on," she said, shoving her pile onto mine. "Oh, and don't bother trying on some of these darker dresses," she said pulling out the burgundy *lehenga choli*, navy *anarkali*, and about half of the other dresses I had selected. "I can already tell these colors won't look good against your skin tone."

I groaned and clumsily staggered into the dressing room, dropping the pile of outfits onto the small leather ottoman. Outside, I could hear my mother ask the saleswoman if she was married, and the disappointed "I see" that followed when the woman replied in the affirmative. *Great*, I thought miserably. *One more person to whom my mother can compare me.*

For the next forty-five minutes, I squeezed and sucked my body into every single dress from my mother's selected pile as she waited eagerly by the dressing room door to shower me with a slew of criticisms about why none of them were right.

"No, no, no. This one looked much better on the hanger."

"Leila, can you try making your hips smaller?"

"It's a pretty dress, but just not on you."

"Does this come in a color that doesn't make you look so dark?"

"Why are your shoulders so broad? You must get that from your father."

At one point, she turned to the saleswoman and asked her if she had any dresses to make my breasts look more "shapely." As the two of them wandered back into the store to find another round of options for me, I pulled out the final dress tucked beneath the others—it was one of my picks: a beautiful white sari with dazzling crystal accents along the border, an elegant high-necked blouse, and a teardrop back covered in sheer netting. I carefully draped the silky fabric across my body and stepped out to the dressing area to get a better look at myself in the floor-length mirrors. My heart skipped a beat as I glanced at my reflection.

"Hey, *salaams*," said a familiar voice behind me. My heart jumped again and I quickly turned around to see Hisham carrying a stack of dresses so high that only the top of his forehead was visible. "Your mom wanted me to drop these off to you," he said, his voice muffled behind the fabrics.

I quickly grabbed the dresses from his hands and dropped them on the bench outside my dressing room door. "Wh— what are you doing here?" I asked, blushing nervously as I redraped the *pallu* to make sure everything was properly cinched and concealed. The butterflies in my stomach fluttered as flashbacks from last night flooded my mind. *This is so unexpected. I didn't think I would see him again until Meena's reception.*

"I came here with my—" Hisham paused midsentence. "Wow," he exhaled, his expression quickly shifting. I looked down, suddenly feeling very self-conscious.

My face flushed as I spun back toward the mirror. "I'm not sure if the fit is right . . . Do you think it might be too much?" I tilted my head, trying to look at it from all angles. As much as I loved the sari, I knew my mother would find a million things wrong with it, which was causing me to question my judgment.

"No, not at all," he stammered. "It looks beautiful," he added, looking at me through the mirror. Our eyes locked briefly in the reflection and he smiled shyly.

"Leila, look who I ran into!" My mother's voice pierced through the dressing room as she walked in with the saleswoman and a fashionably dressed aunty carrying large shopping bags in each hand. "This is Shabana aunty—Haroon and Hisham's mother!" she exclaimed.

"*As'salaamu Alaikum, beti.*" Shabana aunty leaned in and kissed me on both cheeks. "I was just here picking up some items, and what a pleasant surprise to find you both here! Your mother tells me you are shopping for a dress for the reception?" I nodded, glancing quickly toward Hisham, who was now leaning against the wall, his face lowered while he looked into his phone screen.

"What a beautiful sari! *Wah!*" Shabana aunty turned toward my mother. "What I would give to be young and thin again!" she remarked wistfully, while my mother smiled in agreement.

"Yes, yes," my mother concurred. "Leila can pull off almost any dress with that tiny figure of hers!"

"*Masha'Allah!*"

I bit my tongue and tried not to roll my eyes. *Tiny figure?* That wasn't the tune she had been singing for the past forty-five minutes.

"So, have we selected a dress then?" The saleswoman motioned toward me as I glanced in the mirror one last time. I carefully watched my mother's expression, waiting for her reply.

"I think it's just lovely on you, Leila!" Shabana aunty bobbled her head. "Nida, what do you think?" My mother looked from her to me, with a thin, forced smile plastered across her face. I could tell it was killing her to not be able to say what she *really* thought.

"I think if Leila likes it, she should get it," my mother finally said through clenched teeth.

"I like it," I stated without hesitation.

Hisham looked up from his phone and gave me a lopsided smirk.

"Okay," my mother said, still smiling awkwardly. She turned toward the saleswoman. "We will select this one."

"Very well, madam."

"But first we must agree on a reasonable price," my mother said, leading the saleswoman toward the registers. "I could buy the whole store for what is written on the tag . . ."

"I'm going to change." I grinned at Hisham as he and his mother exited the dressing area.

When I finally rejoined them, my mother had already completed the negotiations and was sliding her credit card into the machine. By the look on her face, I could tell she was pleased with the outcome—which was great since I knew she wasn't so thrilled about the outfit. I handed the sari to the saleswoman, and while we waited for her to wrap it up, my mother and Shabana aunty began talking about the wedding.

"These preparations are so tiring, Nida! The reception is tomorrow and there are still so many things left to do!"

"I can only imagine!" My mother shook her head sympathetically. "It's good you have Hisham here to help you."

"Yes, he has been so very helpful," Shabana aunty said, shoving all her shopping bags into his arms. "I don't know what I would do without him!" she exclaimed, throwing her hands up. "You know how it is here, Nida. Everything has to be *just so*."

"You probably can't wait for it to be over!"

"Oh, yes. We have already decided for Hisham's wedding, we will not go this extravagant."

"No, no. Of course not. The expectations are much higher for the first child's wedding."

The saleswoman handed us our bag, and the four of us exited the store, walking onto the bustling sidewalk outside. Shabana aunty and my mother continued chattering away while Hisham and I trailed a few steps behind.

"Looks like they're already planning your wedding, huh?" I gave Hisham a playful nudge. He shot me an embarrassed look and shrugged. I laughed.

"And it is much more work for a daughter! All the clothes and the jewelry." Shabana aunty shook her head. "*Ya Allah*. I don't envy your position, Nida."

"Trust me, I would happily shop for jewelry and clothes if it meant my daughter was getting married." My mother glowered disappointingly in my direction.

"It will happen in its own time, Nida."

"That's the problem. With Leila, I'm afraid that time will never come!"

I could feel my face burning.

When we finally reached the corner, Shabana aunty turned toward Hisham. "*Beta*, will you pick up the sweets from the shop, and I will wait for you here?" she asked, fanning herself in the afternoon sun. "I am feeling very tired all of a sudden."

"Come, Shabana, let us take you home," my mother offered, pointing to Sahil's car parked across the street. "You should take some rest. We will give you a ride back."

"No, no." Shabana aunty waved her hand. "There is so much left to do. I will just take a break for a few minutes."

"Aunty is right, *Ammi*. You should go back." Hisham placed the bags in her hand. "Just let me know what still needs to be done, and I can take care of it while you go home and rest."

My mother looked at Hisham with a satisfied smile. She loved when others agreed with her.

"*Beta*, there are three different sweets shops you must go to, and a long list of others. How will you manage alone?"

"Leila will accompany him." My mother pushed me forward. "If there is anything Leila knows, it is her way around a sweets shop."

I looked down at the ground, wishing a sinkhole would magically appear and swallow me whole.

Shabana aunty hesitated, but after a few moments finally acquiesced. "Okay, I will come with you, Nida," she said, nodding. My mother grabbed her arm and we watched the two of them cross the busy intersection and climb into Sahil's parked Suzuki as he tried to fit all their shopping bags into the small trunk. The sound of thunder rumbled in the distance.

* * *

"Shall we?" Hisham said, motioning his arm forward. I followed his lead, still feeling deflated from my morning with my mother.

"Everything okay?"

"Yeah," I mumbled, my mood reflecting the dark gray clouds forming overhead.

"Wedding pressures getting to you?" he said half-jokingly.

"Why is everyone so obsessed with marriage?! And by everyone, I mean my mother."

"That's *every* mother, Leila."

"It's like she turns every conversation into a discussion about why I'm not married. I can't catch a break!"

"If it helps, I can tell you, we've all been there."

"Yeah, but at least you don't have the same pressures that us women have," I replied testily. While all South Asian mothers badgered their children about marriage at some point, it was a known fact that they were always less judgmental toward their sons. No one would bat an eye if a South

Asian man chose not to marry until his mid- to late thirties. Women, on the other hand, were expected to bear children, so they couldn't be afforded the same leniencies. The younger a South Asian woman married, the more desirable she was in the eyes of her husband and her in-laws. Therefore, even though Hisham was trying to relate, I couldn't help but feel that the pressures faced by Indian men were minuscule compared to their female counterparts.

"That's not true. At least you live in America. You probably don't have it nearly as bad as we do here."

"It's even harder in America!" I cried. "We're the minority population. Imagine how difficult it is to find a good Muslim, who is of a similar ethnicity, whom you like, who likes you back, who meets all the criteria on your list, *and* whom your parents approve of. Here, all you have to do is walk outside, and you're met with a million options. We don't have it quite as easy as you think."

Hisham cocked his head. "So if there are so many options here, why haven't you found someone yet? I mean, all you have to do is walk outside, right?" He wiggled his brows playfully. "What about him?" he said, pointing to a turbaned man on the street tugging along a wooden cart filled with boxes. "Or him?" He pointed to a young man wearing tiny shorts and a tank top on a scooter.

"You know what I mean," I said, rolling my eyes.

"Oh, look at that one!" He directed my attention to a

stocky, middle-aged uncle spewing chewed-up *gutka* onto the curb, leaving behind a reddish-brown stain.

"Gross." I turned away, disgusted.

Hisham continued pointing out every ridiculous "prospect" he could find for three blocks until my sullenness subsided and I finally cracked a smile.

"*Okay*, I get your point. You can stop now." He gave me a lopsided grin. "So where is this sweets shop, anyw—"

A giant drop of water suddenly plopped onto my forehead and I peered upward at the grayish-white sky. Hisham glanced in my direction, amused, as I wiped it away.

"What?" I snapped, flicking the moisture from my fingers toward him. Just then, sprinkles of wetness hit us both on the backs of our necks. As light scattered drops painted the sidewalk a darker shade, we looked overhead and watched as the billowy clouds suddenly broke and a flurry of rain showered down upon us. I squealed and lifted my hands over my head as Hisham quickly pulled me across the street into the small *mithai* shop at the corner.

We rushed through the small glass doors, setting a tiny bell jingling as we entered. My cotton tunic had soaked all the way through; I pulled on the fabric but it clung stubbornly to my skin. Hisham stepped in beside me and shook his head, spraying droplets of rainwater in every direction. "Hey!" I protested, holding my hands up as a shield. He laughed.

Inside, the familiar scent of ghee and coconut filled my senses. Every wall was lined with glass cases, and behind them, heaps of *laddus*—in every color and variety—lay on beautiful silver trays. I turned toward Hisham.

"This is just like a dream I once had!" I remarked incredulously. He looked at me with a huge smile across his face.

"You're not the only one who knows her way around a sweets shop." He pointed toward the cases. "Shall we give some of these a try?"

"I really shouldn't . . ." I hesitated, staring at the beautiful globes of sugar beckoning me from behind the glass.

"Meena and Haroon deserve the best. We should personally make sure they get it." His eyes twinkled.

"I suppose if it's for Meena and Haroon—"

"Consider this a familial sacrifice." Hisham grinned, gesturing to the uncle behind the counter.

For the next half hour, we waded into the waters of *laddu* paradise as we tried *boondi laddus* and coconut ones. We tried some with almonds and others covered in pistachios. We ate *laddus* made with pure ghee and some made with brown sugar. Hisham knew all the good ones to try, and not once did I feel him judging me for my massive appetite for sweets. By the time we were finished, we had selected more than two dozen boxes for Meena and Haroon's reception party.

As the uncle carefully wrapped our selections in beautiful red boxes decorated with gold foil, Hisham went outside to hail a taxi. I gazed through the shop window at the rain, watching all the people running along the side of the street. Some were wearing *dhotis*, long yards of fabric that were tied baggily to form pants, and brown leather *chappals*. The women wore rain-soaked *kameezes* and carried newspapers, flour bags, or whatever they could find to cover their heads. The vendors were bringing in baskets of fruits and spices they had laid out earlier in the day, while cascades of water gushed forcefully from the flimsy roofs of their street-side shops. I couldn't believe how quickly the weather had shifted.

"Here you are," the uncle said, breaking up my thoughts. I thanked him, grabbing the boxes, and ran outside to where Hisham was waiting with a cab. I jumped into the back seat as he held the door open for me and placed the sweets carefully on my lap.

Hisham climbed in beside me and leaned forward to give the driver directions to the next stop. As the car pulled out slowly into the crowded streets, Hisham scooted back, wringing out the edge of his rain-soaked T-shirt. "So, I'm guessing you've never experienced monsoon season before?"

I shook my head. The rain was coming down heavier now, and the sound reverberated through the small car as the water pounded steadily against the roof.

"Do you have rain like this back home?"

"Not really," I said, thinking back to the always sunny,

moderate climate of Southern California. "It usually only rains a few times a year, and even then"—I glanced out my window at the deep pools forming along the street—"it's never like this."

"This is my favorite season of the year." Hisham grinned and interlocked his hands behind his head. He took in a deep breath and closed his eyes. "It brings back so many fun memories, you know?"

I returned my gaze to the window. There was something so romantic about the pitter-patter of rain as it drummed against the glass. I could no longer make out what was happening on the other side. The steady rain had created a heavy sheet that blocked all visibility beyond a few inches. I leaned my head against the cold glass and felt my eyelids descending. My mind wandered to scenes from old Bollywood movies where two young lovers danced among tall trees in a forest during a rainstorm. I imagined myself lifting the *pallu* of my sari over my head to shield me from the rain as the hero grabbed me by my waist, wrapping his strong arms around me and pulling me close. Fully drenched in our love for one another, we peered into each other's eyes—those soft, brown eyes, that chestnut-colored skin, that smile that melted me with the flash of a single dimple . . .

"Leila!"

I jolted awake from my daydream.

"Leila, wait here." Hisham opened the door and stepped

outside. "I'll just run in and grab the sweets," he shouted, then dashed across the flooded streets into the well-lit bakery on the other side. With the rain slightly abated, I watched through the windows as Hisham walked inside and peered at the displays. As he leaned against the counter, the outline of his jaw curved gracefully down his neck, showing off the twining cords of muscle that shaped his strong, chiseled arms and firm, broad chest. His wet T-shirt clung to his biceps as he casually ran his fingers through his damp hair and gave the saleswoman a dimpled smile. I looked away, blushing.

A few minutes later, I heard a knock at the window and leaned across the seat, unlocking the door.

"Another few shops." He sat down, placing the bags near his feet. "I sure hope we can finish everything in this weather," he said, sneezing.

"Me too," I said, handing him a tissue from my purse.

For the next hour, Hisham and I took turns braving the storm as we ran into different shops, checking off every stop on his mother's list. We were soaking wet, freezing cold, and sneezing like banshees, but he wanted to keep going until we had everything we needed, and I wanted to savor every moment of time spent with him. "Where to now?" I asked, toweling off my hair with a scarf I had in my purse.

"*Now* we get lunch."

I looked outside at the torrential downpour.

"Is there a drive-through option?" I scrunched up my nose.

"Not this time, but trust me, it'll be worth it."

* * *

We zigzagged through side alleys and small streets until the taxi finally stopped in front of a narrow structure wedged in between a bank and a shoe store.

"Here?" I said, pointing to the white sign hanging over the front door that read CANTEEN in handwritten black letters.

"Yup," Hisham said, opening his door as I scooted out the other side. We grabbed all of our shopping bags and waddled up a narrow flight of stairs into a cramped dining hall on the second floor. Tables and chairs lined the peeling light blue walls, and a nineteen-inch television set was mounted in the corner playing slightly fuzzy videos of classic Bollywood songs. The kitchen was blocked off by a beaded curtain, and the smell of coriander hung thick in the air.

"*Aaye, aaye*," said a craggy-faced uncle with tufts of orange-white hair sprouting around his balding, mottled scalp. He grabbed a notepad and led us to one of the many empty tables.

"This is the place you were talking about?" I sat down, dropping the bags on the floor and glancing at the chutney-stained menu in front of me.

"We don't need these," Hisham said, stacking the menus at the edge of the table. "We will take two orders of *keema pau*, *ek* kabab platter, *ek* samosa platter, *ek* order of chicken *tengri*, a plate of *rumali rotis*, and two rolls of mutton *bhuna gosht*." The uncle nodded, quickly writing everything on his notepad. "And could you please bring us some extra lemon pieces with the *bhuna gosht*?"

"Is that all?" I asked, teasingly.

"Oh, and we'll also take two special *faloodas*." Hisham turned toward me and grinned.

"What makes you so sure I'm going to like everything you ordered?" I asked as the uncle walked away. "What if I wanted something else?"

"Leila," he said with a serious look on his face, "you are about to experience the best street food in all of Mumbai. This is going to be a life-changing experience for you. A culinary journey of the senses, so to speak. The only question you should be asking is, 'Am I ready?'"

I leaned in and stared directly into his eyes. "Oh, I'm ready," I said, rolling up my sleeves. Normally, I would have been turned off by the idea of someone ordering for me without asking for my input, but I was attracted to Hisham's confidence. He had proven he knew his way around the *laddu* shop; I trusted this experience would be no different.

"I knew I liked you," Hisham said, breaking into a grin.

I blushed and looked away.

On the television screen, a song was playing that I hadn't heard in years: "*Tip Tip Barsa Pani,*" from *Mohra.* The heroine, played by Raveena Tandon, looked sizzling as she danced through a rainstorm in a bright yellow sari while the hero, played by Akshay Kumar, chased behind her. As the two clung to each other in a passionate embrace, I couldn't help but think how strangely similar it was to my daydream earlier. I wondered if it was a sign.

"I used to have such a crush on Raveena Tandon. Especially in this song," Hisham said, his eyes fixated on the screen. "I must've watched this movie about a hundred times."

"Me too. But Akshay Kumar was the object of my crush."

"*Oy hoy*, a Bollywood fan? I wouldn't have guessed."

"Guilty as charged." I put up my hands.

"Speaking of crushes, I heard that Asad really took a liking to you. Any chance the two of you might reenact this song?" He wiggled his brows.

"Stop it." I threw my napkin across the table at him.

"Imagine how thrilled your *ammi* would be."

"My *ammi* would be happy with anyone at this point." I rolled my eyes, laughing.

Just then the waiter, a young boy wearing a Gap T-shirt with brown trousers that ended four inches above his ankles, emerged from behind the curtain carrying two drinks on a plastic tray.

"What is this?" I asked, staring at the delightful concoctions as he set them down in front of us. They were tall glasses of pinkish ambrosia, each topped with a generous scoop of *pista kulfi* decadently covered in chopped almonds, coconut, cardamom pods, and strands of fragrant saffron.

"*This* is the moment your life changes forever," Hisham said. "Go on, have a sip."

I leaned forward, taking a mouthful of the sweet, refreshing, rose-flavored syrup coupled with velvety ice cream, silky vermicelli noodles, slithery black basil seeds, and crunchy almonds. It was psychedelic.

"Oh my goodness." I closed my eyes, letting the cool liquid run down my throat as it filled my mouth with the most delicious tastes.

"And that was just the *falooda*. Wait until you try the rest," Hisham said as the waiter returned, balancing multiple trays of mouthwatering kababs, rolls, samosas, barbecued chicken, and everything else on the order. I took Hisham's lead and dived right in as he explained each item to me. The flavor combinations exploded in my mouth as we devoured plate after plate—each tastier than the next.

"So, what exactly are you looking for? If you don't mind my asking," Hisham said as he squeezed fresh lemon juice onto his *bhuna gosht*.

"If you had asked me this question about three months ago, I would have had a very specific answer for you. I might have even provided you with . . . a *list*." Hisham lifted his eyebrow, clearly intrigued.

"And now?" he said.

I shrugged and looked up at the screen. As I bit down on a samosa, my mind drifted toward the list. It was the first time I had thought about it since I had been in India. Back home, it was what I relied on to measure my feelings for someone—the point of reference for all my past relationships. But I hadn't needed it to measure my feelings for Hisham. I liked him. From the moment I first met him, there was no doubt in my mind.

"So when was the last time you had an Akshay Kumar–worthy crush on someone?"

Right now; at this very moment. I looked into Hisham's eyes. "I don't know, I guess it wasn't too long ago," I replied.

"Really?" Hisham said, his body inching forward. "Tell me, what was he like?"

Sweet, smart, charmingly handsome. Great sense of humor with an unbelievable taste in food. Can cheer me up—even after a morning spent with my mother—and knows the ins and outs of Indian wedding ceremonies like no one I've ever known.

I wanted to tell Hisham all these things. About the butterflies I felt each time he was around; how even though I had only just met him, I could already feel myself falling for him . . . But instead, I told him about Zain. How we met. How our mothers had ambushed us with a date. I told him about our night at the jazz club. The feelings I had for him and how he had ghosted me. I told him everything as he listened intently to every single word.

"Do you still think he was the one for you?"

"A few weeks ago, I would've said yes. But after hearing stories of how my parents met, seeing Meena and Haroon together, and even talking to you—" I paused. "I'm starting to question a lot of the things I used to be so sure of."

"The best part of life is realizing you don't need to know all the answers. Sometimes you just have to trust that you'll figure it out when the time is right." Hisham smiled, popping a bite of chicken *tengri* into his mouth. I sipped my *falooda*, silently lost in my thoughts.

* * *

After our meal, Hisham and I walked outside to wait for a taxi. The rain had stopped, and the humidity left a stickiness in the air that was almost oppressive. We leaned against a wall, feeling full and lazy.

"Can I ask you something?" I said.

"Sure."

"Love—before or after marriage? What is your opinion?"

Hisham thought for a moment. "If I'm being perfectly honest, I've only ever seen it occur—successfully—the former way in the movies. But that's not to say I don't believe it's possible. I think when it comes to love, anything is possible—regardless of what our mothers may tell us."

"That's because love before marriage is not the *Indian way*."

"I know it's hard for many people to wrap their minds around, but I guess I always considered the idea of love after marriage to be quite romantic."

I gave him a look.

"Wait a second, hear me out," he said with a laugh. "Think about it: two people who are willing to take a blind leap of faith and commit to each other for no other reason than for the intention of marriage—there's definitely something special to that, don't you think?"

I inhaled slowly as a warm breeze swept through the air. I had never really thought about it in that way before. The risks involved always seemed far too great, but I supposed there was something slightly romantic about such a giant leap of faith . . .

"Can I ask you something?"

I nodded.

"Zain. From what you told me, he wasn't the one for you."

"That's not really a question," I teased.

"It's not." Hisham smiled, leaning in toward me. "But I just thought you should know."

"What makes you so sure he wasn't the one?"

"Easy," he said, gently placing his finger under my chin and lifting my face up to his. As he pulled in closer, my body instinctively gravitated toward his until we were no more than a few inches apart. I could feel the coolness of his breath. Hear the sound of his heart beating. Or maybe it was mine. I couldn't really tell. "He let a girl like you go." My knees weakened as I felt myself being swallowed in his soft brown eyes.

I turned away, suddenly feeling nervous. *What is happening right now? Is Hisham flirting with me? Does he feel for me the same way I feel for him?* Maybe it was the food, or the touch of his skin so close to mine, but I felt sort of in a haze, like my thoughts were all jumbled together.

"Leila," he continued, speaking gently, "maybe all the answers you are looking for are right in front of you. You just have to be willing to take that leap."

I looked up, this time allowing myself to get lost in his gaze. We stood there for a moment, our faces almost touching, the sound of my heart pounding against my ear.

Suddenly, a taxi pulled up. Hisham quickly stepped back and cleared his throat. We stood there awkwardly for a second and then got inside—the driver placing our bags in the trunk—as the sound of thunder roared in the distance, closely echoing the rumblings in my heart.

Bombshell

"I like him," I whispered, sitting up on the bed. It felt liberating to actually speak those words aloud.

"What are you going to do?" Meena asked, rolling onto her stomach. Her eyes sparkled with curiosity as the moonlight from the windows cast faint shadows across her face. It was one in the morning, and everyone else in the house was fast asleep. I had been thinking about Hisham ever since I had returned home from our afternoon together—the touch of his fingers against my face; the warmth of his skin; the sound of his heart beating against mine. I desperately needed someone to help me make sense of the feelings racing through me.

"I wish there was some way of knowing if he feels the same about me!"

"Maybe you should tell someone."

"Who?"

"Your *ammi* . . . my *ammi* . . . someone who could speak to his parents for you."

"No way!" I said, plopping down on the pillow. "Meena, I've gone that route before. It only makes things worse."

"But this is India. This is how it is done here."

"I think I'm just going to tell him."

"When?"

"Tomorrow."

"Are you sure?" she asked, hesitation in her voice.

"Yes, I'm sure." I nodded matter-of-factly. I was going to tell Hisham how I felt. No games. No waiting. No outside interference. This time, I would take matters into my own hands. I would blindly leap and trust that love would take its course.

* * *

The next morning, Meena had her *nikkah* ceremony. The local imam came to the flat to see the bride at her home. In the presence of several witnesses, the imam read selected verses from the Qu'ran, asked Meena a list of questions about Haroon, and once she said "*Qubool Hai*" three times, she was officially married. She signed the marriage contracts, and the imam left to deliver those same contracts to Haroon, who was already waiting at the mosque.

With the *nikkah* completed, everyone breathed a great sigh of relief and focused their attention on the grand reception that was being held at an upscale hotel that evening. As

I helped Meena slip into her traditional red *lehenga choli* and watched her mother adorn her with lavish jewels, I had to admit she was the most gorgeous bride I had ever seen.

"Meena, you're beautiful," I whispered as I straightened out her headpiece—a gold-and-pearl *tikka* with a red ruby drop that came down to the center of her forehead. "Just like a Bollywood heroine, *masha'Allah*." I stepped back to admire her.

"Thank you, Leila." She smiled back at me shyly with red-painted lips. "How are you feeling? About *you know* . . ."

"Good," I said, thinking back to our conversation last night. The more I thought about it, the more sure I was about my feelings for Hisham. I was ready to tell him. Tonight at the reception.

"You're still sure you don't want to talk to—" She gestured with her head toward my mother, who was helping Jamila aunty fix a pin on her sari.

"I'm sure," I said, giving her a reassuring smile. Although I wasn't certain yet of what I would say to Hisham once I saw him, I figured I still had hours to figure it out. Right now, my focus was Meena.

"She needs more liner around the eyes," Jamila aunty was telling the makeup artist, a middle-aged aunty with bright pink fingernails and a gap between her front teeth. "And make the shadow a little brighter. Her eyes should really come alive."

As the aunty quickly grabbed her brushes and got to work, there was a knock at the door.

"*Salaam*, Shabana! Come in, come in!" Jamila aunty motioned her in. "Nida, this is Haroon and Hisham's mother," she said as the two of them embraced emotionally.

"Yes, we met yesterday," my mother said, leaning in to give her a kiss on both cheeks. "How are you feeling, Shabana? Were you able to get some rest?"

"Oh, it is impossible to rest with all this excitement!" Shabana aunty touched my cheek affectionately. "*Salaam*, Leila *beti*. Hisham told me you were of great help yesterday. Thank you so much." I smiled at her. Just the sound of Hisham's name made my insides flutter.

"Shabana, I was just telling Jamila what a nice boy she has found for her Meena, *masha'Allah*," my mother remarked. "As mothers, what more can we ask for?"

"Yes, yes." Shabana aunty nodded in agreement. "We are very lucky to have gained such a lovely daughter as well," she said, lifting Meena's hand and giving it a kiss.

"So tell us, Shabana, is it true what we hear?" Jamila aunty interrupted with a teasing wink. "When is the next wedding going to be?"

Shabana aunty waved her hands and laughed. "We must get through this one first!"

I stood next to Meena as the makeup artist carefully applied another layer of dark kohl above her upper lash line. I tried to appear occupied, but my curiosity was eating away at me. What was this talk about another wedding?

"A second wedding? You never mentioned this," my mother asked eagerly.

"*Oy*, everybody's talking about the good news!" Jamila aunty exclaimed. "Shabana, you really *must* confirm . . . is Hisham engaged?"

Meena popped open her eyes and turned in my direction.

"*Beti*, you must sit still," the makeup aunty scolded her, shaking her head in irritation.

"Sorry," Meena muttered as she leaned back in her chair. I turned toward Shabana aunty, holding my breath, desperately waiting for her response.

Shabana aunty gave a sly smile. "*Haan*, it's true. Hisham has recently been engaged!" She beamed with pride.

Jamila aunty squealed.

My heart dropped to the floor.

"*Mubarak! Mubarak!*" my mother exclaimed. "When did this happen?"

"Just less than a month ago, with a girl we have selected for him. *Alhamdulillah.* We could not be happier," Shabana aunty replied.

"You are a very lucky woman indeed!" my mother said, a tinge of envy wrapped around her words.

I pressed my body against the vanity mirror. Every muscle tensed with shock. *Hisham is engaged. He's getting married.*

To a girl his parents have selected for him. The noises around me faded into one long whirring sound. My head spun in circles, and I started to feel light-headed.

"Leila," Meena said, touching my hand gently, her beautiful eyes fraught with concern. "I-I-I'm so sorry. I had no idea—"

"I know," I whispered, nodding weakly. Meena's eyes glistened with tears.

"I'm going to get some air," I said, rushing out of the room. My mother was so busy discussing wedding details that she barely took notice of the fact that I had left.

I ran to the living room and leaned my head through the open window above the ledge. The sound of cars whizzed past from below. I could feel the warm air against my face.

Breathe.

Breathe.

I kept repeating this mantra in my head.

Hisham is engaged! I can't believe he's engaged. It felt like I had been kicked in the gut.

What did you expect to happen? Another part of my brain screamed. *You just met him two days ago!*

I squeezed my eyes shut, drowning out the voices.

It wasn't like I imagined us getting married tomorrow . . . I just thought . . .

I wasn't really sure what I thought. I knew I liked him. And up until a few minutes ago, I thought he liked me back.

I just never saw this coming. I focused my breathing, trying to ignore the lump in my throat.

Inhale.

Exhale.

Inhale.

Exhale.

Thunder clapped in the distance. *He's engaged. Engaged!* Those words kept reverberating in my ears. Suddenly, I felt a drop of water plop down on my forehead. And then another. *Plop. Plop.* I looked up. The dark, ominous clouds stared back at me—chastising me for being so foolish. I shut my eyes again, breathing in the wet air. Even as the clouds split and neat, parallel sheets of rain threatened to drench me through the open window—I remained frozen, unable to move until the sounds of my heart eventually steadied.

* * *

The ballroom of the Trident Hotel was filled with guests. Beautiful ivory silks hung in loose, graceful folds, and the tables were adorned with elaborate centerpieces—gold vases filled with decadent white roses and jasmine blooming over the edges. There was a dance floor in the center of the room where guests were already celebrating under the warm amber lighting emanating from the ceiling.

I smoothed out the drapes of my sari and readjusted the

pallu. My mother had initially been so resistant about my selecting this ensemble, but given that she had spent the majority of the evening bombarded with inquiries and proposals about her "highly desirable daughter," I figured she may have had a change of heart. As I watched her converse with a line of aunties who kept glancing in my direction, I couldn't help but think of the fresh stack of bio-datas that would soon be coming my way.

The mood of the room quickly shifted with the arrival of the bridal party. Haroon sat nervously on a stage, waiting to catch sight of his blushing bride. He was wearing a black-and-gold *sherwani* with a red turban on top of his head. As the clock struck seven, the double doors finally swung open and Meena entered atop a beautiful golden palanquin. She looked like Bollywood royalty perched on the shoulders of relatives and friends in her traditional red garb.

The moment her litter lowered to the rose-petaled ground, Haroon rushed toward it, extending his hand to help his new bride onto the stage. While the guests collectively whispered "*Masha'Allah*" under their breath, I stood off in the corner, watching the newlyweds as they merged into a couple right before our eyes.

Everyone around me seemed to be having a wonderful time, but I just couldn't bring myself to do the same—not after the bombshell that had been dropped earlier. Every time I turned around, there was Hisham—running his fingers through his hair or smiling with that lopsided grin of his. As much as I wanted to remain cool and collected, inside I was a total mess. A part of me wanted to talk to him and get some answers, but I didn't trust myself to do so without breaking into tears.

Our afternoon together kept replaying in my head: *the way he held me close . . . the sound of his heart beating next to mine . . . Why wouldn't he tell me he was engaged?* We had spent so much time talking about love and relationships; I couldn't understand why he would have withheld this information from me. *Did he simply forget? Or was it intentional?* Either way, I felt hurt. More than hurt, I felt foolish. Betrayed. Rejected. The knot in my stomach wound tighter and tighter.

"I found you."

A thin voice broke up my thoughts. I turned to see Asad smiling broadly.

"Wow, Leila." He took a quick glance over me from head to toe. "You look ravishing!" he exclaimed, touching the tip of his mustache.

"Thanks," I mumbled, still distracted by my thoughts.

"I was actually hoping we could continue our conversation from the other day. We hit such a momentum, and it was unfortunate we got cut off."

Unfortunate was hardly the word I would use, but I needed to get Hisham off my mind.

"Sure," I replied. "What did you want to talk about?"

Asad's smile slightly wavered.

"I just think you and I are very compatible, Leila. I think you feel it too."

I forced a polite smile.

"We share the same values and worldviews. We have similar expectations when it comes to a life partner. I just thought with you and aunty leaving soon, perhaps we should consider moving forward with this. What do you think?"

"Moving forward? As in . . . ?" I knitted my brows.

"I already spoke with my parents about you." Asad looked at me eagerly. "They would be open to an engagement. That is, if *you* are."

An engagement? My heart pounded in my chest. This was it. My final chance to successfully meet my parents' deadline . . .

Directly behind him, I noticed Hisham out of the corner of my eye. Hisham, the man of my choosing, versus Asad, my mother's pick. The choices offered two very different futures: a life of arrangement versus a life of love. The only problem was, only one of these choices had selected me.

A sharp pang sliced through the center of my chest. Asad was my *only* chance. I opened my mouth to speak, but only a brittle sound escaped.

"What do you say, Leila?" Asad pressed.

A wave of nausea washed over me. Was this what it had come to? Was this the only way to satisfy my parents' expectations? I couldn't believe *this* was the ending to my Bollywood fairy tale all along.

"I . . . I don't know," I stammered. My head spun in confusion. "Can I have some time to think about it?"

"Yes, of course." Asad smiled; however, the disappointment in his voice was obvious.

"I-I'm so sorry," I said, unable to look him directly in the eyes. "I think I just need to get some air." I touched my hand to my forehead and took a step back. "I'm sorry. I just . . . I really have to go."

"Leila? Leila . . . are you okay?" I could hear Asad's voice calling out to me, but I needed to get as far away as possible. I moved past the crowd, pushing against a sea of bodies, refusing to look back. I kept moving, straight through the double doors and down the long carpeted corridor until I found myself outside in the hotel gardens.

Dizzy and breathless, I sat down, trying to regain my composure on the steps of the marble fountain. I shut my eyes, listening to the rushing flow of water—synchronizing my breath with the steady rise and fall of sounds. From across the gardens, I could hear footsteps walking in my direction.

Closer. And closer.

He must've followed me. My heart sank. I knew I owed Asad an explanation, but it wasn't a conversation I was ready for. With my eyes still shut, I braced myself.

"Hey," said a voice from the other side of the fountain.

I opened my eyes as he made his way around. Within seconds, I was staring into a set of familiar brown eyes.

It was Hisham.

"Hey," I said softly. He kneeled down until his face was directly across from mine and grazed his fingers across my forehead, straightening out my *tikka* as the diamonds sparkled reflectively in his eyes.

"Something tells me you might be breaking some hearts tonight." He grinned. "Or maybe you already have?"

I swallowed the lump in my throat and said nothing.

Hisham cleared his throat uncomfortably. "I might be crazy here, but why do I get the feeling that you've been avoiding me all night?" I looked at him, the confusion in his eyes mirroring the same confusion I felt inside. "Leila, what's wrong?"

"You're engaged," I said bluntly, standing up. He looked at me with his mouth open, trying to articulate a response.

"Leila, I was going to tell you . . ." he began, his voice taking on a flat tone.

"Really? Because there were at least a dozen opportunities to tell me yesterday, but you never did."

Hisham jammed his hands into his pockets and looked down. "I'm sorry, Leila. You're right. I should've said something."

"So why didn't you? Why did you make me believe that you . . ." My voice trailed off.

"That I what?" He looked up, taking a small step toward me.

"That you liked me," I whispered.

"I do like you, Leila." He shrugged. "I think you're amazing. But I shouldn't have allowed myself to get caught up like that . . . I should've told you."

I looked into his face, searching for answers. Those same eyes that once felt so warm and promising suddenly looked distant and unfamiliar.

"So that's it? You're still going to go through with it?" I asked, trying to steady the tremble in my voice.

"It's not like that, Leila. It's . . . it's hard to explain."

"Try."

"This is just how it is here. Not everything is like it is in the movies." Hisham sighed. "People don't end up with whoever they want, Leila. There are obligations. There are compromises to be made."

"You don't think I understand compromise?" I scoffed. "Trust me, we *all* make compromises. But that doesn't mean we don't have a choice."

"A *choice*? Leila, look around you," Hisham exclaimed. "Do you think Meena and Haroon had a *choice*? Do you think our parents had a *choice*? As much as you'd like to think you have control over your life, you don't."

I stared at him, hot tears pressing against my eyes.

"When it's all said and done, we will eventually end up with who our parents choose for us. *That's* our only *choice*."

I wiped my face and looked away.

"Leila," Hisham said gently. "I'm sorry. I just—"

"It's fine." I shook my head, taking a step back. "Congratulations on your engagement—"

"Leila." He reached out to touch my elbow, but I quickly slipped away.

"Goodbye, Hisham," I said, just as the tears began flowing down my cheeks.

"Leila . . ." he pleaded as I hurried across the garden, refusing to let him see me cry. My name was the final word I heard as I ran back inside, leaving my shattered heart on the other side of the glass doors that shut behind me.

* * *

"How could you turn down such a good boy?" my mother cried as we waited to board our plane. "*Ya Allah!* Sometimes I really don't understand you, Leila." She shook her head.

I stared at my boarding pass and remained silent. Meena's reception had ended with a teary *rukhsati* ceremony, and then she and Haroon had left immediately for their honeymoon. Her final words to me before she left were "I'm so sorry, Leila."

The next evening—on our final night in India—my mother and Jamila aunty invited Asad and his family for dinner without so much as asking my opinion. As irritated as I was, I found a quiet moment to finally tell Asad that I had thought things over and felt it was best that we didn't move forward with an engagement. Although I could sense his disappointment, he took the news better than I had expected.

My mother, on the other hand, did not.

"You keep saying you are finding someone on your own, Leila, but I don't see you putting in any effort," she said as people began lining up.

"We are now boarding rows one through fifteen. Also any families traveling with small children and any disabled or elderly passengers needing a little extra time on the Jetway . . ."

"In case you forgot, *Ammi*, Asad was not someone I chose on my own."

"Okay, so I helped a little. Is that so terrible? And what have you done? It has been almost three months, Leila, and you haven't brought home a single person. Your father and I have agreed to give you time, but all you keep saying is 'This one is too old. This one is too this. This one is too that.'"

"I don't know what to tell you, *Ammi*, but I'm trying," I mumbled.

"Pfft," my mother sneered. "Be honest, Leila—you are not trying at all! You are just wasting all of our time!"

"Ladies and gentlemen, we thank you for your patience. We are now going to begin boarding rows sixteen to twenty-eight. I repeat, rows sixteen to twenty-eight."

As groups of people pushed past us, my mother and I

remained still, glowering at each other. How could she be so inconsiderate? If only she knew how much I had wanted things to work out with Hisham, and even Zain, but they just hadn't. It was beyond my control.

"How can you say that?" I fumed back. "You don't even know what I've had to go through these past few months!"

"What have you had to go through, Leila? A few bad dates and your life is ending? You don't realize how difficult it is for me to see everyone's children getting married, and you are still here. Think of what *I* have to go through!" she retorted.

"This isn't about you!"

"Thank you again for your patience. We are now going to board the remaining passengers. All remaining passengers can now come forward."

"Just because I'm not doing things your way, *Ammi*, doesn't mean that I'm doing them wrong!"

"*Bas!* I am done talking about this." My mother held up her hand. "I have given you three whole months, and you have done nothing in that time. Enough is enough, Leila. Either you find someone like you keep saying, or it is time for us to take over again." She grabbed her purse and stormed off, leaving me in the empty gate alone.

Revelations

"You fell for the groom's twin brother?!" my friends cried, stupefied by this admission.

It was Tuesday night—a week since I had returned from India—and I had accidentally made the mistake of telling my friends about Hisham as we pored over pictures from Meena's wedding.

The past seven days had been more or less a blur. My mother and I had managed to cool off from our argument on the twenty-hour flight back home, but the harshness of her words still left behind a bruise, even though I tried my best to forget them. Instead, I busied myself with preparations for my parents' thirtieth anniversary party, which was set for the following weekend. My mother had coercively transferred everything event-related over to me, so in between negotiating venue prices, picking floral arrangements, and taste-testing cake options—the only silver lining—I had barely any time to mull over my fallout with

Hisham. But now that my friends knew, they of course wanted all the details.

"How did that . . . how did you . . . ?"

"It just kind of *happened*," I muttered, my face burning with humiliation.

"I can't believe you didn't know he was engaged!" Hannah exclaimed. "That's the first question you should've asked!"

"What, you mean like, 'Hi, how are you? Are you engaged?' "

"Not like that! But you know what I mean."

"What about *him*?" Tania asked, shaking her head. "Why would he not tell you about his engagement? I can't believe he led you on like that."

Hannah and Liv nodded in agreement.

Hisham's reasons for concealing his engagement were still unclear to me. *Maybe he didn't realize he was leading me on? Or perhaps he did and he simply didn't care?* All I knew is it would've saved me a lot of tears and heartbreak had I known sooner.

"I know this wasn't the outcome you were hoping for, Leila," Tania said sympathetically. "I'm so sorry."

I thought about where I was when I first started this process—my Bollywood fantasies, my unrealistic expectations about finding love—and where I was now. It felt like an entire lifetime had passed in between. There was actually a time when I believed I was incapable of falling in love, and now here I was, having had my heart broken twice in the span of three months. It might not have been the outcome I wanted, but in a way, it was kind of remarkable.

"Now that you've experienced love *twice*," Hannah said, "do you at least feel like you have a better sense of what you're looking for?"

I thought about my list and how far I had come from it. For the first time in my life, I had surprised even myself with my openness to being with someone who grew up in India. I'd always assumed that because of the differences in cultural upbringing, I would prefer someone American versus Indian-born. However, after spending time with Hisham, I realized that was not true. Our differences actually brought us together, and it was through him that I was able to appreciate aspects of my culture in a way I never had before. My feelings for Hisham went beyond a cursory list, and they taught me more about myself than I had ever expected.

"I do. I feel like I've grown," I said softly. "But . . ." I could feel the lump rising in my throat as the thing that had been nagging me for the past week finally formed itself into words. "I may have fallen in love, but I wasn't able to convince anyone to fall for me. So at the end of it all, I feel like I've failed."

I closed my eyes tightly as my mother's words replayed in my mind.

If you do not succeed in finding a suitable boy by our thirtieth anniversary, it is in our hands from there. No more excuses.

"My future now rests with my parents," I said, looking at my friends. "And there's nothing I can do about it."

"Leila, of course you can!" Liv said.

"This is still your life, regardless of what your parents tell you!" Hannah added.

I looked at Tania and she remained silent.

"It's complicated." I shook my head. "Yes, I've grown. Yes, I've learned about myself, but what does it matter? When it's all said and done, perhaps we do just end up with who our parents choose for us. Maybe there is no greater purpose. Maybe that is our kismet. Maybe that is our only choice."

* * *

That night as I lay in bed, I began scrolling through the photographs from Meena's wedding once again. There was one in particular that I was looking for. My fingers moved quickly, swiping through each image on the iPad until finally the photo I wanted came onto the screen. I held it up.

It was a picture of me and Meena on the night of her *mehendi* ceremony. I tapped the screen to zoom in closer.

Everything in the background was blurred except for the two of us. We were sitting on the stage while she was getting her *mehendi* applied. I was leaning in close as if telling her a secret, and Meena had both her arms outstretched, her head tilted back, laughing. She was radiant. I closed my eyes, thinking of her in that moment. Where would the girl in that photograph be if she had had the choice to live out her life the way she wanted? Would she have become an interior designer? Would she be traveling the world? Living in some glamorous city? Would she still have married Haroon? I looked once more at her image. There was something captivating about her smile. It was so full of . . . hope.

I swiped to the next image. It was a photo of Hisham with his mother. He had his arm wrapped around her shoulders and they were both grinning from ear to ear. My fingers gently grazed the outline of his face as I thought about the deal I had made with my parents nearly three months ago. I would have to tell them that I had failed to deliver on my promise. I just needed to figure out when the right time would be.

My phone suddenly buzzed. It was Annie.

"Hey!" I said, setting the iPad down. "How was your trip?"

"Incredible!" she said, her voice energized. "I was on a remote island off the coast of the Philippines snorkeling through shallow hidden caves with manta rays, sharks, and stingless golden jellyfish. It was surreal!"

"When did you get back?"

"I think a week ago? Everything's a blur. My body reacted to one of the delicacies I ate at my homestay, and I spent the first couple days confined to my bed."

"Oh, that's awful. What did you eat?"

"Bat soup. At least I can say I tried it, right?"

"Your life is so much cooler than mine," I said, laughing wistfully.

"I don't know about that. From what you told me last time, your life doesn't seem to be lacking in excitement either. So, how did your dating dilemma work out? Did you find what you were looking for?"

"Unfortunately, the odds didn't work in my favor," I said, glancing at the photo still on the screen. "Was I crazy for thinking they would?"

"Honestly . . ." Annie paused. "Yeah."

I cringed at her bluntness.

"You do have a habit of setting yourself up for disappointment, Leila," she said. "So what now? Are you finally going to let go of these fantasies and move on with your life?"

"I have to. I've agreed to let my parents choose someone for me."

"You're not serious, are you?"

"It was part of the deal."

"Leila, I've always tried to make sense of some of your choices, but you've really topped yourself with this one."

"There's nothing I can do, Annie."

"You can stop living the life you think you should, Leila, and start living the life you want."

"What if this is what I want?" I asked.

Annie remained silent. I could imagine her absorbing my words on the other side. She finally let out a small breath and sighed.

"If it really is, Leila, then maybe I'm not the one you should be convincing."

Deadline

Saturday morning—the day of my parents' anniversary party—I woke up earlier than usual. In less than eight hours, my three-month deadline would be coming to an end, and I would have to inform my parents that my plans to find a "suitable boy" had backfired. In less than eight hours, the fate of my future would lie entirely in their hands, and they would have free rein to arrange my marriage with whomever they pleased. I should've been panicking, but instead I felt strangely calm. There was comfort in knowing there was nothing left to do. I walked into the kitchen and was greeted by both of my parents eating breakfast at the table.

"Good morning, Leila!" My mother smiled, pulling out a chair for me. "Come, eat some warm *chapatis*. I made fresh ghee to go along with them."

"Happy anniversary," I said as I kissed her and my father on the cheek.

"Happy anniversary, *beti*," my father said as he sipped his chai and glanced back at the morning paper.

"It's not my anniversary, *Abba*," I said, sitting down. "Have you wished each other?"

"Oh, Leila. We don't do this *wishing smishing* stuff." My mother waved her arms, blushing. "Besides, that is what tonight is for." She looked over at my father and smiled. "Thirty years. Can you believe it?"

My father shook his head. "How you lasted with me so long, I have no idea," he said, laughing.

"You know, Leila," my mother began. "Twenty-nine years ago, and I can still remember my and your father's very first anniversary. Do you remember it?" she asked nostalgically.

"Of course I remember, *jaan*," my father said, putting down the paper. "We were living in that tiny apartment next to the university."

"Right, the one with the broken faucets in the bathroom. We could never figure out which was hot or cold! Everything was freezing!"

I smiled as I listened to them recall this story that I had heard countless times over the years.

"Your father was studying late that night, so I wanted to surprise him with something special when he returned."

"Your *ammi* learned early on that I had a weakness for

sweets, so that year, she wanted to show me how American she was by making me an American dessert. Cupcakes." He smiled at the memory.

"I found a cookbook with a recipe for chocolate cupcakes. I went to the grocery and bought all the ingredients on the list. Except, I forgot to buy the measuring spoons. When I went home, I couldn't understand the teaspoons versus tablespoons," she explained. "We only had one kind of spoon in the drawer, and I couldn't tell if it was for the tea or the table." She placed her hand on her head. "It was so confusing!" she said, laughing. "Anyways, by the time your father came home, he found cupcakes that had exploded in the oven and me crying on the kitchen floor."

"I had no idea what happened, and when she finally told me, I laughed . . . which made her even more upset!" he said, shaking his head. "But after she finally calmed down, I broke off a piece of her American cupcake from the oven and tried it. It tasted so bad!" He laughed. "But I ate them all, just to keep her heart."

"And that was the moment." My mother looked at him, smiling. "That was when I knew that you were the one I wanted to spend every anniversary with for the rest of my life."

I looked at my parents as they gazed happily into each other's eyes. It was rare to see them outwardly express their affection for one another—in fact, in my twenty-six years, I couldn't recall them ever kissing or even holding hands in my presence. However, listening to them reminisce about their life together made me realize that love was meant to be subtle. It wasn't found in the grand gestures you saw in the movies, but rather in those small moments that might not seem like much to the eye, but meant everything to the heart.

"So that was the moment you first fell in love with *Abba*?"

My mother blushed and smiled.

"But what about before that?" I asked.

"Before that, he was my husband. I still cared for him, but it was different."

"Love after marriage. It is the only way we know." My father bobbled his head. I smiled, remembering our conversation right before I left for India.

"You know," he said, leaning back in his chair, "that was also an important year for one more reason."

"Oh?" My mother leaned forward. "And what reason is that?"

"That was the last year you ever baked me an American dessert," my father replied, his eyes twinkling.

I shook my head and laughed.

"Well, maybe that is because you are no longer a skinny man!" My mother clucked her tongue as my father puffed out his belly and made a sad face.

"If I am fat, it is only because of all the fatty foods you've been feeding me for the past thirty years." He winked at me.

"Oh, really? And will you eat a salad if I make it for you? No, it is you who likes all these oily foods!"

As my parents continued blaming each other for their poor dietary habits, I couldn't help but smile at their relationship. They bickered nonstop, they hardly ever agreed on anything, but they were more in love with each other after thirty years than any other couple I knew. Despite all the disappointments I'd faced these past three months, a part of me still remained hopeful that I would one day find the kind of love they had . . .

I cleared my throat. I couldn't hold it in any longer. I needed to tell my parents that I hadn't met their deadline. There was no point in waiting until the evening when I could just break the news to them now.

"Um, can I talk to you both about something?" I interrupted their banter. My parents stopped and turned toward me.

"Yes, Leila. What is it? Are you sick?" my mother asked, suddenly concerned.

"No, it's about something I've been meaning to tell you both—"

Briiiing.

"One second, Leila." My mother held up a finger. "Let me just get this." She picked up the phone, and a few seconds in, I could already tell that it was not good news.

"What do you mean the flowers haven't arrived? The party is tonight!" she cried, handing the phone over to my father and rubbing her head.

"Hello? Yes. Okay. Okay. Okay. I will let her know." My father calmly hung up as my mother and I stared at him.

"Leila, the florist is sending you new arrangements in your email. Will you check the pictures and let her know which one we want?"

"Sure," I said, feeling a bit frazzled. I still wanted to talk to them, but I wasn't sure if they'd be able to handle more upsetting news.

"Can you believe they haven't arrived yet?" My mother turned toward my father. "I must call the decorator and make sure everything else is set for tonight."

I could sense a degree of panic in her voice.

"Will you go through the guest list and confirm the final numbers with the caterer?" My father nodded and quickly got to his feet.

"Can I just tell you guys something real quick . . . ?"

"Not now, Leila. We will discuss later. Go check the pictures and email the florist. She is waiting for your message."

"But . . . but—" I stammered helplessly as my parents cleared the table in a hurry. Within minutes, they had gone into the other room and the kitchen was empty as I sat there alone. *What now?* I thought. *I should tell them before the party, but when?* I shuffled back to my room.

What if I wrote them an email? I pondered half-seriously as I opened my laptop, searching through the inbox. As I scrolled through the messages, my cell phone vibrated. It was Tania.

HEY! What's up? Ready for tonight?

Ugh. I responded.

Lol . . . party problems or personal?

Both.

Can I help?

Maybe. The florist was supposed to send me new pictures for centerpieces, but I don't see her email in my inbox.

Weird. Have you checked the junk folder?

Let me look. I clicked on JUNK and waited for the messages to download. There it was, at the very top: Floral Arrangements, it read in the subject line.

Got it! You're a lifesaver! I texted her as the emails continued to download. All of a sudden, one by one, the messages appeared as I sat there dumbfounded. Dozens of unread emails staring back at me from behind the screen. With trembling hands, I grabbed my phone and dialed Tania's number, waiting impatiently for the sound of her voice.

"You'll never believe what's in my junk folder," I said when she finally picked up. "How soon can you get over here?"

Prayers Answered

"His phone bricked . . . Lost all his contacts . . . Got your email from your school website and has been trying to get in touch with you ever since . . . I just . . . I just don't believe it," Tania kept muttering under her breath as she read through each email. "We all just assumed he wasn't interested."

"You said he ghosted me!"

"I know, I know," Tania said, shaking her head. "All the signs pointed towards it being a classic case of ghosting. But really, he zombied you instead!"

"Zombied? Wh-what does that even mean?!"

"It means he came back from the dead. Popped up out of nowhere. He resurrected your relationship—"

"Okay, okay," I interrupted, feeling a headache coming on. I stared at the screen, rubbing my temples. A month ago, this was exactly what I had wished would happen. That Zain would come back into my life. That I would finally receive an explanation for why he had vanished. That he would whisk me away from a life of arrangement, so we could live out the ending to our Bollywood fairy tale. But now that the answer to all my prayers was staring me in the face, I didn't feel the elation that I once thought I would.

"So what do I do now?" I asked, facing Tania. "Do I seem like a total jerk for not responding all this time? Should I message him to explain? Or should I just let it . . . dissolve?"

"I don't know." Tania bit her bottom lip. "I mean, this has never happened before. At least not to anyone I know." She knitted her brows in deep thought. "We need to really consider what this means."

I nodded, scrolling through all the messages once more.

"What if he's at the party tonight?" Tania asked. I hadn't even thought about that possibility. I knew my parents had invited Yasmeen aunty, so the idea of Zain coming was not entirely impossible.

"I don't know. I guess we'll just have to wait and—" I stopped, suddenly distracted by the name on the screen. "Tania, there's also a message in here from you," I said as I clicked on the email to open it up.

"Yeah . . ." Tania shifted nervously, watching as my eyes quickly scanned the screen. "I sent that from my cousin's phone. But I wouldn't worry about that right now—"

"What is this?" I said, looking at her.

"It's . . . it's nothing. I was going to tell you—"

"You and Zeeshan broke up?" I exclaimed.

"Yeah . . ."

"When? Why? Oh my God, why didn't you say something?"

"It happened while you were in India." She sighed heavily. "Look, Leila, I shouldn't have sent that email. I don't want to bother you with my stuff because I know you have a lot on your plate right now—"

"Tania . . ." I suddenly felt incredibly guilty. I had been so self-absorbed, so consumed by my own failures that I hadn't even noticed that my best friend had just gotten her heart broken.

"Why would you think that would be a bother to me?" I said with a pained look on my face. I wrapped my arms around her and gave her a hug. "Tell me everything. What happened?"

Through muffled tears, Tania told me the whole story. How the day before she was supposed to meet Zeeshan's parents, she had decided to share everything about her past with him. Her previous marriage, the fact that her parents had arranged it without any input from her, her inevitable divorce: she put it all out there for him. At first, he seemed understanding—even comforting, reassuring her that things like that happen and it wasn't her fault. But the next day, when he was supposed to pick her up to drive her to his parents' house for lunch, he never showed up. She had left him dozens of texts and voice mails, but she got nothing but silence from his end. Three days later, he finally called her back and told her that his parents could never accept a girl who had already been married—regardless of the circumstances—and even though he still cared for her, he couldn't go against his parents' wishes.

"I sent you the email because I needed to tell someone," she said softly.

"So none of the other girls know?"

She shook her head.

"Oh, Tania!" My voice cracked as I thought back to when I saw her at Liv's house. How selflessly she had comforted me and offered words of solace. No one would've guessed that there had been two broken hearts in the room that day.

As I watched her wipe her eyes with the corner of her blouse, I thought about how different her situation had turned out from my parents'. My parents were fortunate to have found love within their arranged marriage, but Tania was left with nothing more than a painful scar from her past. She would forever bear the blame for a choice that wasn't even hers. It didn't seem fair.

"Listen, Leila," Tania finally said. "I've been thinking a lot about this, and I've come to the conclusion that we, as South Asian women, are constantly having to prove our worth. We are constantly having to prove that we are good enough. And for who? Our parents? Our future husbands? Our potential in-laws? The entire South Asian community? No matter how hard we try to please others, we are always going to be judged because of our past, our age, our marital status, our career, or whatever. You know better than anyone that it's a double standard that only applies to women. I say we put an end to it." She grabbed my hands. "I should've said something to you the other day, but I'm going to say it now. This is no longer about them, Leila. Your parents, Zain, Hisham, every goddamn *rishta* aunty. This is about you and what you want. It's about doing what is right for you in this moment, regardless of what anyone else expects of you."

I let her words sink in. She was right. Even Annie was right. I had spent so much time focusing on everyone else's expectations that I had lost sight of what I truly wanted. I buried my face in her shoulder as we hugged. "Thank you," I whispered into her ear. She gave me a squeeze. "But what about you?" I leaned back to look at her tear-streaked face.

"What about me?" She shrugged. "Zeeshan might not have chosen me. But *I* choose me. I'm going to be just fine." She smiled. My beautiful, resilient, incredibly brave, and wise-beyond-her-years friend just gave me the last push of courage I so desperately needed, and for that I was grateful.

* * *

After Tania left, I sat there staring at the laptop, a million thoughts rushing through my mind. I thought back to what

Hisham had said about not having a choice. About all of us eventually doing what our parents wanted. He was wrong. Ending up with who our parents wanted us to was the easy option, but it prevented us from acknowledging how we truly felt . . . from going after what we really wanted. The more I thought about it, the more it seemed like a cop-out. Like nothing more than a lame excuse. I still believed in love before marriage, but I suddenly realized that it wasn't romantic love I was lacking. It was self-love.

I looked over Zain's emails, reading the messages again and again. This wasn't about my parents. This wasn't even about the deadline anymore. This was about me. And I couldn't choose something simply because it was my only option. That wasn't choosing. That was settling. And I loved myself enough to know I was worth more than that.

For the first time in a long time, I knew exactly what I needed to do. I placed my fingers over the keyboard and started typing.

Dear Zain,

First off, I'd like to apologize for not getting back to you sooner. Your emails were placed in my junk folder, and I am just discovering them now. A lot has changed since the last time we saw each other, and I think it's only fair to let you know what's been on my mind . . .

Final Toast

The banquet hall at Shalimar Restaurant was teeming with guests. Despite all the last-minute changes, it was a relief to see everything finally come together. All throughout the restaurant I had displayed blown-up photographs of my parents over the past thirty years. There were images of the two of them on their wedding day—my mother in a beautiful red sari and my father in a dark gray suit with thick, neatly parted hair and a mustache that even Tom Selleck would be envious of. There was a photograph of my mother eight months pregnant, with my father's arm around her shoulders. They were both grinning widely into the camera, excited and hopeful for the future that lay ahead. There were pictures from various family vacations like the Grand Canyon and Disneyland, and most recently, a photo of the three of us at my twenty-sixth birthday dinner, the night this whole journey began for me.

As I made my way around the hall, I took my time greeting

all the aunties and uncles who had known my parents over the years. Some of them I had seen frequently at our home or various events; others I hadn't seen in years. I smiled and nodded as they inquired about my job, my trip to India, and of course my marital status. I had grown so accustomed to these rounds of questioning that they didn't even faze me anymore. From the corner of my eye, I noticed my girlfriends hanging out near the buffet table. I politely excused myself and headed in their direction.

"Leila! You look beautiful!" Hannah, Liv, and Tania showered me with compliments as I gave them each a hug.

I was wearing a dress that Meena had gifted me the night before her reception: a powder-blue *lehenga choli* with ivory and gold embellishments. My hair was curled into long, loose waves, and I had placed a delicate gold *tikka* across the center part.

"Have you talked to your parents?" Tania asked.

"Not yet." I bit my lip.

Between the flower snafu, Zain's unforeseen return, and my earlier talk with Tania, I hadn't found time to inform my parents about the outcome of their deadline. After ruminating on everything I had endured over these past three months—the frustration, the hopelessness, the love, the heartbreak—there was only one choice that felt right in my heart; however, I had no way of predicting what their reactions would be when I finally told them. All I knew was that when I had crossed off the last X on my calendar that afternoon, I'd felt a sense of relief rather than dread, along with an overwhelming confidence about my final decision.

"*Salaam, beti!* How are you doing?"

I turned around to see Yasmeen aunty holding a small plate of appetizers in her right hand. She leaned in and gave me a warm kiss on both cheeks. "What a lovely party you have thrown together for your parents, Leila! May Allah bless us all with such kind and loving children, *Masha'Allah*." She squeezed my hand.

"How have you been, aunty?" I asked, shifting uncomfortably.

"Very good, *beti*."

"And how is Zain?" I asked, trying to keep my voice steady. Although my mind had already been made up, the possibility of seeing Zain at my parents' party, especially after the email I had sent refusing his offer to "see where things could go," was slightly nerve-racking. I held my breath as I waited for her response.

"*Alhamdulillah!* He's been so busy getting everything prepared for his L.A. office opening. But he will be back for another visit in just a few weeks!"

I exhaled a sigh of relief.

"I must let your mother know when Zain comes, so the four of us can get together once again, *insha'Allah*."

I nodded and forced a small smile. Although I felt somewhat guilty about giving her false hope, I reminded myself that I was doing the right thing. I politely excused myself just as the buffet lines cleared and made my way toward my parents' table near the center of the stage.

During dinner, several friends and close acquaintances of my parents took turns saying a few words. Everyone agreed that thirty years of marriage was an extraordinary feat, an accomplishment worth celebrating. As each speaker lauded my parents with praises and countless blessings for the years to come, I felt proud. My parents were happy. They were still in love after thirty years of marriage. They had found the thing that people spend their entire lives searching for.

From inside my purse, I pulled out a single notecard. Wiping my sweaty palms on a napkin, I glanced at the speech I had prepared four days ago for this very event. So much had changed between then and now. As I quickly skimmed over the words, I realized there was still so much I wanted to say. To express. *But how?*

When Bushra aunty and Mohammed uncle finished the final words of their speech, I took a deep breath and stood up. My legs felt like jelly as I walked toward them. I prayed my knees would not buckle underneath me. There were collective murmurs among the audience as my parents' only child took the microphone.

With the notecard clasped tightly in hand, I cleared my throat.

"*As'salaamu Alaikum*, everyone," I said, my voice slightly cracking. "Thank you all so much for coming tonight to celebrate my parents' thirtieth wedding anniversary."

Everyone applauded enthusiastically. I drew in a deep breath.

"My parents have always been the embodiment of what a successful marriage looks like," I read from my card. "They have taught me so much over the years about love, hard work, and compromise through their example. And I hope that I can one day follow in their footsteps . . ." My voice trailed off.

I looked out at all the familiar faces—a roomful of aunties and uncles smiling back at me, their expressions brimming with expectation. There were the Rehmans and the Dhakkars from that very first awkward dinner date. There was Seema aunty, the matchmaker, placing a sweet *gulab jamun* into her mouth, and Yasmeen aunty with her husband giving me a wave of encouragement. There were my father's cricket buddies and my mother's friends from her monthly *halaqa* classes at the mosque—they all stared at me, waiting expectantly to hear what I had to say.

I glanced down at the notecard with trembling hands and pounding heart. Tania's words echoed through my mind: *This is no longer about them, Leila . . . This is about you and what you want. It's about doing what is right for you.*

I took another deep breath, folded up the card, and began once more.

"*Ammi, Abba*," I said, facing the center of the room, toward my parents. My mother, in a lovely blue sari, and my father, in a suit, smiled back at me, beaming with pride. "You've only ever wanted the best for me. And I may not have always understood your ways of showing me that, but I see it now. Marriage is a beautiful thing. It takes two separate people and unites them into one, and there is nothing more special than that. The proof is right before us."

I paused. "Knowing what you two have, I understand why you've been pushing so hard for my own marriage. You want for me what you've found for yourselves, and as your daughter, I can appreciate that."

"But I also understand that marriage is not the only thing that defines our worth. It is a choice. It is one option of how we can choose to live our lives, but it is not the only one. And our worth should not be determined solely by that choice." I looked directly at my parents as the rest of the room blurred into the background.

"I hope that one day, I can find the kind of love you both share. I truly do, *insha'Allah*. But I've realized that my life doesn't begin once I'm married. It's already begun—whether I'm married or not—because my happiness comes from within me as well as those around me, not from those whom I have yet to meet." I drew in another breath.

"You both are amazing parents, but this has nothing to do with you. This is about me and the life that I want. That is the reason I have decided I will no longer spend my life waiting for someone to come along and 'choose' me. Nor can I allow you to choose *for* me. *I choose myself.* And that is a decision that I am okay with. I just hope that you can be okay with it too."

I placed the microphone on the stand and walked back toward the table. The room fell quiet. The only sound came from the clacking of my heels. I stared at the floor, refusing to look up. With each step I took, my heart felt lighter. Freer. Like a heavy burden had been lifted. Despite the silence in the room, there was a thunder roaring in my chest.

As I made my way to my seat, there was a sudden clap in the back of the room. Then another. After a few hesitant seconds, the rest of the room joined in with broken applause.

"Yeah, Leila!" I heard Tania yell from the back.

I looked at my parents and saw pain in their eyes. As I braced myself for all the guilt they would no doubt inflict on me, this time, I felt ready. No tears, no lamentations over cut noses and absent grandchildren would change my mind now. But to my surprise, my mother stood up and quietly took me by the arms and pulled me in close.

"Oh, Leila, we have only ever wanted your happiness,"

she whispered into my ear. "How could you think otherwise?"

My father got up and wrapped his arms around the both of us. "Leila, we are proud of you, *beti*," he said. "Marriage or no marriage, you are our daughter and we love you." And with those words, everyone and everything in the room seemed to fade and the three of us just stood there, locked in an embrace.

Despite all their craziness these past few months, my parents loved me, and I'd never felt it more than I did in that particular moment. Would they continue to pester me about marriage? I had no doubt they would. But this time I felt stronger, more certain of myself. This time, I wouldn't allow myself to succumb to the pressures like I had before. Because I, Leila Abid, realized that not all happy endings need to include a Bollywood hero. Sometimes the scene ends with just us, on our own, picking up the broken pieces so that we can start over again. Sometimes it's letting go of cultural expectations in order to pave our own paths for the future. Or sometimes, the happy ending is simply moving forward.

Regardless of what happened, I had grown. I had learned. I had discovered my own self-worth. Hero or no hero, I was still the heroine of my story, and truth be told, my story was just beginning.

Acknowledgments

I've always believed that every person has a book within them. For me, this was the book I carried with me long before I even began writing it, so to see its transformation over the years into the very thing you are now holding has been one of the most rewarding experiences of my life.

A part of me wants very much to thank every single person I have ever come into contact with because I feel that every presence, interaction, and moment has in some way led me to this exact point. However, for the sake of those reading this, I will resist that urge and focus on the specific few, without whom this book would not have been possible:

To my parents, both of whom I owe more to than words can ever express. My mother, whose unconditional support and love (and endless supply of chai), has always been my greatest source of strength. My father, who taught me the importance of patience and perseverance, and who never once discouraged me from following my passions.

My sister, Zunera, for being the first one to (voluntarily) read this book from cover to cover and for dubbing herself my "biggest fan." Your sincere enthusiasm toward everything I've ever written motivates me more than you know. To my nieces, Ahyana and Amanah, my sources of light, you both are the inspiration behind everything I do.

Some say writing is something that cannot be taught; however, I owe so much of my writing accomplishments to the amazing teachers I've had the fortune of learning from throughout my life. Peggy Keller, I'm so grateful that our paths crossed when they did, and that you were willing to take the time to advise me even when this book was nothing more than a distant dream. Ellen Kleiner, thank you for your keen eye during the beginning stages of this manuscript. Your encouragement and guidance instilled a sense of confidence in me that I didn't even know existed. Nick Taylor, you gave me an opportunity to take part in my first writing workshop at SJSU after reading a sample chapter from this novel, and for that I am forever thankful. To my professors in CSULB's MFA program, my heartfelt thanks for your always kind generosity toward me and my work, and for shaping me into a better writer. Au-co Tran, my most trusted writing partner, I can always count on you for your honest feedback, and I thank you for being the perfect sounding board to all my rants and raves.

My deepest appreciation to Maria Cardona—my agent,

my friend, and my closest confidant through this whole process. Thank you for your unwavering belief in this book and for helping this dream come to life. To Anna Soler-Pont, Marina Penalva Halpin, Leticia Vila-Sanjuán, and everyone else at Pontas who read an early draft of this manuscript: thank you for seeing its potential and for always being in my corner. To my editor, Lucia Macro, you took a chance on me, and I cannot tell you how honored and grateful I am to have been given the opportunity to work with you. To my copyeditor, Laura Cherkas, thank you for your patience and diligence while working out the kinks in this manuscript. Asanté Simons, thank you for taking care of all the details. I truly couldn't have dreamt of a better publishing house or team of people to work alongside with.

My immense gratitude to my friends who have supported me through this process in innumerable ways: Lexi Solesbee and James An, for always lending an ear and for helping me maintain my sanity through all the ups and downs over the years. Helen Netramai Mollenbeck, for your constant encouragement and words of wisdom, most of which were imparted on our "early" morning hikes. Atinuke Adediran, for your selfless support and love through every major milestone. And Amy Patel, my long-lost twin, for blessing me with your friendship for the past seventeen years.

Last, but not least, to my husband, Matheen: you have held my hand through every major disappointment and celebrated with me even the most minor successes along the way. I am in constant awe of your unconditional belief in me, and without you, this book—this dream—could not have been possible. Thank you for being my biggest supporter, my most loving critic, and my best friend. I would not have had the courage to embark on this journey with anyone other than you.

About the author

About the book

Insights, Interviews & More . . .

Meet Zara Raheem

Nang Ngoc Pham

ZARA RAHEEM received her MFA in fiction from California State University, Long Beach, and has been teaching English and creative writing for the past nine years. She resides in Southern California. *The Marriage Clock* is her first novel.

The Inspiration Behind *The Marriage Clock*

Like many South Asian American children who grew up in the nineties, I feel very much a product of what I consider to be the golden age of Bollywood. Bollywood in that era was dominated by the Khans and the collective belief that Prince Charming wore ripped denim and yellow hoodies with oversize Gap logos across the front. The predictable story lines, saturated with sequins and cheesy song-and-dance numbers, were my first glimpse into the world of romance; however, it was not until my twenties that I finally realized that IRL love stories rarely—if ever—begin with dimpled, floppy-haired men serenading you in a field of bright yellow poppies.

The idea for *The Marriage Clock* transpired somewhere in the midst of this realization. After witnessing many of my closest friends find love the arranged way, I couldn't help but question why it was not happening for me. I had spent several years entrenched in the matchmaking process, ranging from *rishtas* to arranged dinners without so much as feeling a spark or a flicker, and I wondered if perhaps I was doing something wrong. So, I began keeping ▸

The Inspiration Behind
The Marriage Clock *(continued)*

a journal that documented details of every "date" I went on in an effort to make sense of the various emotions that arose throughout the process. At first, it was only a way of analyzing my experiences and viewing them from a different perspective; however, it wasn't long before I started sharing these details with other single friends and discovered that I was not alone in the confusion and frustrations that I felt.

Dating is hard. Finding love is even harder. But the most surprising thing I learned is that the pressure to satisfy cultural and familial expectations is not exclusive to South Asian communities. The challenges of finding love within a traditional framework also exist for those across a wide range of ethnic cultures. And once this became apparent, I began to view my incessant journaling as the beginnings of a universally complicated love story that needed to be written regardless of how my own story panned out.

When I began writing *The Marriage Clock*, I had no idea how I wanted the story to end. All I knew was that I wanted it to be told from the point of view of a female protagonist who resembled the women I saw around me. Leila Abid does not fit within the stereotypical narrative of a Muslim

South Asian American woman. She is outspoken and strong-minded. She is complex and multidimensional: unapologetic in her Americanness, yet simultaneously possessing a sense of pride in her culture and traditions. Seldom in mainstream media do we see women like Leila step into the spotlight. South Asian American women are often seen straddling one of two extremes: they are either too South Asian or too American—rarely do we allow them to simply occupy the space in between. Thus, Leila's existence in itself redefines what it means to be a Muslim South Asian woman living in the West because her story does not hinge on her willingness to sacrifice any part of her identity, but instead acknowledges and celebrates that she is *both* South Asian and American, a true conglomeration of Eastern and Western values.

My hope with *The Marriage Clock* is that it will entertain readers and allow them to see a part of themselves through Leila's journey. Most importantly, however, I hope that this novel will challenge women to resist the social pressures of marriage and family placed upon them, and step outside of these expectations in order to discover their own definitions of happiness. ~

Q&A with the Author

Q: You mention how the idea for* The Marriage Clock *stemmed from your own experiences. How much of the story would you say is fact and how much is fiction?

A: I would say that the majority of *The Marriage Clock* is fiction. While there are minor details interspersed throughout the novel from my own life, I would not claim Leila's journey to be a full reflection of my own. I think the aspect that is most autobiographical is perhaps the range of emotions that Leila experiences throughout her journey—her frustration, disappointment, confusion, and self-doubt. Having Leila grapple with these feelings was incredibly cathartic for me to write because I drew upon precise moments when I felt those same emotions during my own process. However, while the emotional threads of the story can be said to come from a more intimate, personal place, the same cannot be said about the various characters and situations that Leila finds herself in.

Q: In what ways does* The Marriage Clock *shed light on some of the larger issues existing within the South Asian community?

A: On the surface, *The Marriage Clock* is a story about modern dating and the difficulties of finding love within an arranged process. And while that alone is a challenge that many South Asian women (and men) face, there are also other, less talked about issues embedded within the culture. Even today, there still exists a preference for lighter-skinned brides; there are still biases and assumptions made about unmarried women over a certain age and negative stigmas attached to women who have been previously married. Yet, since the tone of the book is fairly lighthearted, I didn't want this information to be presented in a way that was too prescriptive or heavy-handed. However, from a storytelling aspect, I felt it would be impossible for readers to fully comprehend the challenges of Leila and Tania's struggles without at least touching upon these issues in some way. ▸

Q: Why was it so important for Leila to seek out a love interest who shared her same culture and traditions?

A: I think oftentimes when you have a protagonist who is South Asian or belonging to a nondominant culture, the story revolves around that character falling in love with someone outside of their culture in order to be accepted into dominant society. I didn't want Leila's story to perpetuate this narrative by reinforcing the hierarchal binaries between South Asians and their American counterparts. I wanted to show Leila making a conscious decision to be with a South Asian man (even when presented with other options) because I feel it is important to shift this mind-set that nondominant cultures are somehow less than or secondary to white, mainstream culture. Therefore, teasing out Leila's relationships with Zain and Hisham was especially important because both characters subvert stereotypical perceptions of South Asian men by proving themselves to be equally desirable and viable love interests for Leila.

Reading Group Guide

1. Leila's friend Annie says about the search for love, "The longer you hold on to these notions of perfection, the more disappointed you're going to feel when you don't find it." In what ways do you think Annie might be wrong? Are there ways in which she might be right?
2. Leila's parents clearly just want her to be happy. Are there ways that their hopes for their daughter's happiness are reasonable? Are there times when they cross the line, and do they even realize it when they do?
3. When Leila agreed to the three-month deadline, did you believe her parents would really hold her to it? Why or why not?
4. Would you ever try speed dating? If you have tried speed dating, what was your experience like?
5. Were you surprised that Meena agreed to get married after knowing her fiancé for such a short time?
6. Leila's parents are undeniably happy together. Are there times that "love after marriage" might actually work? How do you think they made it work out? ▸

Reading Group Guide ***(continued)***

7. Leila says, "Hero or no hero, I was still the heroine of my story, and truth be told, my story was just beginning." In what ways did you think Leila would get to this point? Did you ever think that she was waiting until she was engaged to start her own life? In what ways did she seem more independent than that?
8. Describe Leila's relationship with her mother. Do you think they have a close relationship? Are they always as honest with each other as they should be? Do you feel that their relationship is stronger or weaker than most mother/daughter relationships? Why or why not?
9. Family and cultural tradition play a strong role in this novel. In what ways do you feel the generational differences between Leila and her parents influence the *rishta* process? Do you think Leila is genuinely open to the process, or is she agreeing just to please her mother and father?
10. Describe the most embarrassing date you have ever been on.

Extra credit for the book club: Watch a Bollywood movie and enjoy! You can even pick one of Zara's favorite Bollywood romances from the nineties and early 2000s:

- *Dil To Pagal Hai*
- *Hum Aapke Hain Koun . . . !*
- *Dilwale Dulhania Le Jayenge*
- *Hum Dil De Chuke Sanam*
- *Kuch Kuch Hota Hai*
- *Mohabbatein*
- *Pardes*
- *Dhadkan*
- *Kaho Naa Pyaar Hai*
- *Devdas*